SHE WAS PALE, SO PALE THAT THE VEINS STOOD OUT LIKE BLUE TRACING ON HER SKIN

Her black hair was bound by a thong interwoven with copper coins and blue stones. The kohl on her eyelids made her smoky green eyes large and luminous. Her mouth was too wide, giving her a generous smile, but she allowed cruelty to twist it. She was the evil sorceress Rodeka!

Sharlin halted, bitterly afraid.

Rodeka lifted her hands. "Welcome, spirit, whoever you are. Come closer so that I may see you better."

If Sharlin could see the woman, why couldn't the woman see her? Sharlin looked at the floor and saw that she threw no shadow. . . .

WHERE
DRAGONS RULE

WHERE
DRAGONS RULE

R. A. V. Salsitz

A SIGNET BOOK

NEW AMERICAN LIBRARY

NAL BOOKS ARE AVAILABLE AT QUANTITY DISCOUNTS WHEN USED
TO PROMOTE PRODUCTS OR SERVICES. FOR INFORMATION PLEASE
WRITE TO PREMIUM MARKETING DIVISION, NEW AMERICAN
LIBRARY, 1633 BROADWAY, NEW YORK, NEW YORK 10019.

SIGNET, SIGNET CLASSIC, MENTOR, ONYX, PLUME, MERIDIAN
and NAL BOOKS are published by New American Library,
1633 Broadway, New York, New York 10019

First Printing, December, 1986

1 2 3 4 5 6 7 8 9

PRINTED IN THE UNITED STATES OF AMERICA

To Pat Peal
with respect and gratitude.

Chapter 1

He dreamed of dragons. He stood in a deep canyon of red and pink, as the sky filled with glimmering scales and leathern wings of green and brown . . . but the color that dazzled him was gold, a gold more molten and full of life than the sun itself. They, he and his companions, had just awakened the dragons from their graveyard sleep, and this was their joyous flight. His sword grip warmed in his hand as he held it tightly.

The air filled with the hiss of their tongue and the swoop of their wings against the sky. Wheeling about the canyon bowl, they began to leave even as the golden dragon looked to him and drank him in with eyes of amber.

He flinched, afraid, knowing that a black shadow would down him once again.

Pulse roaring in his ears, Dar pivoted on one heel. He held the sword up defensively as he looked for the black dragon. Sweat pooled his brow. Nightwing would come, as he always came, and Dar would have no choice. Again, he'd die. Convulsively the swordsman gripped his weapon. If only he didn't have to die!

Gold Turiana spat as the black shadow cooled him, and he spun around again, striking as the dragons struck at each other. *By dragon's claw, you will be freed*, whispered the Swamp Witch of Kalmar in his memories. He'd spent years searching for an oracle who could tell him that. Tell him how to escape from the sorcerer king Valorek. Now the moment had come. Dar trembled.

A claw curved at him. A claw the length of his body. A claw of obsidian, shaped like the crescent of the moon. He screamed silently, "No! I want to be free, not dead!" Though he dodged, it sliced through him with cold fire. He twisted and fell and lay there, sweating and cursing, and felt the dampness of his blood run out of him.

He lost sight of the canyon as an unlit tunnel swallowed him whole. This part he didn't always remember, but the dream tonight had a relentless hold and wouldn't let go. The swordsman tried to breathe. A brilliant light blazed at tunnel's end. He staggered to his feet, drawn by the light as a moth is drawn to the flame . . . but this flame would heal, not burn. Dar moved toward it. The fear evaporated suddenly. He saw more than he had ever seen before.

A shape eclipsed the brilliant light. His breath caught in his throat as he thought he recognized that soldier's stance with the span of heavy shoulders, unbowed by years of dairy farming once the sword was put away.

"Father?" he asked tentatively.

The figure responded, moving forward.

Dar felt a kindling in his heart and thought that if he was indeed dead, he would welcome it.

The aura sprang out again, suddenly illuminating the gloating face, set off by closely cropped dark hair and beard, so like the silken pelt of an animal. Flat, cruel eyes gleamed, and the olive skin creased as his enemy smiled. "Thought you were rid of me, eh, boy?" Valorek reached for him.

The oracle wrong. His life and soul still gripped in the witch king's greedy hands. Horror flooded him at the thoughts.

Then his heart jumped, and the tunnel opened under

his feet, dumping him into midair. He fell, hurtling downward, and then he was alive again, and awake.

Dar woke. He lay still a moment as his pulse slowed to a dull thunder, and his body realized it lay curved under a warm coverlet. Spooned to his side was another form, warm and slender. Her honey-colored hair tumbled over her shoulder carelessly, and one bare breast was showing. He reached and covered her again, his hand trembling, wondering that Sharlin could still be asleep after the nightmare he'd had.

The cave was still dark. Dawn hadn't quite yet lightened the mouth. As he held his breath and tried to still his fear, he heard the snore of another being, the golden behemoth resting across the exit, protecting them against the wild.

How many slept with the queen of all dragons to protect them? And yet, even that was not enough to save Aarondar from the death in his sleep.

Dar brushed his hair back from his forehead. Nightwing was gone. Turiana had cut him flaming from the sky, and with the death of the black dragon, gone was his sorcerous tie to the witch king Valorek. Even Valorek should be dead, though Dar couldn't accept that. Not in his dreams and not while awake.

He creeped out of the covers so as not to awaken Sharlin. Turiana had conjured up a goose-down bed from somewhere, she called it borrowing, and it offered some comfort in the abandoned cave. From the post of its frame hung his trousers and shirt, and a new set of leathers to replace those Nightwing had ripped to shreds. He pulled them on as quietly as he could, though the leathers creaked a little.

Two wine-red nostrils pushed into the cave. Amber orbs glowed on either side of Turiana's wide forehead, crowned with spines. Awe of the dragon's beauty flooded him anew.

"Awake, fair son?"

"Yes, but she's not." He drew on his swordbelt and fastened it, before stooping and leaving the cave. Outside, he sat on a flat rock and pulled on his boots.

"It's good for the hunter to be up early." Turiana craned her neck. Her ears swiveled forward. "The sun comes."

"Good." He'd known that by the tinting of the sky, but the golden dragon had an imperious way of assuming that no one knew the world of Rangard as she did. And perhaps, even three hundred years after her death and resurrection, no one did.

"That one inside would do well to stay here with you and build a nest."

He smiled slightly. Turiana had been obsessed with nesting the past few days. "That one," he answered, "is determined to return to her people and free them from Rodeka's tyranny."

At the name of the sorceress who was Sharlin's enemy, Turiana frowned, a rather odd sliding together of the scales that knitted her brow and rattled her spines. "I don't know of Rodeka," she answered. "But I swore a lifedebt and will honor it. Then, perhaps, you can talk that one into nesting."

"Maybe," Dar answered as he stood and adjusted the swing of his sword on his left hip. "But I doubt it. Sharlin will nest if and when she wants to."

Turiana reared up suddenly, as a dark green shape swooped overhead through the lightening sky. Her nostrils cupped, and she settled back down. "A green," she muttered. "Scarcely worth noticing."

Dar tried to ignore the prickling hairs along his neck. Dragonfolk were all too common. The green Turiana scorned had probably come from decimating a crofter's herd. The rapaciousness and spitefulness of an immature dragon were legendary. It couldn't be allowed to go on. Dragonfolk and humankind were going to have to determine perimeters of existence before both died out.

Normally he wouldn't have given a rusty knifeblade for a dragon. Back in the days when he scorned them as gods, he had rarely thought of them as intelligent beings either. Now, with Turiana firmly imprinted on his mind, he found his world upside down.

The golden dragon scored a claw into the dust as though she might be privy to his thoughts.

"It cannot be allowed to go on."

"What can't?"

Her eyelids half-lowered as the sun inched upward in the sky. "My people have grown arrogant and shiftless. The codes must be reestablished. Rule must be returned." She curled her paw as though she might hold all of dragonkind within. "Else man will rebel against gods they learn are false, and look to slaughtering us." She looked suddenly at him, intensely, and he swallowed, unable to avoid the glittering eye. "Eh, swordsman?"

"To protect themselves," he answered reluctantly.

"Yes. And if not that, vengeance. No nests will be safe then, yours or mine."

Nesting again. Dar thought uneasily of the golden dragon's rape by the evil Nightwing. He hesitated, then said, "Turiana, you speak a lot about nesting. Are you carrying a clutch of eggs?"

The amber eyes flared, and her head jerked back with a spat. "Fool! What kind of an idiot do you think me—a dragon's spawning is her death! Do you think I would allow conception now, when all the world is against us? I was given resurrection. Be assured I will hold on to it with the tightest clutch of my claws!"

A talon sliced the air just under his nose. and he froze before the anger of a dragon god. Still, he did not quite believe her. He would have to watch, and wait.

Sharlin appeared at the cave mouth. Dar swallowed

and looked away from her less than modestly dressed form, until she shrugged into a riding skirt and a blouse. "What are you two whispering about?" the princess asked as she buttoned the blouse and tugged on her soft leather boots.

"Where to find softfoot for breakfast," Dar answered.

Turiana snorted. A blurry gray smoke ring issued as she did. "And I told him—over there." She pointed with an elegant clawtip.

Sharlin fastened back her hair with a shell comb. "Then I'll come with you." She smiled as she crossed the rocks. "Turiana, you lie here and soak up the sun." The girl ran her hand critically over a ridge of scar tissue along the dragon's flank. "It looks better, but I think you still need to rest."

"Of course, daughter," Turiana said placidly and laid her head down upon her paws. "I shall sleep. Bring a few softfoot back for me, please."

Leaving the dragon queen asleep like a very large lizard among the rocks, the two of them proceeded down into the valley. If Turiana had said softfoot could be found, Dar had no doubt they'd be there, even if Turiana had charmed them to their deaths.

Indeed, as sunlight spilled over the tiny valley, they found an open patch of sweet grass filled with softfoot dozing on their haunches, eyes closed to their peril. Dar sighed.

Sharlin put her hand on his wrist. "It's just until she regains her strength. You don't have to kill them all."

He drew his sword, and the sound of the blade scraping free woke not a one of his twoscore prey. He frowned. "But how many softfoot do you think it takes to appease a dragon her size? Not less than ten for a fair bite, and I know she'd rather have a side of gunter."

Sharlin's mouth curved. "I love you for that. All right. There's at least five baby-fat softfoot here, and two more that look as though they've been nursing. We'll leave them and take the others."

"Fair enough." Dar dispatched the victims as quickly as he could. Sharlin knelt in the grass by his side, her dagger busily working at skinning and cleaning the carcasses.

As they worked, the litter-fattened softfoot awoke, twitched their noses, and hopped away in alarm. Sharlin watched them go, an odd smile on her face. Then she bent over the small bodies they skinned, her knifeblade busy.

Dar straightened and arched his back. Sleeping in a cave, goose-down bed or not, was not his idea of a way to spend the night. Dampness from the rock seeped into every bone, and he felt the stiffness. Or maybe it was the dragon flight from Glymarach, the cradle and deathbed of the dragons, that stiffened him. Riding Turiana as she raggedly sailed the skies was not his idea of transportation. Nor could he put aside his doubt of the beast, and the aid she offered to Sharlin.

In the shaded glen beyond, he could hear the contented cropping of his horse, Brand, and Sharlin's horse, Cloud, both of them somewhat recovered from their hair-raising trip clutched in the dragon's claws. Though Turiana had charmed them to sleep, Cloud had awaked before journey's end and struggled, whinnying in high-pitched fear. His sides were scored where Turiana had gripped him tighter. The scratches looked nearly healed as Dar looked the horses over and decided they were well enough to ride again.

"I'm nearly done with my stack," Sharlin called out.

"Good." Dar cut a flexible switch from the tree shading him. He'd string up the bodies to take them back.

A dark shadow grazed him, and he flinched, then looked up and saw nothing but blue sky and wispy clouds overhead. *Dragon-shy*, he thought wryly, as he whittled a point.

He strung the bodies up quickly, ignoring the bloody forms. He hadn't gutted them, as the dragon showed a marked preference for eating her meals whole. Sharlin wiped her hands clean on a tuft of grass. Without a word from him, she shouldered her end of the limb and followed him out of the glen.

Dar carried his end of the rack with a sigh of contentment. This was what it was like to be whole, this partnership without words or bickering, but a quiet assent that what was to be done would be done together. He liked it. He was growing used to it . . . and that, in the wake of what Sharlin required of Turiana, bothered him a little.

As strong as Turiana's legendary past had been, Dar had seen no great sorcerous feats from the dragon queen yet except for sleep-charming. True, the golden had nearly died at the talons of the black, and that's why all of them sought solitude for now, to heal and grow rested. Yet he could not shake his feeling that, although resurrected, Turiana was not yet whole. Nor perhaps could ever be. He feared to say anything to Sharlin.

As they crossed the sunlit expanse to the jumbled rock mountain where Turiana lay, a shriek pierced the sky. Dar pulled his sword and went to his knees, as a shadow again darkened him.

"Get down!"

Sharlin tumbled to the grasses, the rack of softfoot at her side. He watched the shadow glide over her and looked up. Too small to be a dragon, but—

The bird screeched again and darted at him, claws out. He sliced at it, and the creature pulled up, wheeled, and rose in the air out of his reach. A vystra. But how could the enormous and vicious bird of prey even be in this region? The vystra nested in the Goblin Reaches, not here in lower Kalmar.

Sharlin let out a cry and then muffled it as the bird dove at her, talons curled and raking through her hair.

It caught her up, and then its claws slipped through the amber strands as Dar reached out and swung with his sword. The vystra had been known to carry off sheep and young gunters. Black feathers flew as the blade swept through the tail, missing the flesh of the creature's body.

"It's the softfoot," Dar said. "Leave them and run!"

Sharlin got to her feet and bolted past him toward the nearest tree. Her dagger flashed as she clutched it in her hand. He glimpsed her pale face and launched himself after her, to protect her back.

Darkness brushed him. He stopped and dug his boot heels into the ground, ready to face the bird. It winged above him, circling far out of reach, even if he had had a bow.

The swordsman glared upward and realized that the pile of softfoot bodies, still warm and pooling blood, had no lure for the bird. They, he and Sharlin, were its intended prey. The vystra swooped downward, wings spread like ebony fingers against the azure sky, its red eyes glittering.

"Dar! Get out of there!"

Sharlin's voice echoed thinly. He tightened his grip on the sword. Anger rushed through him—rage at being a target. He stood his ground as the vystra plunged at him, talons ready.

With a *ker-rack*, a golden bolt split the air and pierced the vystra through the breast. The bird curled up with a whistling shriek and hit the ground not a man's length from Dar. It flailed its wings and then balled up and died. The magic arrow faded from the carcass.

Turiana lumbered up. "Can I not trust you two even to fetch a sleep-charmed breakfast?"

"Thanks, Turiana." He sheathed his blade reluctantly.

"Don't mention it, fair son. Was it after our softfoot?"

He closed the ground and nudged the body with his boot toe. "No, I think it was after us."

A wattled yellow leg convulsed, then grew limp, and he saw the message scroll tied to its limb. Sharlin tossed him her dagger, and he slit the thong holding it. She joined him in the curve of his arm as he unrolled the parchment and read aloud.

" 'I am coming after you. Valorek, the king.' "

An icy feeling stabbed through his chest and fled, that suddenly. He crushed the missive in his fist.

Chapter 2

"Let me see if I have this straight," Turiana said, licking her bloody lips with a forked tongue. "You think this Valorek was looking for you."

Dar also licked his breakfast off his lips, though his meal had been thoroughly roasted first. "I have no reason to doubt it."

"Well, if the king had been dead when Sharlin performed the resurrection spell, it would have acted on him the same as it did on any of us. However, if, as you say, he was merely an aging king and wounded when taken to the graveyard by Nightwing . . . no, the spell wouldn't have had any effect. Resurrection spells only affect the dead. They are not healing spells." Turiana changed subjects. "I examined the craw of the bird. It's been eating lightly for some days now. I would say Valorek has no idea where we are and that the creature has been on a search pattern at random."

"That's reassuring." Sharlin tore a leg off a roasted softfoot and nibbled at it with her even white teeth.

Dar shifted. He had wanted the chance to look at the vystra again, to see if Valorek had fastened a magical amulet to it or some such, if the bird might be tied to the master by more than a scroll. But Turiana had devoured it promptly after her examination, pronounced it delightful if stringy, and that was that.

17

Turiana added, "I would say that your link with the king has been severed. You face his spite now as any other would who'd crossed Valorek, but he can't hope to convert you into a shell for his soul."

"There's that, at least," Dar said, drawing comfort where he could. He sliced a hunk of meat off and tossed it lightly between his hands, cooling it, before biting into it deeply.

"Not that anyone would want Valorek for an enemy," Sharlin said. "At least before, he had a reason for keeping Dar alive."

"There's that," considered Turiana. She reached out, plucked another softfoot body off the rocks, and plopped it into her mouth. "Of course, there's no way of knowing how healthy Valorek is. He could be on his last legs. In your terms, fair son, you might only have to flee for a year or two."

Dar choked, coughed, turned red, and then caught himself as Sharlin pounded on his back. To a dragon, of course, a few years were a relatively short span of time.

Turiana continued with a wave of one claw. "I'd say there's nothing to worry about from his quarter." She bared her fangs and delicately picked a ligament from between her teeth. "But when I have my council set up, if Valorek is still alive, he shall have to answer for a few things."

"What council?" Sharlin.

"Ah . . . the council of dragons, of course, child." Turiana arched her brow. "It will be the only efficient way to rule Rangard."

"Rule the world?"

The dragon stretched a paw toward Dar, reconsidered, and drew it back. The swordsman sat quite still, wondering if it was an affectionate gesture or a hostile one.

"Naturally. You don't think we could continue to leave that to humans, do you? With the various powers at our disposal, dragons must have a checkrein, and you certainly aren't equipped to do it. The only being that can handle sorcery is another sorcerous being. Even this Valorek, powerful as you described him, obtained his power from a dragon . . . and though Nightwing is gone, the king remains behind to work what sorcery he can. It will take one of us to deal with him." Turiana nibbled at another softfoot, her tenth. Her leisurely pace indicated that she was growing full, thanks to the appetizer of vystra. "And he will be dealt with, make no bones of that. The taking of a Face is no light matter, even among dragons."

As Dar looked at her, she caught him with the glimmer of her amber eye. He remembered the massive expanse of her bleached bones stretching across the floor of the graveyard. No, taking another's life to prolong one's own would not be a light matter, even among dragons. He shifted.

Sharlin wiped her hands clean. "Rodeka is no less powerful."

He heard tension in her voice. She worried about her family and people, and knew the delay for them all to heal chafed at her. He licked the last of the softfoot off his blade. "Another day or two at the most, Turiana? Then we'll be off after the sorceress?"

"Ummmm," Turiana said. Her inner, transparent, eyelids closed. The amber fire of her eyes muted. "Back in time. Yes. That's a problem I must consider." She rolled belly up in the sun and shut her eyes the rest of the way. After a moment, a thunderous snore filled the air.

Sharlin kicked the fire down vigorously. "That's another day lost."

Dar approached her, but she turned her back to him. He hugged her shoulders. "When we go back, we'll go back to the same time, no matter how much has passed here. You'll be all right."

"Maybe. None of us even knows if it's possible—not even Turiana."

"And how possible do you think it would be without her?"

Sharlin quivered between his hands. "Never," she whispered. "I could never go back."

He thought back to the girl he'd met at a backwater border inn. She'd been disguised as a pallan then, one of the mysterious veiled and shrouded race, to save her life. A peddler had left them a map to the graveyard of dragons, and Dar, demon-pursued, had thought it the answer to severing his ties from Valorek, the riddled prophecy from the oracular swamp witch. She'd thought the map the answer to her plight. She'd left her kingdom in the north on griffin-back, seeking sorcerous aid to fight Rodeka, and had been struck down, her griffin thrown across the seas to land and die, abandoning her in the wilderness. The map, though, brought her the promise of her original goal—to find the legendary Turiana and resurrect her, and ask her aid.

Sharlin never knew until the graveyard was nearly reached that she'd been thrown not only across land but across time. The time of her people's crisis lay over and done several hundred years ago. Still, she'd not given up, even when she saw that the pallan temple at the gateway to the graveyard of dragons held the defeat of her people written in stone. No, not even then—though she had nearly lost her mind.

Dar swallowed. Sharlin was tough and soft, all at once, and he knew that he loved her more than life itself, but he couldn't solve her problem. Only Turiana could attempt to do that. Still, he said it. "Sharlin, if I could fight it for you—"

"I know." She twisted in his hands, turning to face him. She hugged him tightly. He bent his neck to gently kiss the red birthmark on the curve of her throat, the mark of her lineage from the house of Dhamon. "I know." Letting go, she walked briskly away to where the tethered horses grazed, and he did not follow.

Baalan rested in the afternoon sun, his purple bulk stretched across the rocks, and gloried in the newness of his life. He watched a pair of greens on the wing overhead as they fought and spat like two angry cats. As they passed from ear range, he rumbled a sigh. Yes. Life was good. Almost as good as power. His claws flexed unconsciously.

A whisper of rustling robes reached him. He opened an eye as an acolyte approached. The manbeast went to his knees and bowed until his forehead struck the ground.

"Lord Baalan. A visitor wishes to speak to you."

Baalan had seen the rider come up the mountainside hours ago. He knew the visitor by reputation, for the dragon had wasted no time in sizing up the current situation in the various lands of Rangard. The witch king Valorek, late of Nightwing's power, stirred as the acolyte's soft words woke him. The dragon's right nostril flared a little. Too bad Nightwing had perished. He would have been a worthy opponent.

"What is it he wants?" Valorek asked.

"Silence," Baalan ordered. "I know what it is he wants." His talon bit into rock. "Tell the manbeast I wish to make no further alliances at the moment." He knew what the visitor wanted, just as he knew what it was Valorek wanted. Sorcery. More power. Just what he, Baalan wished, though on a different scale.

The acolyte got to his knees. His face was very pale. Baalan smelled the fear as he began to sweat from his pores. The dragon sensed that the servant was nearly as frightened of Valorek as he was of the great dragon. Odd. Perhaps Baalan would have to convince him otherwise.

But the servant began to back away, stammering, "Yes, my lord."

Baalan stretched. "Have you finished with the count yet?"

"N-no, my lord. It is difficult to weed out the duplicates. But I should have it fully prepared in another two days."

"Excellent. Remember how I want it broken down . . . colors as well as magical alliances."

"I remember, my lord." The acolyte bowed and turned to go. He hesitated as if remembering something else. "My lord . . ."

"What is it?"

"The visitor said to tell you something, if you turned him away."

The dragon's spines went up, crowning his shrewd head. "What was that?"

"That he knows of Turiana, and her whereabouts."

Baalan's newly born heart flexed a little. The two stomachs rumbled. "Perhaps I should see this manbeast after all," the great dragon said. "Bring him forth." His blood heated and raged. *Turiana! Most ancient of enemies*, Baalan thought. "This should please you, too, Valorek."

The man stretched out a hand and gently scratched the slightly ticklish underplates of the dragon's jaw. "Pehaps. If Aarondar is with the queen. But how can a petty wizard know what all your spies, human, pallan, and dragon alike, haven't been able to tell you? Even my vystra could not locate them."

"Patience," the dragon counseled. "We are not all perfect." He watched the greens span the distance above them. To his keen eyesight, the riders perched on their backs were clearly visible, though he knew the man beside him could see only small specks. "Just as dragonriders are not trained in a day."

Valorek said nothing to the dragon's gentle jibing. He watched his lieutenants and knew that they clutched fearfully to their sanity as well as the harnesses which secured them. He clenched his free hand even as the other gently stroked the dragon's sensitive spot. Why could they not open their eyes and sense the sheer possibility of it—of leading an army from the air, or *through* it? They would be unstoppable!

"Patience," Baalan rumbled again. "Not every man is a Valorek," and the witch king recoiled at the reading of his thoughts. No, this dragon was no Nightwing. The great black dragon would have been pale next to this monster.

There is no way, Dar reflected, to travel rough country comfortably. The horses picked their way through the mountainous terrain carefully, but it only took the merest scent of dragon from upwind to send them plunging and bucking through the underbrush. If Turiana charmed them, then he and Sharlin rode mounts that sleepwalked—and in this terrain, could walk them right off a cliff. On the other hand, if they rode dragonback, the horses were subject to injury, and Turiana could not sustain a pace carrying both humans and horses.

A swift-flowing brook cut off their path. Sharlin spat out a curse as Cloud dipped his dappled gray neck and refused to cross it. Dar heeled Brand past her and urged his horse through the foaming blue waters.

The chestnut stallion also dug in his heels. As Dar whipped his rump lightly, the horse turned his head to look at him, as if to say, If you want across, why don't you go across?

"Hang on," Dar muttered. He dismounted and took firm grip on Brand's chin strap. Dust littered his boots, covering even the black stains from goblin blood, as he stepped into the brook.

Narrow and swift it was—and much deeper than it looked. It swept Dar right off his feet. The only thing saving him was his hold on the horse's bridle. He swiveled in the water and flailed, his shoulders heaving, and pulled himself back onto dry land. Brand rolled his eyes, snorted, and backed up a step or two. As he dragged his master out of the river, the watching Cloud let out a whicker.

As Dar found his footing again, he looked at Sharlin. She bit her lower lip and looked away. "All right," he muttered. "Maybe they're not so dumb after all. Let's go downstream."

Turiana crossed overhead, her wings in full gliding sail. She blotted out the sun with her own golden glory.

Sharlin frowned, then said, "Turiana says there's a crossing about a quarter of a league down, and a big meadow beyond. She wants to land and rest awhile."

Dar swung up, his leathers dripping with icy water. "Sounds fine to me."

True to her word, the dragon queen awaited them at the meadow's edge when they finally reached it. Though the horses threw up their heads and snorted, their nostrils flaring wide, they soon quieted. Dar helped Sharlin dismount.

Turiana stretched lazily. She gazed through pleased slit eyes. "Not far from here is a pallan city. We will be met with great honor there, and I expect to find out much history that I need to know."

Sharlin looked at Dar. "Pallans?"

"Yes."

Dar wasn't familiar with lower Kalmar, but from what he knew of pallans, there was no love lost between them and dragons. How could Turiana expect to be welcomed by them? "Most of the pallans I've met are nomads," he said. The sun worked on drying his leathers and, uncomfortably, shrinking them. He kept on his feet, doing deep knee bends to keep the armor from becoming unwearable. Turiana watched with great amusement.

"Surely you saw the great pallan city as you approached the Pit?"

"Of course—but it's been abandoned for decades."

Turiana nodded. "With the vast decline in dragon population, I should have expected no less. But here, in the rich wilderness, the pallans should still be doing well. And, as we dragons say, there is no history untouched by pallan pen. They have no fear of being judged."

"Maybe we should go ahead and scout—"

"Have you pallan veil and robes?" Turiana snorted. "You wouldn't get far."

"As a matter of fact," Sharlin declared, "I do. The hood and veils, anyway."

"Well. Surprises all around. Then wear them, fair daughter, if you wish, though it won't take much for the pallans to see through your disguise. Yet it might be enough to get you through the gates."

"How far is the city?"

"I spotted the outlines of it from the air. About tomorrow dusk, at your pace, I estimate."

Dar flexed his shoulders. "You will do as you wish, as always, Turiana—but it will please me if you stay behind, at least until Sharlin and I are at the gates."

"You worry about me? How quaint."

He frowned. "Dragonbane isn't quaint. Times have changed since you ruled the skies, and I don't trust in the kindness of strangers." Not to mention Valorek, out there somewhere. Why not in a pallan city? "Besides, with your wings, you could catch up with us in no time."

"This is true. Very well. I'll settle here until Sharlin summons me." So saying, the dragon queen curled up. One eyelid popped back open. "There is wild gunter grazing downstream," she said wistfully.

Dar could not help smiling. "I'll check on it," he answered.

It had been a great city once, carved and terraced from the mountain. As he and Sharlin rode in, he could

see that much of the city was now abandoned. It rode
an immense plateau, much of which was kept cleared.
It was scored and raked, and he puzzled on it until
Sharlin made a tiny noise and then said, "Dragon stage."

Of course. He saw now the markings on the rock
boundaries and read the sign she did. At one time, a
massive number of dragons had landed here. He looked
down over the sloping valleys. Greenery clutched the
far side of the plateau. Terrace gardens would provide
what farming the pallans needed—the valleys lay too far
away.

No sentries watched the plateau. He rode through
the decaying outer gates with Sharlin at his side, hooded
and veiled. Had they been seen and he hadn't noticed?
Did the disguised girl give them clear passage? He
touched his sword hilt uneasily, testing it one more
time to be sure the weapon was loose in the sheath.

A breeze blew across the plateau, bringing with it the
hint of crisper nights ahead. Indian summer long gone,
winter edged into the seasons. Dar breathed deeply.
Only high in the mountains did he sense the kind of
winter he was used to in the north. Sharlin pulled her
cloak a little tighter about her slim body.

He sensed eyes watching from the shadowed corners
of the old city. When he looked, however, he saw no
one. That meant nothing. The pallans were aware, finally, that the two of them rode in.

He noticed Sharlin looking about as she also tried to
pin down the onlookers, without success. The same
dark blue veil and hood she'd worn when they first met
hid her long amber hair and the stormy gray-blue eyes he'd
grown used to looking into when he woke in the morning.

As they rounded a corner, their horses kicking up
dirt in the broken street, a veiled pallan appeared from
the stonework. It blocked the road silently.

Sharlin's veil puffed as she breathed. The pallan eyed

the two of them as they reined up in front of it. It lifted
a gloved hand palm outward, and then turned aside.

Dar kept his hand on his sword casually as they rode
past, but the pallan did nothing. He sensed growing
numbers behind them watching them enter the city.
He let out a tensed breath. "All right, Sharlin . . . call
in Turiana."

The girl nodded.

A second group of pallans crossed their path. Brand
snorted to a halt and pawed the street impatiently. This
group, however, was not as easily appeased as the
other.

"You are not pallan, as you pretend to be," said the
leader. "But neither are you enemies."

Sharlin put aside the veil and let down the hood.
"You have brothers in Kalmar who took me in."

The pallan assessed her from behind its own veils. It,
like most, wore a gauze face mask under the veil. Dar
could detect nothing of the creature behind the fabric.

The being shrugged. "It is sometimes done." He
waved another pallan close, this dressed in shimmering
white veils. "We will bring you water and food, such as
we can offer you."

Dar shook his head. "There's no need. We've found
plenty on the trail here. What we ask is hospitality for
our companion, for she needs access to your histories."

"Companion?" If there had been an eyebrow to see,
it would have arched.

"She comes in a moment—the golden dragon Turiana."

A hiss of surprise. The streets cleared of all pallans
but the one in black and and the one in rainbow white.

Then: "Dare you this?"

Dar felt Brand move uneasily as he answered, "Turiana
assured us she would be met with honor in your city.
She remembers it of old."

"And we, her, if she is the Turiana of the past.
However, dragons are no longer welcome here. We

refuse you hospitality." With that, the black—veiled pallan turned away.

Before Dar could protest, a shadow wheeled overhead. He looked up, expecting to see Turiana, telling Sharlin, "Send her off. I don't like the tone of this," but green, not gold, scales met his eyes.

Two immense green dragons flew above them.

The pallan in black snapped, "The trap is sprung. They have been awaiting the dragon queen." It disappeared then, into the rubble of its forgotten city, the pallan in white at its heels.

Cloud let out a whinny of pure fear. He plunged and bucked under Sharlin's hold. She fought to gather in her reins.

"Take cover!"

"Not in here," she protested. "I don't like this."

There would be scant cover on the plateau, but Dar had no chance to argue as Cloud pivoted and bolted, Sharlin little more than a burr in his saddle.

As the horse streaked to the outer gate, Dar kicked Brand after him. He watched Sharlin hunch in the saddle, her shoulders working as she sawed the reins. She fought to regain the bit from his teeth, but Dar had ridden the gray, too, and knew his mouth was like iron. He heeled Brand, urging the chestnut to overtake the gray. He had to stop her before they made the flat of the plateau.

A green flew down, hazing her, with a screech that cut the mountain air. The gray stallion faltered, then dodged away, even as the dragon's talons cut toward them. Dar cursed and drew his sword. Where was Turiana?

Rising out of the sky as if blossoming from his thoughts, the golden dragon appeared above the plateau. She spread her massive wings and let loose a trumpet of challenge, her tail whipping the air.

Two greens answered the challenge. Dar caught up

with Cloud and wrestled the stallion to a halt. He grasped the headstall. Sharlin fought to regain her stirrups.

Both horses backed, trembling, into the shadows of the broken city, as the dragons fought overhead.

Sharlin put her hand to her mouth. "Dar! There are two of them!".

"I know." He craned his head back and watched the two green dragons bait and slash viciously at the golden dragon.

She outflew them. She curved and chased them down, lashed out, and slipped away. Fire danced in the open sky as the greens retaliated. Turiana beat powerful wings, ascending nearly straight up. Then, as they pursued, she balled her wings and body and plunged earthward. As she passed the greens, she cut at one of them. A cloud of blood fountained. With a keening shriek, a green tumbled from the sky.

Turiana plunged toward the mountaintop. She caught herself on the wind at the last possible second, her wings unfurling and billowing. For a second she drifted.

The second green swooped down, talons out. It raked her back. Turiana wobbled in her glide, then slipped away under him as she regained momentum once more. Sharlin sucked in her breath.

The golden dragon rolled, slowly, presenting her soft underbelly to the green.

"No," Dar muttered. He clutched his sword uselessly.

The green saw the vulnerability and dove again. It screeched in angry triumph—and then Turiana struck, golden spears of energy arching upward.

"Magic," breathed Sharlin softly.

Yes, magic. Turiana struck the green dragon down just as she had the vystra, only this time with more vigor. The bolts speared the green, knocking him tumbling from the air. He disappeared in the trail of the first, down the mountainside, to oblivion.

Scarcely breathing heavily, the golden dragon sculled and landed, then waddled up to Dar and Sharlin.

The watching pallans faded silently from the wreckage of the city.

Turiana craned her slender neck. "What happened here? Who set the greens after us?" She ignored the long crimson scratches down her back.

"The pallans have refused us and you. As for the greens . . ." Dar twisted in his saddle, overlooking the city. "I don't think they sent them, but they knew the greens were here. They knew the greens were searching for you."

Turiana's eyes narrowed. She shook her head, rattling her spines. "I could smash into their libraries if I wished."

"Turiana, don't—"

"No. I won't, daughter. No, if the pallans have turned against dragonfolk, Rangard has changed more than I reckoned. It is time for me to act. I will find the answers, and now, before dragons are pitted against themselves, and dragonfolk and humanfolk wade in each other's blood. I'm yours now, but beware. The time is drawing near when I must forsake you and put my house in order."

With that, despite Sharlin's soft cry of dismay, the golden dragon launched herself.

Chapter 3

Turiana stood over the fresh rack of bones, her throat stretched in a keening of agony. Sharlin stood nearby, the corners of her mouth white as she held back nausea.

Dar paced the site of the kill, despite the shrill noise Turiana made steadily. He noted the number of men and horses—and dragons—who'd made the kill, skinned the beast, and left it. Later, when Turiana calmed, he would discuss the site with her. It was not the first such they'd found, and he doubted it would be the last. And the most disturbing factor about all of the dragon kills they'd found had been that Turiana knew the beasts, and counted them as friends of herself and dragonfolk.

The three of them had flown on dragonback across Kalmar, crisscrossing, searching out contacts with benevolent beasts. Turiana had wasted much time in finding out the status of her kind. Someone else worked ahead of her, steadily decimating the ranks of dragon who could be considered benevolent.

He took a last look at the great head of the creature, the only portion not skinned and butchered. It had been a bronze beauty of a male. Wide through the forehead. Eyes of glimmering cat green. Spines of deepest sable. It must have been a massive beast, larger by

half again than Turiana—and it must have taken a full
wing of lesser dragons to bring it down.

Turiana's keening stopped. She put out a wing and
gathered Sharlin close, seeking comfort. A great tear-
drop shimmered in her amber eye. She put her muzzle
down to the head.

"Goodbye, firstborn," she whispered. "Seek out your
father and fly higher than dragon ever has."

Unable to bear the agony of their combined grief any
longer, Sharlin buried her face on the golden dragon's
neck. Dar pretended not to hear her muffled sobs.

Firstborn. Turiana had more than known this bronze,
then, she had laid the egg it hatched from. Perhaps
even nurtured it, if dragonkind nurtured their young,
before her death. He cleared his throat.

"With lyrith . . ."

"No." Turiana looked at him. "No resurrection for
this one. Dragons have done that which will make it
impossible. And, besides, death is death. To tempt it
too often is to tempt the gods themselves."

Wings trailing the ground, Turiana moved away from
the carcass. Sharlin lifted her wet face and met his
glance.

She looked away. She did not often discuss the bond
between the dragon queen and herself with Dar, but he
knew they sometimes thought alike, and that Sharlin
could send calls for help across the leagues with silent
thought. Now he knew they shared a part of their
hearts, as well.

He put his arm about her shoulders. "What's done is
done."

The princess nodded. She took a deep breath. "But
how many more will we find? That's four in nearly as
many days."

He shook his head. "Whoever is doing this is just
ahead of us. Turiana will catch up sooner or later."

"And if they catch her first . . ." Sharlin's voice trailed off.

He held her tight and kissed her temple. "The golden dragon will live to see you back home. I promise you that."

She gave a short laugh. "If only you could."

"I'll do what I can."

"I know you will, Dar. But somehow, right now, it doesn't seem enough." Sharlin stepped away from him. Her gesture took in all of the kill site, but her next words were interrupted by Turiana.

"We must go now."

Dar let Sharlin step away and mount the dragon first. As for himself, he'd as soon be on horseback, and he knew that the ones they tracked traveled by horseback. He could have made a case for it, but it would do him no good now. They weren't even on the same continent where they'd left Brand and Cloud behind, hobbled loosely and protected by wards in a valley of sweet water, grass, and clover.

He mounted the dragon's withers behind Sharlin, settling among the spines and taking hold. Turiana squeaked, and he moved, to find that his leg had pinched a tiny fold of her wing.

"I'm sorry."

"Never mind, fair son. You are not used to dragon-riding."

No, he thought. Nor will I ever be. He gripped a dragon spine tighter in each hand, preparing for the unsettling jump that would launch them into the air.

Each takeoff put his stomach in his mouth. Sweat beaded his forehead and would have clouded his eyes if he had left them open to see. Dar could not control his fear until the dragon leveled off and the icy wind dried his beads of fear. He clutched the spines and clenched his jaw, waiting for this one.

Moments later, he opened his eyes and swallowed

down bitter vomit yet again. Sharlin did not seem to mind dragonriding. He had not discussed his own violent qualms with her.

He did not recognize the lands under them. "Where are we going?"

"I don't know."

Turiana's voice, thinned by the wind, rumbled back to them. "Have you any suggestions?"

"Yes," said Dar suddenly. "Back to the Nettings."

He felt Sharlin's back tense. Returning to the harbor city of northern Kalmar meant returning to a city where pallans were treated as slaves . . . and thrown to the waters of the sea in return for safe fishing from sea serpents, cold drakes, and other beasts. It meant returning to earlier memories when they had been accompanied by the wizard Thurgood and his dwarf valet Toothpick, now both dead.

Then Sharlin nodded abruptly. "You're right, Dar. I'll give her the picture."

After a moment, Turiana said, "I see." Her wings fanned out on the wind, as she swung about, and they headed in another direction.

"What good will it do us to go back there?"

Sharlin had twisted about, her mouth close to his ear, and even then had to practically shout to be heard. He did likewise.

"I'm not sure—but if Turiana can alleviate the pallan plight there, I think the Nettings has a large enough colony of them that we can get some help. Since the pallan history seems to be a key for all of this, it's worth a try."

Sharlin considered. Her lips were a thin blue line as she nodded briskly then. Dar wrapped her cloak and his arms about her as Turiana swept the skies.

She flew nonstop for two solid days, and when she gained the mountains outside of the Nettings, the golden dragon was a pale shadow of herself. She crawled into a cave and rested there, only her eyes still glowing with life. Dar raided a stray herd of woollies and brought her meat.

The next morning Sharlin awoke him gently. She shook her head. "She's still too exhausted to go down with us. All she wants to do now is nest."

"She has to be able to back us up." Dar hadn't forgotten that the last time he'd left the Nettings, he did so as a royal sacrifice to placate the dragongods.

"Maybe they won't even remember us."

He smiled grimly as he got to his feet. "Is there much chance of that?"

She smiled in return as she remembered the blasphemy Dar had shouted on the dock before sailing . . . and the desire of the crowd to send Dar out dead rather than alive. "Maybe not. But Duke Mylo is a good man, basically. I have an idea."

He frowned as she told him. "I don't like it. First of all, we have to go on foot. Secondly, sneaking into the duke's manor will be more difficult than it sounds. And thirdly, we should be able to count on Turiana as a backup."

Sharlin's eyes flashed gray. "I'm the one taking the risk, pretending to be the ghost of his dead sister, not you. And you rely too much on Turiana. Where's the swordsman I remember?"

He flinched.

Instantly, she knew she'd said too much. She paled. "Dar. I— I'm sorry."

He turned away, so as not to see her face any longer. "Forget it." He picked up his sword and belted it on. "I'm going to bring back another woollie for breakfast, if you can stand more mutton."

"I can. And besides, she needs it."

He nodded. "I'll think more on the plan. But we will need the dragon, sooner or later, to liberate the city. Even if all she does is make an appearance."

"I understand."

Dagger clenched in her right hand, Sharlin took the leg-up from Dar and scaled the clay brick wall silently, despite the veil of darkness that obscured her handholds.

"You should have been a thief, princess," he whispered, as he took her hand and joined her.

They sat atop the wall. Turiana had conjured up a long veil that shrouded Sharlin from head to toe. He could vaguely see her face through the thin fabric. It gave her an ethereal quality that sent a chill down his spine regardless of her familiarity to him. The haunting just might work.

The duke of the Nettings was a devout man. He believed in the dragons as gods with all his heart. When he lost his sister to the oceans and then most of his ocean harvest as well, it had become apparent the dragons no longer smiled on him. Of all beings, the pallans revered the dragons least, and so the population of the Nettings suffered, being scorned and humiliated for their lack of piety. After beating a certain amount of piety into the pallan servants, the Nettings still suffered. It was in desperation that the duke had sent a ship of sacrifices, human and beast, and goods, to the seas to appease the dragon gods.

It wasn't the duke's fault that the anger of the gods was actually a wounded dragon that had taken to the seas to travel south in search of Glymarach, the dragon's graveyard. Being injured and rapacious, it had killed and eaten whatever it might on the ocean waters, including the duke's sister, who had been boating at the time.

Dar knew that the duke had seen a great deal of his sister in Sharlin and that it was with a great deal of remorse that he'd sent Sharlin in search of the same watery grave to make the gods happy.

Her plan to return as his sister's ghost seemed as likely to work as anything Dar could think of.

He held his breath as a guard and a massive dog passed by below. The dog had not winded them. He counted off as they went by, then nudged Sharlin.

"Now. I'm right behind you."

She nodded, then shinnied down the wall and sprinted across the courtyard. He caught up as she had climbed halfway up the rain gutter, onto the second story. The shuttered windows fell open quickly to a twist of her knifeblade. The two of them wasted no time getting inside.

He refastened the shutter behind them. The inside of the manor house was pitch-dark, it being the dead of night. It smelled of clean rushes and fireplaces, still smoldering with evergreen wood. The duke lived a comfortable life.

He caught Sharlin quickly and drew her back into the corner with him as a clinking sound came near them. They held their breaths and watched as an ankle-chained pallan shuffled past and disappeared down the hall.

Sharlin muttered something vicious under her breath. He kept hold of her arm and waited for her to calm before stepping back into the corridor.

He pointed down the passageway after the pallan servant. "It carried a bedwarmer. That way, I think."

Sharlin considered, then nodded. Only the duke was likely to be important enough to rate a bedwarmer in the middle of the night.

Silently, they padded through the house. The chain-clinking pallan disappeared in a doorway, and they halted, until it reappeared and left the way it had come, seemingly unaware of them.

Sharlin had turned to squeeze through the door when Dar caught her arm.

"Wait a moment. Let him get a little drowsier."

They poised for a few moments longer, then slipped inside the room.

The duke, it seemed, slept in lush, secure quarters. A banked fire cast a low light. His canopied bed occupied the warmest corner of the room. Dar took out his sword and found an obscure corner to wait in while Sharlin walked to the foot of the bed and drew the curtains aside.

The lump under the bedcovers did not stir.

"Aaaaaawaaaake, my brother."

The coverlets twitched a little, rustling.

Sharlin took a breath. "Awaaaaaken, brother dear." The veils puffed about her as she spoke.

In the gray twilight of the room, she looked marvelously ghostly. So the duke must have thought also as he sat up and strangled to catch his breath.

She waited patiently.

"Have you forgotten me so soon?"

"N-n-no, Adele. By all the gods . . ." the duke lowered the edge of his coverlet from his face. He wiped a tear from the corner of his eye. "Have I offended you? Don't you rest?"

"No. Not as long as pallans suffer for my folly."

That brought a little color back to the man's graying face. He straightened. "Pallans are nothing but dirt under your footstep, Adele. Trouble yourself about them no further."

"Broooother . . ."

He brought the coverlet back up to his chin and clutched it there. "On the other hand, you have evidently returned to give me good advice."

"Yesss."

Dar thought her hiss a little too snakelike. The duke was not a stupid man—and how long would it be before sentries passed this way?

The duke lowered his bedcovers to his waist. "Adele, think well of me. What do you want me to do?"

"Free the pallans and both the dragongods and I will remember you kindly."

The duke leaned forward suddenly and grabbed her wrists, pulling Sharlin onto the bed. Before Dar could spring to her aid, he'd torn the veil from her body and collapsed, lying back with no less a frightened look on his face.

"You!"

And as Dar stepped from the shadows, blade in hand, the duke's glance flickered to his face. "And you as well. Two ghosts substituted for another."

Sharlin rolled and got to her feet. "No ghost, duke, but flesh and blood. But the offer of dragon favor still goes—if you free the pallans."

The duke swung his feet to the edge and balanced there, holding onto a bed curtain. His face twisted. "Ah, yes, Dragons have returned to Rangard in force— but have any of them graced the Nettings, most faithful of all Rangard's cities? No, but you know the answer already. None! And all because of the miserable, blasphemous pallans. If you want them freed, take them with you— to hell!"

A stiletto winked in his hand. Dar leaped forward, cut neatly, and the duke dropped his weapon with a cry and clutched his nicked wrist.

Sharlin stepped back, her eyes wide. She swallowed. "Duke, listen to me. You only grind yourself further into the dirt. Let the pallans go. They will stay here, this is their home . . . and all of you will prosper. I have a golden dragon who will come and tell you so."

The man held his face in his hands. He looked up briefly. "Is this true?"

"As true as anything I hope to say. Assemble the town in the morning, proclaim your edict, and a golden dragon will come to favor you. Of course, you must be prepared to receive her. She especially likes gunter."

Dar looked at Sharlin. "Will she come?"

"For gunter," and the girl smiled mischievously, "Turiana will fly anywhere."

"And what is in this for you?"

"We wish the favor of the pallans."

The duke tried to grasp this and failed. Why would one who had the gods on his side want the aid of the lowly pallans? His face showed his bewilderment.

"We want to read the pallan histories," Sharlin explained further.

"Ah." The duke nodded. "The pallans have always been merciless in their histories. Nothing escapes their pen. Let us hope you find what you need."

Turiana found the dawn, the city, and the fatted gunter to her liking. As she landed, still stiff and awkward from her journey to upper Kalmar, she looked about. "Not a bad place for nesting," she commented, as she vigorously slaughtered the gunter and gulped it down.

Dar watched uneasily. He looked down the sleek flanks of the golden beast and found bulges where there should be none. He shifted as the crowd of the Nettings, human and pallan alike, jostled forward to see their dragon patron. Uneasily, he remembered the mating/death flight of Turiana and Nightwing. Could there be a maternal instinct behind Turiana's nesting comments?

He did not like the dark shadow he saw nudging her golden flanks.

Chapter 4

Duke Mylo had a huge canopied festival pavilion set up at the outskirts of town for Turiana's behest. The pallans came and went in a solemn line, their robed arms filled with the scrolls and tomes of the histories they had kept, and they sat at the feet of the dragon, reading solemnly to her until their voices grew faint and another came to take their place. The townspeople also came to watch when their jobs were done. They brought blankets and baskets and jugs, and even their children, and lay about on the grass knolls, talking quietly and listening to the murmur between dragon and pallan. It was an unheard-of event, to picnic with a god, and not one of the inhabitants of the Nettings wanted to miss it.

The duke gave over an entire wing of the manor to Sharlin and Dar. Dar was too uneasy to stay there. As he overlooked the canopied tent and the meadow of picnickers, a bad feeling gnawed at him. Turiana, already a target, now became an event. News wouldn't take long to reach the dragonhunters and possibly even Valorek. He might as well paint a target on her and say "Come and get it." He regretted their course of action, but now that they were embroiled in it, there was little he could do.

So he stood on watch, ignoring the occasional child

that toddled up and hung on his boot tops until he nudged it about in another direction. He stood and watched and flinched whenever a dark shadowy cloud graced the fall sky, and battled his own cowardice with a sense of duty.

Sharlin watched him from a narrow slit window from the manor wing. The duke had had the tent pitched just so that it could be observed from this wing. She had not left in the three days ensuing.

She dropped her hand from the windowsill and wiped it on a handkerchief. The window was dirty, as much of the manor was. A whole wing had been boarded up. Without his sister to run his household, the duke was at a loss how to maintain it. Running the Nettings had been his job. The spare man had mentioned more than once that what he needed was a wife to help him, and Sharlin had ducked her head and walked away refusing to heed what he hinted.

She returned to the massive desk in their sleeping chambers. The great piece of furniture looked like some squat beast on tiny legs. Sunlight and candlelight glowed in its highly polished surface. Tiny etchings from quill scratches bit across the pattern, irregular lightnings in the wood. She ran her fingers over it. It reminded her of her father's desk.

She knew that Dar slept poorly at night. It ached at her now that she was ill-using him. Should she have let him go, after the resurrection? Their quest together had been finished. She told herself it was not duty but love that kept them together. Yet if she had loved him enough to bring him, shouldn't she have loved him enough to let him go?

Robe hems whispered on the rushes. Sharlin looked up swiftly, startled, but she sat back in the chair. A pallan stood framed in the hallway. This one was dressed in seafoam green and gave not a hint of its age or sex, though she sensed perhaps it might be female. Even having lived among them briefly, Sharlin knew little of the mysterious people.

"May I come in, princess?" the being said lowly.

"Yes. Yes, please." With the toe of her boot, she edged a side chair toward the pallan, though she doubted if it would seat itself.

The pallan entwined fingers and stood at the far side of the desk. She'd had a parade of them in the last three days—some of them still hoarse from reading to Turiana. It seemed that every last pallan in the Nettings was going to come and thank her for freeing them. Sharlin waited for this one to speak further. The gratitude left her with a hollow feeling, but she steeled herself for one more thank-you, while wondering if she'd really done the pallans any good. When it came time for Turiana to leave, what would happen to them then?

"When I spoke with the golden queen yesterday," the pallan began softly, "she told me of your lineage. Our histories, alas, do not cover the reign of your people. She has asked me to tell you this. I searched the libraries further before coming, in case I was mistaken. My apologies, Princess Sharlin."

The sibilant s-sounds faded away. Sharlin was a little surprised at the speech, then considered that this was a pallan she might have seen yesterday. She smiled. "Then it's my turn to thank you, for looking. I saw the temple at Glymarach, and read most of what was etched there. It's not necessary to read it again." And she doubted if she could stand to. She knew already her mission had failed, and Rodeka had conquered her father's lands. But she hadn't read the end of the story, and perhaps, just perhaps . . .

The pallan spread its gloved hands. "You are most gracious, savior-of-pallans. You have amply repaid your debt to my people."

The girl looked up, and locked eyes with that unreadable gauze facing. How had they known . . . "How did you—"

But the pallan cut her off with a brusque movement of the hand, a brutal gesture to the graceful and sinuous pallans. "There are questions that can never be answered."

"Perhaps. But then I will ask another, and hope for an answer. Did you know me . . . did your people know who I was and what had happened when they took me in? Did they know what would happen to me?"

A long silence fell in the chamber. Sharlin was aware of the sound of her breathing, but not that of the pallan. Then it stirred. "I have no real answers for you, but you carry your destiny with you, like an aura. Be it known to you that we pallans are not like you, and we can sometimes see what you cannot. And because we study history so diligently, because of our familiarity with the past, it's not always difficult to predict the future. We saw the griffin fall with rider, and the funeral pyre fit for a god, before we watched and gathered you in. We knew of your ancient lineage, though how it could be so, we did not know."

Sharlin gripped the edge of the desk as the pallan talked of Gabriel. It spoke as if by rote, and she wondered for a moment if it heard its fellows in its mind, as she sometimes heard Turiana. How else could it know the intimate details of her servitude in lower Kalmar, when it had never left the Nettings? The voice of the pallan faltered to a halt as it ended, "And so you were guided to the inn, where travelers from many roads cross paths, and it was hoped you would find your way."

And she had. Sharlin stood. Her voice caught in her throat, and she cleared it huskily. "For that aid, I can never repay you and your people."

The pallan inclined its head. "Then you remain in our debt, as we remain in yours. This is perhaps better, a bonding, which will last beyond mere words." It hesitated. "And now I must say to you, princess, that which you will not like to hear."

She had not braced herself for what followed, and she sank back onto the chair as it said, "You must let the swordsman Aarondar go. Your love is an unfortunate happening, as it ties the two of you together, and we have seen that it cannot be. As I have told you, you carry your destiny, just as we see that he carries his. He must be set free to follow it."

With words that sliced into her heart like a knife, the being left, and was gone before even the murmur of its voice had finished. Sharlin clutched the arms of the chair with hands gone icy-cold.

She bolted out of the chair and to the doorframe. The hall was already empty.

"Wait! Pallan! What do you mean?" She never thought to hear an answer, but it whispered down the hall, quiet and deadly upon the air, like a snake rustling across the flooring.

"Your destiny is the past, and his is the future—the future of all Rangard." And then the pallan was gone, truly gone this time.

Sharlin balled her hands into fists. A broken nail bit into her palm, but it drew no blood. It was as though all blood had left her flesh.

The pallan had told her fortune, as surely as if she'd asked it to. She would find a way back . . . a way back, and perish there, with the rest of the house of Dhamon. And she must not take Dar with her!

She found herself at the window and looked out of it, unseeing, until dusk began to gather its folds about the town, shutting out the sun.

Dar stirred. Birds shot overhead, winging their way back to their nighttime sanctuary. He felt the chill tang of the sea wind. Turiana gave a slight cough in the pavilion, and he heard an overlarge ledger being closed with a solid thump of no doubt dusty pages. Parents with toddlers had already left the field. The only on-lookers remaining were those without a care for the lateness or a worry to making a meal. In moments they would be gone, too, as the street lanterns were lit and the taverns opened for business.

The pallans came out of the tent. In their somber, jewel-toned veils and hoods, robes and tunics, they left, wind-whisper quiet. A lantern-lighter hobbled into the meadow to light the corner posts at the street's end.

It was a moment that made Dar relax, and so he never saw the shadow until it was too late.

He felt the glide of air and looked up, and thought he saw a portion of the deepening sky blot out, and then the scent came, the musky stink that had grown familiar over the last weeks. But he wasn't sure it was a dragon until the great lamplike eyes opened and skewered him to the spot.

Their liquid light melted over him. His heart thud-ded and skidded to a halt. He fought to swallow the lump in his throat, his hand frozen to the guard of his sword.

The lantern-lighter next to him froze also, bumping into him, letting fall the long-handled pikelike instru-ment with hook and torch fastened to the end, used to open the lanterns and then fire them. The jostling movement jarred Dar from the dragon's gaze, and he lurched forward, grabbing the lantern-lighter's pole.

Its metal coldness woke his hands to life.

"Turiana!" he screamed, and charged at the dragon as it hovered over the pavilion.

The golden dragon erupted from the canvas with a roar, her claws open and her jaws wide. Her own amber eyes lit the deepening sky with golden light, illuminating the bulk of the dragon rampant before her.

Dar ran and drew his arm back, preparing to harpoon

the beast before it could slice open her throat, when the golden dragon trilled, "Pandor!"

It was a cry of welcome. The swordsman dug the end of the pike into the ground and slewed to a halt before he speared the beast by accident, as the tent collapsed in shreds about the golden dragon, and the two bulks settled to the ground, and the night thrummed with dragon-talk.

Dar had barely recovered his breath when a slight form barreled into him, and he caught up Sharlin.

She gasped and held on to him tightly without words. He felt her pulse racing as she held him close. It was the first time in three days she'd come out of the manor, or really touched him, though they shared a bed at night. He took her into his arms now.

"I thought—I thought you'd never see it. I screamed all the way from the garden walls, but nothing carried. Not a sound. It came in so quietly, Dar."

He felt a tremor run through her. He looked at the two beasts, claw to claw, nostrils pressed close as they murmured. "I know," he said, and felt the cold shock of fear leaving his heart. "Next time . . ."

The great beast named Pandor lifted his head. "There'll not be a next time," he rumbled in quiet amusement. "I have come to guard the queen."

"Although," Turiana added, "I think you should see about getting a new tent."

In the morning, though, Turiana waited in the rags of the pavilion, with the bulk of Pandor curled nearby. A group of pallans waited, and Sharlin saw by the lines of their bodies that they were unhappy. She hurried her step, shaking loose the shell comb from her hair as she did, and it dropped to the ground. Dar paused to pick it up. He pressed it into her fingers as he caught up, and she smiled a moment at him, remembering the night.

Then she remembered the pallan's warning and looked away quickly, before he could read her fear in her eyes.

"What is it?"

"There will be no more pavilion," Turiana said coldly.

The pallans shifted, and one in dark blue came forward, arms full of scrolls. "She does not want to be read to, this morning."

Dar stayed back a pace. He looked at the golden creature. In the early-morning light, she looked healthy, even robust. But the dark patterning along her flanks had deepened into a mottling, and he worried a moment. He lost the last of what the pallan said, but Sharlin nodded.

"It's all right. You've not offended Turiana. I think perhaps she has learned what she was seeking."

The golden dragon snorted. "I can speak for myself. Your histories have been magnificent, though boring, to the last detail. I have indeed learned what I came to learn. Go in honor."

The pallans bowed and faded away down the street, hurrying as though expecting to be speared in the back.

Sharlin walked to the beast and reached up, to tickle her under her chin. "What is it this morning? Why are you so snappish? Should Dar go for some fresh gunter?"

He smarted a little, feeling like an errand boy with an overgrown weapon, but he said nothing, and looked intensely at his falroth boots with the goblin-blood stain. The sweet grass of the meadow had been trampled greatly over the last few days.

Turiana rumbled, then lowered her head. "I'm sorry, fair daughter. Snappish is a good word for it. Pandor has brought me news, and that, coupled with what I've read, has told me sad stories about the world since I left it. Dragons have faded. Indeed, had you not awakened the graveyard from slumbering, there might be only two or three left. It was our greed and dislike of each other that brought us to our knees, and it appears that history is rapidly repeating itself."

Pandor blew a warm questioning sound in their direction, and Turiana looked over her flank. "Yes, dear, I know who is probably behind it."

"Valorek," Dar said lowly.

The dragon's ears twitched, and she shook her head, rattling her crown of spines. "No. It is a beast of old, like myself, called Baalan."

"But Baalan is the god of evil!"

"No, Sharlin," the dragon corrected. "A dragon of great evil and power, yes, but no god. No more than I was, or am. But such is the stamp he left on the world."

"Never heard of him," Dar said truthfully.

Amber eyes poured into his, and he felt his face grow flushed. "It's true," he admitted. "I'd never heard of you, either."

Turiana's muzzle twitched. "Nonetheless, this changes my plans. Rest well the day. We fly tomorrow."

Pandor rumbled in disagreement. He reared up on his haunches, his wings arched over him. The golden queen gave him a look, and he quieted.

"You will stay," she said. "If Baalan is gathering forces and hunting us, we must seek one another out and help one another. You will stay, and gather those you can. Baalan is murdering those who fight alone."

"And you?" Sharlin asked. Her voice quavered oddly in the middle of the sentence. The shell comb dropped to the ground unnoticed.

"I will take you to Glymarach. There you must read the history of Rodeka and the house of Dhamon. You will learn, perhaps, if we appeared to alter it . . . or if not. If there is no mention of me, we know before we've begun that time is beyond my ruling, and I will turn my mind to the challenges here and now. If there is . . ." The dragon shrugged. "Then we will have succeeded, in one portion, at least. But time grows pre-

cious. My lifedebt to you must be honored, for I have
other things to do."

"Turiana," Pandor said, "it is too close to go to
Glymarach."

"No."

"You can't do this—"

The golden dragon reared up on her hind legs. Her
sinewy neck twisted as her head turned back toward
the bronze, and she spat, like an angry cat.

The bronze returned it in kind, and the air filled with
their hissing. Dar reached out, grabbed Sharlin from
their midst, and pulled her back against him. So quickly,
shockingly, the creatures turned to violence.

It was over in a second. The bronze drew back and
hunkered down, beaten. He closed his lids over the
lamp of his burning eyes, and gave her obeisance.
Turiana stopped hissing after a moment and appeared
mollified.

Sharlin raised a hand, then dropped it. She felt beaten,
too. She shrugged out of Dar's hands to return to the
manor. Only today. Sometime today, she must find a
way to say goodbye.

She thought she had the perfect out—Dar's getting
so airsick the moment he got on dragonback. She waited
until astride the dragon's neck, then turned to him.

His face, so strong, with wind-burned cheeks, had
grown pale.

"Stay here, Dar," Sharlin said. Her voice sounded
too light, even brittle, in the morning breeze. "Stay
with Pandor. We'll be gone a few days, and he might
need you."

The swordsman hesitated. He'd secured his sword
sheath to his back, and his cloak was wound tight around
him, even as he'd seated her, and tucked her covering
about her tightly against the chill of riding dragonback.

Turiana arched her neck and peered back at them. "What's this?"

"Don't you think Dar should stay?" If ever she wanted Turiana to read her thoughts, Sharlin wished it now. Dar should stay, and the two of them would begin the time quest alone from the temple at Glymarach.

The liquid heat of Turiana's eyes drew her in. Sharlin felt hot and dizzy a moment, then the dragon released her.

"No," said Turiana simply. "I think he should go with us."

Her heart sank as Dar climbed on wordlessly and gripped her tightly. Turiana chuckled meanly.

"I will drop off the cliffs over the harbor," the beast said. "Pray for a good takeoff."

Sharlin pinched the delicate fold behind her legs for spite, and the dragon gave a little squeal. As if in answer, the takeoff was so dramatic that even Sharlin's normally calm stomach pitched a little.

The third day found them winging over the southern-most tip of Kalmar and approaching the island called Glymarach, the cradle. Turiana had paced herself, stop-ping and feeding often, and resting well at night, and even though Dar cared little for flying, he was im-pressed. Even by ship off the coast with the wind at their back, the trip would have stretched into weeks.

He looked down at the jewel-bright ocean. Glymarach loomed under them. No magical fogs hid the bulk of the island from the skies.

He spoke to the dragon, his jaw close to Sharlin's ear. "But why back to Glymarach? Why leave in the first place if the answer was here?"

Turiana rumbled back, the wind thinning her words. "Because we were surrounded by dragonkind. We were both newly resurrected. I could not have protected you, nor you me, if our enemies turned on us then.

Now, most of the dragons will have left the Pits, for
that is a graveyard, and a birthyard, and we have no
business there. And the island is far more barren than it
used to be. In my day, pallans lived well in Lyrith, and
the plains were covered with herd beasts for our feast-
ing. Now it is dust."

She wheeled over the massive plain at the island's
interior, ignoring the mountain range beyond it which
bowled into the region known as the Pit. Dar felt the
gradual spiraling downward which brought the ruins of
the city Lyrith into perspective.

Turiana searched the area keenly, her head weaving
back and forth on her serpentine neck. "There is something . . ." she muttered.

"What's wrong?"

"The island has always been guarded, but not against
dragonfolk. Yet I feel a webbing in the air."

Dar felt nothing but a vague uneasiness.

The dragon swooped down, and the sudden inrush of
air snatched his cloak from about him and lashed it into
the wind. He caught view of their shadow on the ground
below. The airborne cloak gave him a sense of wings for
a disorienting moment, then it was gone, as Turiana
thudded into the dirt and slid to a stop.

"Not your smoothest landing," Sharlin said, as she
swung her booted leg over and jumped to the ground.
She wore a pair of doeskin trousers and a full-sleeved
blouse under an embroidered vest, in addition to the
heavy cloak Dar had gifted her with.

The dragon crouched, taking several long breaths.
Sharlin realized that something was wrong and stayed
by the beast's neck, stroking her lightly.

When at last Turiana raised her head, Dar had already unlashed the harnessing from about her shoulders, removed the pack, and wiped her down with a
light cloth. The dragon nosed Sharlin softly.

"Magic," she said. "Lyrith was guarded."

"Warded?"

"Yes." She stretched herself now, faltered on a trembling leg, and righted herself. "We must do what we came to do, and quickly."

Dar looked at the ruins. The dragon queen had taken them to the far side of the city. It took him a moment to orient himself, then he grabbed Sharlin's hand. "This way."

What must have been a winter's rain had washed some of the dust away. The bluestone shone even bluer, and the whites and pinks were blinding in the sun. Here was a city that had never known frost. As he helped Sharlin over the crumbling blocks and into the deserted streets, the hair rose on the back of his neck.

They had lost Toothpick here, the crusty old dwarf valet of the wizard Thurgood. Did his soul wander the streets along with the thousands of pallans who had mysteriously died away? He felt that pricking of his senses, his soldier's senses, that told him he trod on dangerous ground.

He dropped Sharlin's handclasp and loosened his sword.

"What is it?"

"Nothing," he answered, his eyes busily searching out all the empty doorways and windows. "Nothing and everything."

Turiana's voice carried to them. "Hurry, children!"

Sharlin spotted the round-domed building in the purple shadows of the ruins. "There!"

Bunkers of lyrith plant hugged the back of the building, and a crack in the massive wall had sloughed away an opening. Sharlin hesitated. She looked at Dar. Her eyes were shadowed gray, and he read the pain in them.

"Go on," he said. "I'm with you this time."

She squeezed through the crack, and he followed after, his leathers creaking.

Light filtered down from above, where the stone was so delicate as to allow the sunlight through it. Gold veins glittered as he looked overhead. The temple explained much . . . the pallans' passion for history was a religion. The circular walls were etched with small, painstaking letters and runes, the entire building a book.

They had only to look for the shattered remains of a clay lamp, which Sharlin had dropped in shock the first time she read the terrible fate of her family.

Sharlin went to her knees. Her dark-honey-colored hair had loosened from its knot at the nape of her neck and lay about her shoulders. Dar put his hand out and lifted the wave of hair from its tangle in her hooded cloak. He smelled the fragrance of the herbed shampoo she used, and a feeling of love and contentment surged through him. The past weeks he had felt nearly useless, like an extra left foot or something, but now he knew why he was still at her side. There was nowhere else he could be, not as long as she needed him, and she still loved him.

She felt the warmth of his hand remaining on the back of her neck, and reached back her own hand to cover it. Her vision cleared a little, and she raised her eyes to look at the panel of the wall, searching for the history of her people. She whispered, "And the witch queen Rodeka devoured the village of the countryside in her quest for power until she faced the house of Dhamon itself, and it was powerless to stand before her." The catch in her throat paused her. "King Balforth and his queen Lauren, and their only son Erban, gave themselves over to Rodeka's demands, believing her to have captured their daughter, Sharlin. They found it to be a base lie, but the kingdom had fallen." She tightened her hand about Dar's. "Oh, Dar! They surrendered because I left."

"You may have saved their lives," Dar said, leaning

down. He felt desperation coursing through her hand. "Hold on to me. You have to finish reading!"

She stumbled to her feet then, leaning heavily on him. A boom rocked the building, and she would have fallen but for his grip on her. They both staggered back to the wall.

"What was that?"

Dust rained down on them from the ceiling, and as he looked up, he saw a dark bulk blocking the sky.

"Turiana," he answered, then, as another blast cracked the very stone overhead, he added, "Or another dragon!" The stone crumbled. He swept her up and ran for the arched doorway, as the wall caved in.

As he ran through the darkened passageway to the front of the temple, the noise of the raging battle swept about them. The hissing of enraged dragons, and squeals and trumpets of anger.

"Put me down! I can run!" Sharlin ordered, and he dropped her to her feet lightly, but kept her hand in his and pulled her after him. A great crash behind him told him that the domed portion of the temple had collapsed. The histories of centuries now lay in dusty shards, unreadable.

Columns toppled as they ran past. He spotted the fountain, and beds of lyrith, and knew they were almost on the street. He slowed. The last thing he wished to do was bolt into the open if dragons fought overhead. Black shadows streaked across the open street. He saw two bulks entwined and knew that Turiana fought for her life. Fear quickened his pulse.

Sharlin reached for Dar's sword. "We've got to help!"

"But not from here. Follow me." The swordsman ducked away from the sagging temple and into the alleyway, where the bulk of a two-story building shielded him from the open sky. He looked up as the two beasts broke away, and Turiana pumped her massive wings, aiming for the open sky.

The second dragon was immense, nearly a third greater than Turiana in size, its scales a riot of mauve deepening into a royal purple. He recoiled from the smell of its breath, and from the palpable wave of malevolence that emanated from it.

Sharlin breathed, then said, "Baalan himself."

And high on his neck, the unmistakable form of a rider, a man who twisted about to look to the streets below. The dragonrider in black leathers had a visage he knew well: the witch king Valorek!

Chapter 5

Dar clutched the sword hilt. For a crossbow! Or even a stinger, so that he could try for Valorek from this distance!

Turiana gained the height she needed. With talons outstretched, she plunged downward at the purple dragon and his rider. Sharlin held Dar's arm.

Baalan balked and sculled in midair, as Valorek strained on the harness reins, pulling the drake's neck about with him.

"What are they doing?"

A grim smile creased Dar's face. "Baalan wants to go after Turiana—and Valorek wants to go after us. They're fighting each other, and that leaves them wide open for Turiana!"

Like a golden bolt, she dropped on them and raked across Baalan's back. His answering squeal of pain and anger rattled the stones in the city below. The dragon shook, rocking Valorek on his withers. They dropped after Turiana, who suddenly seemed unable to halt her plunge. She spread her wings desperately and came gliding in over the rooftops.

Dar ducked and pulled Sharlin with him to the side. Baalan came after her viciously. He trumpeted in his eagerness to pull her down in her weakness.

"Stay here!"

"What—"

Dar ran clear of the buildings and stood, his arm cocked back with the sword as though it were a throwing knife. As Baalan swooped low after Turiana, his vast purple bulk shadowed Dar. He swallowed a moment, fighting old fears, then looked up. The stomach paled above him. He tensed and threw, his sword whipping through the air.

It thudded deep into Baalan's underbelly. The beast screamed, and then disappeared! A thunderous crack followed, and what was left of the pallan temple crashed down. Dar's sword fell from midair and clattered to the stonework below.

Then all was silent.

Sharlin straightened from her crouch on the ground. "Dar—"

"I've killed it," he said, though he wasn't sure what had happened. Beast and rider were gone, into thin air, leaving only thunder behind them. He retrieved his sword. Ichor stained the blade, and he cleaned it on a tattered flag hanging from an empty merchant's stall. The fluid ate away what was left of the rotting material. He sheathed it and returned to help Sharlin.

Turiana waddled up the narrow street, her flanks heaving. She craned her neck, breathing like a blacksmith's bellows. "Well done, fair son. Baalan won't be back for a while, though the toadsticker you used isn't likely to have done much permanent damage."

Sharlin took a deep breath. She pivoted on her boot heel to survey the damage. "There'll be no more answers from here," she said. Beside her, she was aware that Dar surveyed the great dragon critically.

"Did you find what we needed to know?"

The girl shook her head sadly. "No."

Turiana hunkered down in the street. "Then we have no choice. My rule here over Rangard must take precedent."

Dar straightened. "There is still a way, possibly."

Sharlin turned back to face the dragon, and crumpled into the dust, to sit cross-legged, her face pale, emotionally defeated. But the dragon queen looked to the swordsman. "Of what do you speak?"

He answered to Sharlin, coaxing hope from her, "The lyrith remains. Remember when Thurgood told you how potent it is. Coupled with Turiana's sorcery, you might be able to reach out, somehow."

Turiana's inner lids closed shrewdly. The beast said nothing.

But Sharlin grasped at the idea. "The pallan said I carried my destiny with me, like an aura. Turiana—surely you could read that for me!"

"If you had the power," Dar prodded.

The dragon said nothing, but Sharlin protested, "Of course she's got the power. She's the most sorcerous dragon in Rangard's history!"

Dar looked at his booted feet, all but hidden in the dust of Lyrith's dead streets.

"I was dead a long time," Turiana finally said. "I have not yet remembered all that I knew . . . and I may never be able to. Still, with the smoke of the lyrith . . ."

"I'll get it," Dar said. He left the two and went to strip the planter boxes about the temple of the yellow-flowered plant. Stone and dust bit at his hands as he rummaged through the ruins.

Though Turiana had denied her pregnancy, he had gotten as clear a look at her underbelly as he had Baalan's. If birthing was a dragon's death, then she approached her own. He would do whatever he had to, to ensure that Sharlin had a chance to fulfill her dream before Turiana's fate caught up with her.

He used his cloak like an apron to carry the herb back to the dragon and his love. He said nothing that revealed his suspicions as he filled Sharlin's lap with the precious herb.

She smiled and ran her fingers through it. "A king's ransom and more," she said. She piled the herb in the dust between her and Turiana.

"Crush the buds between your fingers. When they begin to smoke, lean forward to breathe. Inhale deeply and hold the smoke as long as you can." Before Dar could pull out his flint and iron, Turiana had gusted a tiny flame forth. The buds smoldered a little, then caught.

He blinked at the pungent aroma of the burning lyrith. It was sweeter than incense. Sharlin tucked her hair behind her ears with slender fingers, then leaned forward and inhaled deeply, as did the dragon.

Turiana looked up at him. "Stand guard over us, Aarondar. Some dreams are more deadly than others."

"Deadly?"

"Yes," the dragon said sleepily, unresponsive to the alarm Dar felt coursing through him. "The phantasms of the past are sometimes reluctant to let go."

He stepped forward. Sharlin slumped against his leg. Before he could catch her, she curled gently to the ground, her face curved in a pale smile. "Sharlin!"

"Dar," she murmured. Then, "Home. . . ."

She knew she dreamed. But at the same time, there was a joyous surge inside of her that let go, and she found herself soaring through the skies, with a warm golden bulk beside her.

For a moment she felt terribly afraid, then realized that she rode the seasoned war griffin Gabriel once again. The more concrete her thought was, the stronger the image of the beast. His feathered head turned toward her.

"Gabriel!"

The griffin's beak clacked and he responded, "I remember now."

Sharlin saddened. Even the beast's prescience had

not saved him from death. The wingbeats faltered. "I burned the lyrith for you," she called out, even as the griffin became transparent, and scattered out from under her like a cloud in the wind.

She fell. The golden bulk fell with her, warmed her as the sun warmed her. She tumbled head over heels. The being said, "Spread your wings."

"I haven't got any!"

"Nonsense. We all have wings. You just couldn't sense yours before," the dragon scolded.

Curiously unafraid even as the wind whistled past her face, Sharlin reached out her arms. The scent of burning lyrith wafted up and bore her away. She heard a familiar voice and returned his name from her lips, "Dar," before she looked down on the greener-than-green ridges and valleys of her kingdom. "Home," she cried, and they wheeled downward.

Dar walked on uneasy sentry about the two dreamers. Purple shadows lengthened across the ruined city, and he told himself that Baalan was too badly wounded to come back to Lyrith. He paced until his heels felt bruised. He waited until he had no choice but to relieve himself and then returned, and still no sign that the dreamers would awaken. The lyrith burned down to glowing coals, but never extinguished. Its scent grew more delicate. He bent over Sharlin once, to remove a stray lock of hair from her cheek, the tips of his fingers brushing her skin. It burned.

He thought then of water. He went to the temple rubble and clawed his way through broken stone and pillar until he found the fountain. It still bubbled upward, clean and cool from its unknown source. He had cupped some in his hands to take back to Sharlin when he noticed something bent over her as well.

The water splashed heedlessly to the dust as he reached to his back and unsheathed his sword.

The man-shadow stood, and turned to him. Dar paused. The swordblade caught a glint of the late sun and rayed it through the shadow, but the man did not even flinch, though the beam pierced him. In his features, dim though they were, Dar saw Sharlin.

He searched for, found, and grasped a name. "King Balforth?"

The being watched him steadily. Then the man answered, "I will know you when I meet you." It turned, and caressed the cheek of the girl lying in the dust, and then disappeared.

A cold chill passed over him. Dar flexed his hand about the grip of his sword. Had he seen and heard what he thought he had? And what of Turiana and Sharlin? They were supposed to be the dreamers, not he. What if the lyrith had taken him as well, and they all lay defenseless in the ruins, dreaming?

He shuddered and grabbed the swordblade with his free hand. It sliced him instantly, almost before he knew it would. With a curse, he dropped the weapon and cupped his left hand. Blood welled from the palm.

It took a few moments to wrestle off his leather top and tear a strip off his linen undertunic and wrap the palm. He cursed a few more times, knowing he was lucky not to have sliced his hand clean open, across vital muscles and nerves. He flexed it and watched new blood stain the dressing. At least, he told himself, he was pretty sure he wasn't dreaming. He shrugged back into his leather armor and picked up his sword. He sat down in the dirt and waited.

She drew down to the land of her birth and swept across it, the fresh wind in her hair. It lashed across her face, and she knew when she got home her mother would scold her for ill-using her complexion and getting chapped. But she delighted in the flying.

The sun rode her shoulder, flying with her. The

dragon said, "I can see why you love this land. I had
forgotten its beauty."

"I want to bring Dar here someday," Sharlin answered. Then she frowned. "But the pallan said—"

"What pallan?"

"One of the pallans who read to you. She said that I
should let him go."

"Ahhh." Turiana extended a wingtip, and the leathern sail stretched out under her. "Just remember that a
man is not like a weapon, to be picked up and used
when wanted, and dropped when not. Dar will find his
destiny, never fear. If he chooses to find it with you,
and you choose the same, then perhaps that *is* his
destiny."

"But the pallan warned me . . ."

The wind buffeted her, as though going over a bump.
It took away her breath. She had forgotten what they
were arguing about when she sighted the rock fortress
of her home, hugged close by stables and the eyrie.

The wing disappeared under her, and her feet hit
home with a hard thud that brought her to her knees
and tumbled her over and over across the rocky ground.
But she scarcely felt it, as though she—and not the
vision of her home—were the one who was not real.
Turiana sculled to a stop more gracefully and said, "My
dear, the first thing you must learn about landing is to
slow down first."

Sharlin stood up. She felt as if she were in two bodies
. . . now, and yesterday, when she lived in the high
country, still a girl, not quite a woman. It unsettled
her, and she realized she had been thinking in simple
ways she'd forgotten long ago. Such as Dar . . . nothing
about her relationship with Dar could possibly be as
easy as picking up or letting go.

The crisp air of the plateau stabbed at her. It carried
the scents and smells she'd forgotten, and when she'd
lived there, not noticed. A tiny mouse scurried from

the wispy dried grasses bordering the stone eyrie, and the griffins inside instantly responded. Keen hunters, she thought. Yet they did not seem to hear her.

"Sharlin," Turiana said. "We haven't much longer."

"I just got here."

"I know, daughter. But we were a long time making this journey."

"It's a dream!"

"Yes."

The griffins fussed inside the eyrie again, and she thought of Gabriel. She moved to the barred wooden door and opened it, slipping inside, the last of the sunlight raying in, spilling the gold of the dragon's image across the straw-covered dirt.

The griffins sat on their perches, hooded and jessed, all except for the magnificent old veteran in the corner. He looked up, turquoise and the gold of Turiana's coin, and his flint-dark eyes blinked.

Then he bowed his head. "Great Turiana," Gabriel said. "Sharlin will find you, then. I have remembered properly."

The dragon's head was wedged in the doorway. But her amber eyes glowed warmly, and she nodded her head in respect. "Little wind brother, so you must have. Come, Sharlin."

She put out a hand and scratched Gabriel's feathered chest, then rested her palm a moment on his leonine haunch. "Goodbye," she whispered, and the griffin reached back to nip her affectionately.

Closing the door to the eyrie was difficult. Her flesh kept losing substance and slipping through the wood, but she kept at it until the bar slipped back into place.

A pink sunset began to close at the mountains' edge.

"Come, Sharlin."

"Just a minute. I want to see . . . I want to see inside."

"No."

"Just a minute more." Sharlin twisted away as Turiana grabbed for her, the hooked tip of her talon ripping through the cuff of her blouse, as she raced past.

"No!" the dragon roared, but the sound became nothing more than the wind at her back as she threw herself on the massive front door and pulled it open.

She knew the instant it opened that she had made a fatal mistake. The great hall lay wide open, gutted, sacked . . . furniture scattered, tapestries destroyed, and in the center, a diagram was painted on the stone flooring. In the center of the diagram a brazier sat, and lyrith burned in its flames. A tall woman stood on the far side, stirring the burning flowers.

She was pale, so pale that the veins stood out like blue tracing on her skin. Her black hair was bound back by a thong interwoven with copper coins and blue stones. The kohl on her eyelids made her smoky green eyes large and luminous. Her mouth was too wide, giving her a generous smile, but she allowed cruelty to twist it.

Sharlin halted, bitterly afraid.

The woman lifted her hands. "Welcome, spirit, whoever you are. Come closer so that I may see you better."

If she could see the woman, why couldn't the woman see her? Sharlin looked at the flooring and saw that she threw no shadow. She was the ghost summoned by the woman.

The woman's face grew angry. "I called you here, I, Rodeka. Answer me!"

Sharlin felt the warmth of Turiana nuzzling her back.

"She cannot see you, daughter."

"She senses me."

"No more. Leave now. We have our answers."

The sorceress moved to the side of the brazier. She uplifted something in her hand, a vial that had dangled from her girdle. She poured it over the lyrith. "By the blood of the Dhamons, show yourself, spirit. Show me what lies between me and my conquest!"

Sharlin staggered forward as though shoved in the back. She dug her boot heels into the flooring and grabbed behind her, digging her nails into the wood of the frame. Whose blood? Which of her family had died for the blood Rodeka used? But she wanted the answers to Rodeka's question nearly as badly as the sorceress did, and so she stayed, her throat taut.

A cloud of foul-smelling smoke welled up from the brazier. Rodeka laughed throatily. "We shall soon see you, spirit, and whoever else blocks my path!"

Tendrils reached out, entwined, swelled, and formed . . . two dragons locked in mortal combat. The coloring came, gold and purple. Turiana and Baalan. Rodeka sucked in her breath. "I know you, Turiana," she murmured. "Well I know you! The other, no . . . and it may be I will not have you to worry about." She held the crimson vial over the flames again, and tipped a few more drops out. The liquid spilled out and sizzled when it met the glowing embers. The stench welled up again, so thick Sharlin thought she would choke.

She was pulled at again, so hard and strong she would have fallen into the diagram except that Turiana grabbed her by the back of her heavy vest, and she felt the sharp fangs piercing the fabric and pricking her skin. The pain brought her back.

But there was no Turiana to save the other two who materialized in the vile smoke.

She had no name for the one. A lanky youth, with strawberry-blond hair in an unruly thatch. His nose was long and lanky like himself, with a stubborn bump on the bridge, but he had an engaging smile, which was rapidly fading into bewilderment. He wore simple home-spuns, his one claim to adornment a garish sash.

But the other she knew as well as she knew herself. Dar straightened. The untarnished silver of his half-helm gleamed in the lamplight of the rapidly darkening room as he looked around, assessing the situation.

"Name yourselves!" the sorceress demanded.

The youth started to say something, stopped, cleared his throat, and said, "Hapwith, madam."

The swordsman clenched his jaw, and looked at the sorceress, and gave no answer.

Turiana let go of the back of Sharlin's vest. "Good. He will not speak."

"Is he here? Is he really here?" The cords of her own neck ached in empathy as she saw him tighten, fighting the compulsion Rodeka laid on him.

"I don't know," the dragon answered. "Perhaps. Come on. While she is busy with them, we've got to leave. I can't fight her now."

Sharlin hesitated, torn by the dilemma of the man caught in Rodeka's web. Then she looked, and saw, and found the key.

The half-helm. Dar hadn't worn that in weeks, not since Nightwing had cut him down at the graveyard. He still carried it in his pack, loath to wear it, loath to leave the ancient bit of armor behind, but she knew that when she left him in Lyrith, his light brown hair had curled freely in the breeze.

She took a last look at the youth, who cleared his throat a second time and said, "Hapwith, of Bywater. Perhaps you've heard of me? Philters, amulets . . . ?"

She twisted about and threw herself out the door into Turiana's dragon embrace, saying, "Hapwith of Bywater. Remember him, Turiana!"

Inside the great hall, the brazier sizzled again. Rodeka cried out. Her voice grew shrill and high, and Sharlin stumbled.

"Turiana!"

"I cannot stay this summoning," the dragon gasped. "Her power—"

Sharlin threw herself on the dragon's back as Turiana

broke into a shambling run. The gathering darkness hit the edge of the plateau as the dragon prepared to launch.

The black sky swallowed them whole. A chill colder than frost ripped at Sharlin. She fought with numb hands to hold on to Turiana's spines.

"How do we get home?" The wind tore the words from her mouth, but Turiana heard. The dragon bore down, flying desperately just to keep up.

With a gasp, Turiana lost her battle to stay aloft and they tumbled from the sky.

Dar woke. He sat cold a moment, then cursed himself for sleeping. His knees and neck ached, and he poked his feet out in front of him stiffly, before he saw the apparition sitting across from him.

A dwarf sat, picking his teeth with a stiletto dagger. "Well, bucko. Picked a bad place to nod off, didn't ye? Gud thing I was here to stand watch."

"Toothpick?"

The transparent dwarf flashed him a grin. "An' who else would it be? Now mind ye, I see you're still wi' the girl, as well ye should be. Th' princess needs you now. Lyrith is full of beasties at night. I'm th' least of them. Get on yer feet now, they'll be needing you soon."

"For what?"

"Aye, that would be telling now. But they fight ghosts to get back to ye . . . and I'm thinking ye're the best fighter o' the three o' you. Get now!" And with that Toothpick rose into the air until Dar had to crane his neck to see him, and disappeared.

He found his brow beaded with sweat, and thanked the gods of his youth that he had not awakened to find the ghost of an enemy, such as the demon Mnak, awaiting him. He stretched the stiffness from his joints and strode over to the lyrith, which still burned with a quiet, dedicated glow. He began to crush the embers out under his feet. Orange and red sparkled into the air and flames roared up, biting back at his falroth boots.

Dar danced back in surprise. Then he grabbed Sharlin's limp form and dragged her away from the newly revived fire, so that she could no longer inhale the exotic smoke. The dragon he could do nothing about, but then he remembered the fountain and returned with his hands cupped. The meager splash of water did little at first, then the embers began to wink out.

When the last glowing bud disappeared, so did the firelight. Dar patted his belt to find his flint. When he looked up, he saw a dark bulk move in front of Turiana's sleeping form.

The black demon grinned, his red eyes smoldering. "You picked a poor time to quench the lyrith, man. Damned if you do and damned if you don't." With a guttural laugh, the demon moved forward.

Dar went for his sword.

Chapter 6

"You're dead," Dar told the demon. He could feel it . . . the icy coldness that drifted from the creature's burly form. He knew Mnak, knew him well. The demon pursuer had cornered him three or four times before. Mnak had sweltered with the heat of other regions, breathed steam, glowered with life. This apparition held nothing of the former—except, perhaps, his hatred.

The demon growled softly. "This is a night of dreamers. The dragon here has awakened all of us. That was her mistake. I block her now from coming back and helping you. You must kill me to let her through."

"You died in the mountains."

"Yes. Cold there. Cold here. I have no peace in the cold. But perhaps . . ." He flexed his massive taloned hands. "Perhaps the memory of killing you at last will warm me."

Dar parried the lunge. The sword bit reluctantly, as though there was nothing substantial there to slice. He recovered himself as Mnak paused.

The demon grinned. His smoldering eyes narrowed. The moon was coming up, in its full Shield phase, and Dar thanked it for the silvery light. Mnak said, "I can hurt you, but you cannot hurt me."

"Are you sure of that?" The sword point circled a little, aimed at the demon's chest.

The beast remained still, rocked back on his clawed feet. With a low roar, he dropped his head and charged.

Dar paused a second, wondering if Mnak was solid enough to worry about. Then he dodged and hacked as the demon passed him. But Mnak was ready. He flung out a clawed hand.

It scored, deeply, into Dar's leather-covered ribs. He felt the blow. Heard the rip of the armor. Yes, Mnak could—and would— hurt him badly.

He staggered back to balance himself. Mnak pulled up suddenly. Dar watched him avoid the temple ruins at all cost.

The remaining lyrith, of course. Toothpick and Sharlin had used lyrith juice as a kind of demonbane the last time Mnak attacked in this city. It had not killed him, but wounded him mortally. All Dar had to do was stay moving, and stay alive, long enough to maneuver in that direction.

Barely had he realized it when Mnak dove low, at his ankles. The creature knocked him from his feet, and he found himself with an armful of yowling, spitting demon ghost.

Pain raked his chest as Mnak grabbed his wrists and began to pull his arms outstretched. The far greater armspan of the beast threatened to pull his arms from his sockets. Dar clenched his teeth and fought back. The white fangs glittered in his face, snapping. Then Mnak laughed and pulled harder.

His muscles screamed as he tried to resist the inevitable strength of the stronger. Tears blurred his vision, tears and dust. Dar threw his head back, pulling his throat away from Mnak's cruel bite.

He arched his back and kicked with all his might, throwing Mnak over his head and into the dirt. The demon convulsed and let go. Pulse drumming in his

ears, Dar surged to his feet. His sword lay a man's
length away. As the demon grabbed for his ankles, Dar
knew he could never reach it.

Instead, he dove, sliding into the temple ruins. Mnak
screamed in fury and followed after. Pain in every inch
of his torso, Dar crawled to the nearest bunker of
lyrith, as the demon dropped onto his back. Gasping,
he rolled over, throwing Mnak off.

As the demon laughed wildly and prepared to crush
him, Dar shoved both fists full of lyrith down his throat.

He found himself trying to hold off empty air.

Turiana groaned and rolled to her side. Her wings
and ears twitched violently as Dar got up and staggered
over. Taking a deep breath, he assessed the damage
from Mnak's attack. Bruises, a left shoulder that was
likely to be sore for a day or two, and a new set of
leathers torn beyond repair. His relief intensified when
Sharlin moaned softly and rolled over onto her back.

At night, the blue of her eyes could scarcely be seen
as her lids fluttered open, but he didn't need to see
their color to know she looked at him. She reached out
and touched his face. He winced. Welts which her
touch brought to life crisscrossed his skin. As she dropped
her hand, her fingers trailed across the torn leathers,
and he flinched again, bruises aching.

Sharlin gave a throaty laugh. "By the gods, Dar—
can't I take you anywhere?"

The smell of sizzling sausage and onion cut across the
air. Dar gave an appreciative grin as he took a deep
breath, savoring the festival atmosphere.

"I'd say we came to the right place."

Sharlin frowned, seeing a different Bywater than he
did. Veiled pallans walked quickly through the backways
of the trading village. She sensed the same undercur-
rent here that plagued most of Rangard. Pallans were
abused second citizens. She flexed her shoulders as her

neck muscles tensed. All the same, she found herself arguing with Dar. "We don't even know if he's here."

"It's the only Bywater we found on the maps. As for the time period, well, there's not much we can do about that. Still, all the visions Rodeka brought forth were from now . . . even yourself."

A slight blush colored Sharlin's fair face. She could hardly argue with that. She looked about the many stalls, listening to the cacophony of the sellers' pitches. "What do you suggest we do?"

"Find an empty stall, if there is such a thing. Most of your herbs are common enough, but I'll bet the powdered lyrith will draw the healers and small-time witches like flies."

"That brings no argument." Sharlin resettled the soft leather pack on her shoulder. Dar's suggestion to harvest as much of the precious flower as possible from Glymarach was one of the better things to come out of the near disastrous venture. She let her keen gaze sweep the sellers' field, hoping to spot the town boss. Instinctively, she reached for Dar and clutched his wrist tightly. "Oh, Dar—"

He'd seen it too and drew her away. "There's nothing you can do."

"But Dar—"

"Not here, not now—and not without Turiana!" the swordsman grated and steered her away.

She could still hear the singsong cadence of the auctioneer and the wail of the pallans as their children were sold into servitude. It seemed to follow them clear across the fairgrounds, though common sense told her it couldn't have been possible to hear it still.

"But children," she muttered as Dar plowed to a halt in front of an empty booth. He swung around, and she could tell from the white pinched areas around his nose in his normally deep tanned face that he was angry.

"Look," he said. "There's not one damn thing I can

do about it today. But tomorrow—that's another story. Let's just find a place to set up shop before the buyers go home."

Sharlin had seen the empty booth. She cast about now and saw a woman eying them, an old woman with deep-set dark eyes and skin like rich old oak. A corner of the woman's mouth twitched, as though knowing she drew their attention—and wanting to.

"Let's ask her."

Dar looked over. The woman's thin white hair covered her scalp in a fuzzy aura. It reminded him of a frightened cat. But the look on her face was placid, as though she had bided her time for quite a while. Her shawl was threadbare, her blouse spotted and scrubbed of food stains, and her patched skirt looked to be the remnants of two or three skirts stitched together. He found himself looking at her feet, thinking of the many-warted feet of the ill-fated Witch of Kalmar, but this old lady's feet were as dark as her face, with the pinkish sole barely exposed by the sandals.

"Seen enough, laddie?" she asked, raising her voice to reach them across the row.

"Perhaps." He let Sharlin lead the way.

"An' what would you be askin' of me?"

Sharlin smiled. She let the pack fall off her shoulder and sag to the ground. She felt Dar assume a swordsman's on-guard stance and contained her grin at the solemnity of his gesture. "I have a few wares, herbs and such. We're wayfarers, and this is how I earn enough coins to keep on the road."

The snow-white eyebrows arched a little. "A swordsman and a noble lady? I should not stand in your way . . . not with your father's army probably beating the road after you. Ask away, answers are my job, but you'll have to pay for it, same as if you wanted your fortune told."

Sharlin turned away and put her hand out to Dar,

who carried the money pouch on his belt. As he dipped his head and pulled out the purse, she saw the corner of his mouth twitch. She withdrew a gold half crown. He raised an eyebrow slightly at that, but shrugged.

The old woman's eyes widened, too. "For that, both your fortunes an' your general questions, but, sadly, I still need silver."

"Silver? Why?"

"Th' vibrations, swordsman. Gold is plagued with greed and anger. Silver is clear as th' moonlight it's minted from."

Dar shook his head. The only silver they had on them was his half-helm in his backpack. "If you'll wait until after she's peddled some of her wares—"

"Can't wait. Can't answer th' questions with muddled vibrations about."

"None of them?"

"No, none," she asserted firmly to Dar. He hesitated, then presented his back to Sharlin. "Get my helm out."

"You're not going to give it to her?"

"No, she doesn't want it as payment. She just needs to be crossed with it—purified, sort of. Don't worry about it." Dar had consulted enough fortune-tellers and seers in his day to know a little about it. He felt the weight on his back being tugged out and then adjusted, and turned around when he sensed Sharlin had the helm.

"I'll cross your palms with silver," Dar said, "but not for payment. You'll keep the half crown."

"Agreed. Rajan! Mind the curtain."

Dar started, as a deep-hued figure from the shadows behind her appeared, and he realized he'd never even seen the massive bodyguard standing behind her. "Going soft," he muttered to himself, as he followed the old lady into her stall and the bodyguard secured a privacy curtain behind them.

Three-legged stools and an old drum for a table. Not the height of luxury, Dar thought, as he settled himself. Sharlin perched somewhat warily on her stool, having taken a rickety one. She pushed the helm at him, and he took it as the old woman drew up a high-backed chair for herself. The rotting rushes that made up the seat creaked alarmingly as she settled herself across from them.

Sharlin pushed the gold half crown across the table, and smooth, agile fingers picked it up and tucked it away almost before she had time to blink. The old woman wiped her hands distastefully. "Quick, the silver before I'm so mucked up I can't tell you a thing."

Dar pushed over the Thrassian helm. She sucked in her breath as she placed both hands on it, and her eyes grew wide. She stared at Dar.

"D'you know what you've got here?" She shook her head, white fuzzy hair standing on end. "Never mind, child, I can see that you don't. When you get the weapon that matches it, why then, all Rangard will look to you."

Dar snorted. "I'm no prophetic messiah, grandmother. Tell those stories to another."

" 'Tis true, that's all." But instead of being insulted, the dark woman smiled. "And I'm glad you don't believe old Tessi. I would hate to think these objects would fall into the hands of someone all puffed up with his own importance." Her glance flickered to Sharlin. "Now I know why a princess travels with a common swordsman. You, too, sense the depths within him."

Sharlin's back stiffened. "He's a good man," was all she said, but her eyes flashed stormy gray and Dar steeled himself for trouble.

The woman wagged a finger at her. "Remember, he has a destiny, regardless of the objects. They came to him . . . the destiny doesn't follow the helm and the weapon. The destiny follows him. There is a time when your lives will depend on knowing this, when all else seems dark." Her eyes narrowed and her voice faded. Then, briskly, she pushed the helm back at Dar. "Well. It's done my old soul good."

"Surely that's not all for half a crown!"

The old woman and girl locked stares.

"You said both fortunes and then some for half a crown," Sharlin pressed. Dar looked behind them uneasily and saw the giant Rajan's form outlined against the curtain as if he leaned into the booth to listen. He shifted.

But the old woman smiled then, at Sharlin. "I cannot tell you what you want to know," she whispered. "You are too close to one of those moments when all your fate seesaws. This town and what you do in it will determine much. The gods have blurred it for me." She raised her voice. "I can tell you that the booth across the way is mine. One of my nieces rented it, but she's birthing now, and you can have it for a few days. Two silver pieces. Is that done?"

"How many days is a few?"

"Ah, now, don't you be trusting me after all this? Three days. And I'll have Rajan look after you, too, if your swordsman gets a bit restless. Hard to keep a young man in one place all day, isn't it?" She broke into a bawdy laugh that brought high color to Sharlin's face, and she looked away.

The woman sputtered to a halt. "Bring me the silver at the end of today's sales, if you have it. If not, tomorrow. And if you need a good inn to stay at, try the Flea's Dog. It's cleaner than most, and you'll not be harassed there, milady."

"Thank you." Sharlin stood up gracefully, and not a moment too soon. The three-legged stool collapsed as soon as her weight lifted. She swept aside her skirts and looked in astonishment as the fortune-teller clucked her tongue, snapped her fingers, and the stool gathered itself together.

"No shirking," the old woman admonished it, as she ushered the two of them from the stall. Rajan had pulled the curtain back.

Sharlin stammered. "B-but didn't that stool just—"

"Right across there, and I'd hurry to put your wares out, if I were you," the fortuneteller said. "It's mid-morning, and you've missed much of the crowd already."

Dar took Sharlin by the elbow, and she hissed at him, "Stop it! Dar, that stool just—"

"Forget it," he said. "I think it's wiser."

Chapter 7

As they laid out their packets and bags of herbs, the old seeress amiably watched them, ensconced once more in her rocking chair.

"She doesn't miss a thing," Dar said, as he held out handfuls of the wares.

Sharlin deftly sorted out the herbs he handed her. She noticed, too, her interest in them. "Can you blame her?" she answered. "She's predicted that you're the future hope of Rangard, and my whole destiny hangs in the balance in Bywater."

He made a disdainful noise. "I don't think she believes it any more than we do."

Sharlin paused. The part of her back between her shoulders protested a little, and she flexed to soothe it. "I don't know," she ruminated, watching the seeress a moment. "I think maybe she does. This empty stall is awfully convenient for her to keep an eye on us."

The little shelf was soon covered with the rainbow packets of colored parchment, sealed with wax, and the fabric herb bags. Sharlin eyed a three-legged stool in the corner of the rickety stall. The sun streamed down from overhead, slanting its way through the meager shelter.

"The bait is ready."

Dar eyed a trio of town maidens as they made their

way through the stalls, giggling and talking. One of them had an amulet strung on a ribbon tied about her pretty neck. He grinned as their high-pitched conversation wound its way to them. They squealed as they spotted the table of herbs and ran over, their cotton skirts billowing about slim young legs.

Sharlin was somewhat dismayed by their youth. She couldn't have been much older than they, and yet she felt as ancient before them as the granny seeress across the row.

"Buy another one—what will it hurt?" a fresh-faced dark-haired girl urged the wearer of the amulet.

The amulet wearer tossed her head like a fretting pony. The sunlight caught her hair, giving it auburn waves. She pouted her lips and didn't answer, but trailed an idle fingertip through the packets.

"A love charm, milady, for a reluctant beau?" coaxed Sharlin. "Or perhaps a tonic against the melancholy of the affliction?"

The girls burst into giggles, and Sharlin smiled with them.

The third, a light-haired blonde with a round face and a sprinkling of freckles, looked into the stall. A cunning expression passed over her face. She pointed. "I wouldn't mind a night with *him*," she said.

Sharlin turned her head and saw the finger pointing at Dar. Her composure slipped. "I—I beg your pardon?"

Dar's startled gaze met hers as the girl shrugged and dropped her hand. She said slyly, "I guess it's not true. Not everything in Bywater is for sale, is it?"

"No," Sharlin answered shortly. "Not everything."

The amulet wearer ignored her companions. "What do you have here if I wanted to, say, go to sleep at night and dream of the suitor I will marry?"

It was a common enough method for fortune-telling. Sharlin sorted out one packet and two bags. "Either of these bags, sprinkled under your pillow, will give you dreams. Two coppers each. Or this packet, if you put it into your tea before you retire. The packet is a silver piece."

The three caught their breaths. The redhead said, "That's a princely sum for such a small amount. What is it, anyway?"

"A very rare herb," Sharlin answered. "It is called lyrith in my country."

The girl tilted her head to one side. "All right," she said. "I'll take the packet. But mind you, I'll be back tomorrow if I'm not satisfied."

Sharlin picked up the yellow parchment packet. "Oh, you'll dream, milady—only remember that I cannot control your dreams." A silver coin dropped heavily into her palm. She did not see, but Dar noticed, the seeress sit upright suddenly in her chair at the mention of lyrith. She summoned Rajan and sent the mahogany giant striding through the fairgrounds.

The girls sauntered away, the blonde giving Dar a simmering look over her shoulder just before they disappeared around the row's end. Sharlin noticed Dar had moved to the fore of the booth, his hand on the sword's guard.

"What is it?"

"Our bait's been taken a little more vigorously than planned," he said.

Sharlin laughed softly. "They're just girls! Although they seem to have their appetites and are used to getting what they want."

"Not them." His shoulders stayed in a tense line as he watched, then Rajan came trotting back down the stalls. He helped the old fortune-teller to her feet, and she hobbled across the way to them.

She picked up a yellow packet. "Do you know what you have in these?" she asked, her dark eyes piercing.

"Lyrith," said Sharlin.

"Yes, but what old Tessi asks you is, do you know what you have in these?"

Their gazes held, then Tessi dropped hers downward. "Yes, I believe you do. After all, I read your fortune, didn't I? How much is in each packet?"

"A scant teaspoon."

The old woman relaxed. "Not enough to do any real harm, eh? Well then. What you don't sell, bring to me before you strike out on the road again. I'll give you a fair price. It would be a shame to have your father's trackers find you before you're ready."

Sharlin watched her hobble back to her stall, then she said to Dar, "A subtle threat."

"Yes. She wants the lyrith. And it's my guess she's alerted others. We'll have some action soon."

Dar grinned, looking over the nearly bare table at midday. "I could have been a fortune-teller myself," he said, sweeping a palm over the devastated goods.

Sharlin sat down. Her feet swelled and ached inside her boots. They'd been swamped with buyers, but not one of them looked like the young man she'd seen summoned by Rodeka. Her purse bulged, and she plucked out a few coins. "Do you think you could find that booth, wherever it is, that's grilling the cackles?" The mouthwatering aroma had been drifting throughout the rows, and her stomach rumbled at the mention of it.

"That, and cold cider, and maybe a pickled egg or two?"

"Ah, my lord, you treat me too well," Sharlin said as Dar gave her a whispery kiss on her brow and left the stall in search of a meal. She opened the pack and restocked her table, though sparingly. The lyrith would have to last for another day or two, until Hapwith, or someone who knew of him, took the bait.

The sharp-eyed Tessi had disappeared inside her stall and dropped the curtains. Sharlin thought she heard a snore or two wafting out and was glad for anything that would break the ceaseless stare of the old woman. Friend or foe? Sharlin didn't know, and she didn't like dealing with the uncertainty. Turiana was too far away to summon quickly if they needed help.

Though, Sharlin told herself, she'd lived on the edge of fear and disaster for so long now that it was like a familiar spice needed to liven up everyday meals. What would it be like to live once again between four solid walls, with a guard against thieves and ill-doers, and a crop to harvest every late summer, and rains to brace against every winter? What would it be like to deal with the ordinary things that threaten life, instead of the extraordinary, like demon pursuers and witch queens?

A voice sounded into her thoughts. "Ah, a daydream of love perhaps? Or is that a sigh of weariness? Are you ill used, fair maiden, and can I be of service?"

Sharlin swung her feet around, facing the corner of the stall where a tall shadow blocked the dazzling midday sun. "May I help you, sir?" she asked and got to her feet.

The man leaned inward. "That's not fair. I asked you first." And as he ducked his face in, away from the corona of sunlight that framed him, Sharlin smothered a gasp. She knew immediately the too long nose with the bump of stubbornness at the bridge, the unruly thatch of straw-blond hair, and the gangly height of the shopper. It was Hapwith! Pale blue eyes crinkled at the corners as he smiled at her.

His clothes, if they had always been his, had been outgrown in the way a youth does when he reaches his manhood. Patched and clean, they had once been the garments of a well-to-do wearer, perhaps even a minor noble. Now they were outgrown and out of style. Hapwith smiled wider as he sensed her appraisal.

He reached for her hand as she sorted out the packets in front of him. "Now, my dear, it is I who offered services to you. Forget the herbs. I myself am too well learned in herb lore to fall easily for simple charms. My name is Hapwith. Amulets, philters . . . perhaps you've heard of me?"

Sharlin gently withdrew her hand. "No. We've only just come to Bywater today." Her information rescued his expression from a forlorn look.

"That explains it, then." He leaned on both elbows, unworried by the rickety state of the booth. "Let me offer you a fortune-telling, nothing elaborate, just a sample of what I can offer you later, in more . . . private surroundings. Bywater is a town of many fabrics. Grandmother Tessi, across the way here, and I have reputations, you know."

"I . . . I hardly think so," Sharlin said shyly. Her mind raced furiously. If she made an assignation with him later, could they hire him or would they have to remove him forcibly? Something told her that this Hapwith wouldn't take well to the hardships of the open road.

"Ah, you need convincing of my talent. Well . . ." His gaze took stock of her tiny waist, accentuated by the bulging bag of coins received for the day's sales. "If I can see yesterday, surely I can see tomorrow, agreed?"

"Yes, that's true." This time, Sharlin did not fight him as he reached for her hand.

He touched her hand to his lips and stroked her wrist lightly, a faraway look unfocusing his pale blue eyes. Sharlin felt his touch go from electrifyingly sensuous to a mere formality, as his senses seemed to leave his body.

Then he paled. His eyes bulged momentarily, and he came back with a gulp. "N-never mind," he said, releasing her hand. "Perhaps another time. Sorcery is fickle, you know."

He turned away, but Sharlin caught his sleeve. "Please tell me. What is it you saw?"

"Nothing, nothing at all. It would sound foolish if I

told you." A tiny drop of sweat beaded his brow. He mopped at it with his free hand.

Sharlin swayed closer. "I did so want my fortune told."

"Well, then. Ah. Perhaps. Remember, what I told you. I saw you and . . . and a great golden beast, a dragon."

Sharlin clapped her hands, feigning delight. Shock chilled her blood. How could he have seen? Was there magic here indeed? "My dream! You've read my dream! Wasn't she beautiful?"

The young man took a deep, sobering breath, then smiled. "A dream. Yes, she was magnificent. And what dreams you must have!"

"You must tell me more."

Hapwith seemed recovered. His gaze swept her once again, and Sharlin felt a surge of pride that she could inspire such a survey. When was the last time Dar had told her she was pretty?

"Are you staying nearby?"

"The Flea's Dog."

Hapwith nodded. "Very good, then, ah . . ."

"Sharlin. Sharlin of Dhamon." She looked through her eyelashes. "Will three silver pieces be enough?"

"Assuredly. Till the dusking hour, then, my fair maiden, at the Flea's Dog." Hapwith touched his hand to his brow and turned away, striding through the growing crowd.

Dar, approaching from the other end of the row, saw him. "Hey!" Bundles in his arms went flying. "Stop, you!"

Sharlin caught some of the bundles as the swordsman swept past, in hot pursuit of the magician. The aroma of grilled cackle and pickled eggs filled her senses. She cried out, "Dar!" But he was out of earshot.

Hapwith took one look over his shoulder and burst into motion. With a sigh, Sharlin watched them go.

From Hapwith's reaction, it was obvious he was used to being pursued, and he soon disappeared into the labyrinth of the fair's rows.

Dar came trotting back after a while. His face was mottled pink with exertion, and cackle yolks spotted one knee of his leathers and dripped onto the toe of his falroth boot. Sharlin just looked at him as he handed her a pail. It was half full of eggs, some cracked and some oozing their contents out.

"He took a sharp turn at the end, and I fell into a booth. I had to pay for the damage. Dammit, Sharlin, I almost had him!"

She smiled, and sucked some of the grilled cackle juice off her fingers, as she moved aside to let him finish what was left of the lunch. "Well, I've got him tonight, at dusk, at my room."

"What?"

"He, ah, wants to read my fortune for me."

Dar bit savagely into his portion of the fowl. "I'll bet he does."

Sharlin only laughed softly as she found a rag and wiped the yolk off her swordsman. "We'll soon see, won't we?"

The smoke and din of the inn made it difficult for Dar to keep an eye on the front door. He paused, rolling the dice in his palm, and his neighbor jostled him. "Come on, throw it, man! I've bet you on the quintains again!"

Dar looked down to the pit, then loosed the dice. That rare formation came up, gleaming in the smoky light of the room, and his neighbor let out a yell. Dar shrugged and made some excuse as the dice were taken up and pressed into his palm again. He shot automatically, his real worry the front door.

"Bad luck, soldier."

Dar frowned as the dice cost him half a silver piece

and were scooped away from him. The frown was more than annoyance at losing the dice. He'd heard a great deal about Hapwith in the hour or so he'd been sentry at the pit. Yes, the young man was quite a womanizer, and a poor magician, from all he'd heard. He didn't know how Turiana and Sharlin had come up with his name from Rodeka, but he misdoubted the lad would do them any good. Instead of wasting time selling lyrith at the booth, he should have been gambling at the Flea's Dog. Here he'd learned all he needed to know, and then some.

Not that he could have convinced Sharlin differently. His lady love was headstrong, if nothing else. She'd already put in a summons to Turiana to meet them discreetly at the town borders, if all went well, and they convinced Hapwith to join them.

She'd have far better luck persuading Hapwith to go to bed with her than to join them, Dar decided. He threw down a copper piece on the next throw of dice, just to keep up the pretense of gambling, and looked once more to the door.

A lanky man moved in cautiously through the door, as a trader muscled up his pack and went out. Dar smiled to himself as he noted the effort Hapwith made to be unobtrusive. The magician caught one of the servers by a sleeve and had a room on the second landing pointed out to him. Without looking, Dar knew which room it was.

Hapwith began to back out. Dar frowned, then remembered there was an outside staircase behind the inn. This was beginning to look worse and worse. His neighbor, a balding, chunky merchant, jostled his elbow again as he picked up the dice.

"Wish me luck on the quintains, soldier," the man said, then froze. His eyes widened. "There he is!"

The dice went flying as the merchant shouted. "Get him! Get him! I want that man for my daughter—"

But Hapwith had already sprinted out the front door.

The lobby of the Flea's Dog emptied on his heels. Dar lagged back, jostled by the flow of the crowd. As the room quieted, Sharlin appeared on the second landing and leaned over the railing. He felt a sting of jealousy as he noted her low-cut blouse and the fall of her amber hair over her shoulders.

"What is it?"

Before he could answer, the innkeeper waddled past, his apron drifting away from its tucked-in position in his trousers. He carried a pot of foul-smelling pitch, still smoking, in one hand. "Tar and feathers!" he called in a rumbling voice, and went after his customers.

"Oh, no! Dar, you've got to stop them! Once Hapwith reaches the town borders, it'll take us days to catch up." She turned and raced back to the room.

"If he survives the tar," Dar muttered, turning heel to go after the angry mob.

Sharlin caught up with him, the pack thrown over her shoulder. She'd brought everything, prepared to leave quickly once they had their hands on Hapwith.

Dar took his sword and sheath and buckled them on. He loosened the sword, not stopping, and Sharlin had to take running steps to keep up with his stride. "What I'd give for a fast horse," he said to himself, thinking of his faraway chestnut mount.

Sharlin's answer was cut off by the shouts, and they knew the mob had caught up with Hapwith. They found themselves on the outskirts. Smoldering orange torches illuminated the darkening gloom.

"What's he done?"

The merchant they talked to picked his teeth, then sucked on the gristle he'd loosened. "What hasn't he?" the man answered. "He's been into the pants of half the wives in town, for one."

"Not your wife, I assume," Dar said, noting the man's calm.

The man gave a nod. "I keep mine well satisfied, if you know what I mean. And he's been selling magicks all over town, most of which don't work. The man's a charlatan, and a menace, if you ask me." He held up a sack. "I've got my share of feathers."

"Right," answered Dar, and shouldered a little closer to Sharlin. "Are you sure it's him you need?" he whispered.

Sharlin took his arm. "I only know what we dreamed. He appeared when Rodeka called forth the spirits of those who could oppose her rule in Dhamon."

"Yeah, well, so did I—and I've never met your sorceress."

"Maybe," Sharlin answered. "Oh, Dar! He looks terrible!"

And, indeed, the half-stripped man in the center of the commotion looked abjectly miserable. His hands were tied behind his back, and his shirt had been stripped down off his torso and hung in rags about his waist. Sharlin sucked in her breath. He was little more than a boy! "Do something."

Dar shouldered his way closer, until they were on the inner edge of the mob. He looked about, then leaned to her ear, saying, "I can't fight my way out of here. You just stay with me."

"All right."

The innkeeper had also waddled forward. He swung the pot of tar in his thick hands. Hapwith stood warily, his nose wrinkled at the stench.

"For what you did to my little girl," the merchant said, and struck him. The blow rocked Hapwith back on his heels. Three men grabbed him and stood him back on his feet. He sucked his bloodied lip and looked down with wide eyes.

"I did nothing to your little girl, shopkeeper," Hapwith said. His voice was steady, for all the fear that paled his face. "I have never hurt a child! As for your wives—all of you—I did nothing more than what you were too busy to do yourselves. I courted them. Whispered sweet nothings in their ear. Told them they were still fetching."

"And that's not all you did!" one shouted.

Hapwith colored a little. "Perhaps. But be reasonable, sir—if she'd been happy at home, she'd never have listened to me in the first place!"

Three or four laughs drowned out the man's protest. Dar reassessed his opinion of the youth. He stood his ground well when cornered. The swordsman had expected groveling or worse.

"Either beat him or tar and feather him," another man yelled from the rear of the pack. "I've got work to do."

"Right," muttered the innkeeper. He held out the tar pot.

It had cooled somewhat, but still was hot enough to scorch. In a moment they would slather the tar all over him and plaster the feathers about. Hapwith quaked, thinking of the weeks, months, of dreadful discomfort to come as his seared skin would gradually shed and heal. Then he caught sight of Sharlin watching, one of the few women in the crowd, and his blue eyes sparkled a little.

The merchant pulled a knife. "Down with his breeches, and where's that pole? We're riding you out of town, boy, and don't you come back to Bywater!"

"No fear of that," Hapwith returned and winced as the skinning knife came close to his breeches.

"Wait," Dar said. The merchant paused. "You know me . . . you gambled long enough at my elbow tonight. I'm looking for recruits. So you ride this miserable boy out of town tarred and feathered—what's to keep one of your wives from taking him in out of pity and hiding him? He's a magician, isn't he? Why, he could pull the wool over your eyes for months! Give him to me. I'll quick-march him out of town and into my army, and you know he'll be gone."

"Thanks," said Hapwith, "but don't trouble yourself."

"Well . . ." The merchant hesitated, and the crowd grumbled, talking among themselves.

"Get rid of him, one way or the other!"

The merchant scrubbed his chin. "Don't recruits get signing-up money?"

Dar hid his grin. "That's right, master. Two gold pieces. That should make up for some of the damage he's caused! Of course, you'd have to let him go now—I don't have time to pluck him before I deliver him!"

Loud laughter drowned out the few protests, including a weak one from Hapwith. The merchant held out his hand. Sharlin gave her purse to Dar, who fished around for the gold pieces, then held them up, showing them to the crowd. They shone in the torchlight, and he dropped them into the merchant's hand, who quickly made a fist over them.

Dar took Hapwith by the elbow. "You come with me," he said, "and you come with me quietly."

"No worry," the victim answered. His attention was riveted across the mob. "And if you want to avoid Rajan, we'd best hurry."

The dark-skinned bodyguard of the aged fortune-teller grimaced at them as he tried to shoulder his way through the crowd.

"Uh-oh," Dar said, and took Sharlin by the elbow. "Trouble."

"She wants the last of the lyrith."

"Lyrith? You've got lyrith? Good god, and I tried to con you like the rest," Hapwith said as they steered him off.

"Yes, my boy, you'll like soldiering," Dar said loudly. Quieter, he asked, "How are you in a fight?"

"I'm a fast runner," the charlatan answered.

"Great. Sharlin, pull my sword. Where's Turiana?"

"She's coming in now," the girl answered, and tugged the sword free.

They broke into a run, as Rajan shouted and the mob realized they'd been had.

Dar used his skinning knife to cut the magician's hands free, and they all sprinted like softfoot into the darkness waiting outside Bywater's borders. Torchlight flooded after them. His heart beat like a drum as he sorted out in his mind drawing off the pursuers and sending Sharlin and Hapwith free into the night. She passed him his sword as though reading his thoughts. The night descended on them like a thick, dark cloud, and they plowed to a halt, unable to see anything.

"For a fast horse," Dar muttered again.

"Or a slow dragon?" Turiana gave a throaty laugh. "Don't worry, I've taken care of everything. We're hidden." She blossomed into the cover she'd created.

Sharlin took a grateful breath and threw her arms about the golden dragon's neck. "Just in time."

"Of course. And is this our quarry?"

"Yes. Hapwith, meet Turiana, late of my—and perhaps your—dreams."

Sheathing his sword, Dar added, "I might be wrong about him. He held up well under pressure." Turning, he continued, "Yes, Hapwith, you showed a fair amount of guts back there."

He turned in time to see the youth faint.

Chapter 8

"Actually," Turiana said slowly, her voice slurred with pleasure as Sharlin rubbed her underbelly, "he shows a singular lack of talent for magic of any kind."

"He's not that bad." Sharlin felt the glow of the dragon's warmth through her softer stomach scales. The wind bit at her back in contrast. It reminded her that in this part of Rangard, the world was close to winter.

"Perhaps not by *your* standards," the dragon queen said. Her eyelids fluttered.

The woman stopped, aware of the snub.

Turiana reached around and curled her paw about Sharlin's body and pulled the human close to her throat. "We have different criteria," the dragon prodded.

"I won't be baited into arguing."

The paw stretched and curled about her, kneading gently. Sharlin reached up and scratched the hard scaly base of the spines crowning Turiana's head. "Rodeka did call him forth."

"We don't know that much about her talent either," the dragon said, frowning.

"Then explain what he did for me."

"There's no explanation. A lucky guess, perhaps. Perhaps he read a fleeting thought."

"And if he does it often? If he can read the past? It's the past we have to deal with, Turiana."

The creature rumbled softly, "I don't see the link. I don't see how he can help me solve our problem."

"Neither do I—but I don't want to drive him away until we're sure there's no connection."

A snort blew Sharlin's hair away from her face as Turiana said, "No fear of that, fair daughter. That one is eager to make a nest with you."

"Turiana!"

The dragon let out a series of puffs that Sharlin tabbed as dragon laughter, which soon ebbed away into snoring as the direct sunlight on the rocks lulled her to sleep.

Sharlin rubbed her palms together. She felt on edge. Time. It seemed to be on her side, but she knew she couldn't count on that. Which of her family had died to provide the blood potion Rodeka used in her summoning? If not dead, who was slowly being bled to death? She could not thrust the image and horror behind her, as something that had happened several hundred years ago, and not now. As long as her dreams bridged the gap of time, the events then were as real to her as those now, plunging toward an inevitability she planned to stop.

She moved away from the sleeping Turiana. Dar had taken Hapwith fishing in the morning light. They were camped in the mountains south and west of the Netting, not too far from an area she and Dar had traversed before.

She heard the voices before they appeared. Dar and Hapwith seemed to have settled into a certain camaraderie. Hapwith had overcome his obvious terror of the dragon queen long enough to have her summon up some new clothes, which he wore with ease and elegance. Sharlin hid her smile as he approached, the yellow and spring-green embroidering of his overtunic glittering in the sun.

"Good morning, milady," Hapwith said as he spotted her. He gave an awkward bow. "We have news."

"And that is?"

"That both Aarondar and I would rather catch fish than clean them. We diced for the job, and he, alas, lost."

Sharlin had seen Hapwith's prowess with sleight of hand and dice. She doubted that Dar had lost honestly. But Hapwith paused, waiting for her attention, and she gave it to him. "And what else?"

"Dar says to tell you that he's located a hot spring not too far from here. After breakfast, if you wish, he'll stand guard while you bathe."

Pleasure flooded her. "That's wonderful."

The blond's eyebrow arched. "It would be even more wonderful if you would consider letting me guard while you bathe. There are things that make a bath beyond imagining."

"I'll bet." Sharlin looked past Hapwith and saw Dar making his way to the camp, the newly cleaned fish hanging from a switch. "I think I'll make breakfast instead."

Dar squatted by Sharlin as she prepared the fish for cooking and Hapwith went to see what other goods he could con out of the dragon queen. He watched the youth go.

"If the world could be won by charm . . ." he began, and his voice trailed off.

"Leave it be, Dar. He's harmless enough."

"No—no, not harmless. If we have to count on him, if our backs are ever open to the enemy, I don't know."

"Not everybody can be a soldier."

He looked up and saw her smiling at him. It eased a little of his worry. He returned the smile. "That I know. And I like Hapwith—it would be hard not to.

But I think it would be a good thing to watch him closely when we get to the Nettings. He's got his eye on your store of lyrith. I think he means to take what he can, along with the next ship available."

"Me, too," Sharlin admitted. The pan warmed and the fish began to sizzle. She'd found some wild shallots and sprinkled them in as well. The aroma of the meal filled the air.

Hapwith sauntered down from the rocks. He sniffed appreciatively as he seated himself on a fallen log. "Never wake a sleeping dragon," he said. "What a creature! I never would have believed it if I hadn't seen it."

"What?"

"Their beauty," he answered Dar. "Their incredible beauty. Of course, we've had a green or two scourging the crofters outside of Bywater." He paused, thinking. "I wonder if they're as beautiful. Hard to think of something that nasty as being something you'd want to feast your eyes on."

"I've only seen a few close up," Sharlin said. She deftly turned the fish. "Nightwing was, in his way, beautiful too. Skin like black glass."

"Still," murmured Hapwith. He reached out and pinched off a piece of fish before Sharlin could slap his hand. "Still, I wonder at her coloring. I always thought a dragon's underbelly would be lighter in color. Hers I thought would be a golden cream."

Sharlin looked at Dar. He straightened, leaving her with the meal and the magician, and ambled up the rocky slope to where Turiana slumbered in the sunlight.

Supine without fear, Turiana had exposed her stomach to the warmth of the rays shining down on her. Dar paused. With troubled feelings, he stood taking in the dark amber of her stomach. It patterned itself, reaching like a sunburst out to her rounding flanks.

There was no doubt she was turning color, darkening. But why?

He thought again of a dragon's death upon laying her eggs, and he wondered. But, as one of the few valuable things Hapwith had muttered, it was better to let sleeping dragons lie.

"Your spies are inadequate." Valorek's jaw clenched as he watched Baalan sharpen his talons. He stood behind the dragon's massive head and knew he was, for the moment, out of range. "We've planned an attack. Let's carry through with it before Turiana returns." He was a soldier, and he ached for the kind of action he knew best.

Baalan turned his head. His glowing eyes opened wide, and their silvery color pinioned Valorek to the stone. "Think you?"

Valorek's mouth parted involuntarily. Being bathed in the light of the magnificent beast's attention was an experience close to religious. He forced himself to answer, "Yes. And so would you, if you were paying attention to what we're planning."

Baalan heaved himself to his feet, unsettling Valorek. "You slept too soundly last night. You have missed the latest report."

"What report?"

"Don't agitate yourself, my dear king. I can hear your heart pounding. Have you ever heard the frightened beat of a softfoot just before a vystra gets it?"

"I don't threaten well," Valorek said quietly.

"No. That's true. My spies have reported that it is very likely Turiana has conceived and is carrying a clutch of eggs."

Valorek cursed himself for lack of knowledge about the dragons. Yet no one he knew had chronicled the cycle of the beasts. Gods, after all, were not birthed simply like woollies or the softfoot or even a cackle. This was the first he'd heard of eggs.

Baalan sensed the human's ignorance. "A dragon never mates or lays until it is close to dying. We have few natural enemies except each other. We are extremely long-lived."

Valorek seized the information. "Then Turiana dies after she lays? Good. How soon will we be rid of her?"

"Not so quickly, my dear Val. Don't let your vendetta against the swordsman she accompanies distract you. According to my calculations, two to four weeks."

Valorek did not try to hide his cold smile. "So soon?"

"Perhaps. And then again, perhaps this spawning will not be the death of her. I cannot count on it. She was impregnated against her will and instinct. It would be rare, but she just might survive to see the hatching and raising of her clutch." Baalan's taloned paw clenched. He did not disclose all of his spy's reports. It worried him that something beyond simple conception afflicted Turiana. "That I cannot allow. We cannot wait for then. She must be destroyed first."

"But why? Concentrate on the others!"

Baalan's eyes hooded, and their silvery light became ashen, dim, and malevolent. "I want the surety of her death. I don't want to face the possibility that within that clutch is the dragonet which will grow to challenge me. Another Turiana—or Nightwing. No. I want her dead before then!"

"To get to her you'll have to go through Dar and that girl."

"Precisely. That is why you and I have a visitor waiting to see us. I have my own score to settle with the swordsman." Baalan rubbed his healing stomach. "Put your cloak on. I want to maintain appearances."

Valorek did as he was bid, though he ground his teeth together. Bound to the dragon as he was, he could scarcely leave. He reminded himself to bide his time, that Baalan would serve his purposes yet.

High on the dragon's neck he rode, his cloak wound about him, as they lurched out of the cavern into the sunlight. A man sat in the rocks beyond, and he turned as he heard them. He got to his feet and watched them approach.

Valorek felt excitement course through him. This was a type of being he knew how to face. The man was a born assassin.

Pandor sniffed the late-afternoon air. His ears swiveled. Heaving himself to his feet, he moved to the southernmost end of the Nettings, beyond the wrecked pavilion. His nostrils flared. He heard and sensed dragonwings on the air. His bronze hide quivered in anticipation. Turiana was returning.

A green followed him. She had feathery antennae adorning her brows and was, in Pandor's eyes, nearly as beautiful as the golden queen.

"She will be pleased when she lands," Pandor told her. "She won't expect so many of us have gathered."

Selie had left the huddle of two browns and another green to join him. She had never seen the golden dragon, though they had all left the Pit together, and now she waited eagerly.

A rare turquoise padded forward. His head, too, was tilted to the evening air. The last vestiges of sunlight set off a blue fire among his scales. "More than one," he said.

"She brings others with her!"

Pandor stood, anticipation rocketing through his veins, and yet he was not ready for the sight that dropped out of the sunset clouds and swooped toward him.

The bulk of the lead dragon and rider should have

warned him. Perhaps it was the tinge of the sky, growing toward darkness, that fooled him. Or perhaps it was the sunset clouds, already a kind of mauve, that stalled him on the ground until too late.

Whatever it was, it was the death of the Nettings. With crimson fire and talons of lightning, Baalan and his followers dove down.

Chapter 9

Duke Mylo stumbled out of the casino den, his senses muddled by too much wine and his hearing pierced by a kind of screaming almost beyond his perception. No one else in the den seemed to be bothered, and he attributed it to yet another phase of the melancholy that had gripped him since the gods had swallowed his sister and put a hole into the fabric of his life.

Outside the building, he held tightly to a cornerpost to keep himself upright. He'd sent the guard home, and there was no one now to keep a knife from being stuck between his ribs—or to steady him on his feet. He swallowed convulsively, wondering if he was going to be ill.

It was still light. He blinked at the aspect of sunset. It was the first time he'd left a drinking establishment before dark in nearly a year. The wonderment of it pushed down the nausea, and the world stopped spinning for a moment.

The noise pushing at his ears became audible with a trumpeting that shattered the air about him. As the duke grabbed for his ears, doors and windows banged all over the Netting, from the hilltop to the slopes leading down to the harbor, and the dragons broke into sight.

"By the gods," Mylo gasped. The casino emptied at

his back, and he rolled loosely away from the jostling, as the dusk split, dragonfire raking the heavens.

Before the flames hit, he was ordering the crowd of men about him. "Set up a fire line at the wells!"

They stood, paralyzed, until the gaunt man's voice cracked at them a second time. "Get to the fire lines!"

Then the population of the Nettings began to mobilize, as the sky filled with the might of dragons bent against one another, their trumpets and squeals shrill enough to split human ears. Mylo took a last look himself, over his shoulder, then ran for it as a green beast dived low over the tavern. With a roar, the gases spat out and everything they touched went up in flames. The green's rider let out a cheer and reined his beast across the seaport.

The stench of burning filled the duke's nostrils. As he looked back, he saw the small clay-and-wood huts of the pallans smoking heavily. The dragons seemed clustered over these vulnerable buildings. The duke stumbled to a halt.

He grabbed a man by the collar. "Set up a line by the south end."

"The pallans?" The man spat in astonishment. "Let 'em look to their own!"

"I'm Duke Mylo," his captor ground out. "And you'll do as I say!" But the fisherman shrugged out of his fist and twisted away before the duke could do anything further. With a quick sucking breath, Mylo took his courage into his hands and ran to the south end himself. As he did, he thought of the hundreds of years of books and scrolls hidden there, and what the appearance of Sharlin and Turiana had done to his life. It was not something he wanted to see go up in flames.

A shadow followed him.

Pandor was aware of the panicked crowds running to and fro below him as he chased Baalan's troops. One sail flapped raggedly, a beginning rip hampering him as he pursued. Selie had died in the first sortie. Her beautiful green form lay smoldering on the ground, cindered almost beyond recognition. Pandor bared his fangs. A green swept up before him, his rider calling harshly.

The bronze dragon surged after him. Calling forth his deep magic, he felt his stomachs rumble. He spat out acids and let them fall like raindrops on the evil beast below. The rider screamed and jumped off, flesh melting from his bones. The tougher dragon wheeled, then crumpled in on itself, and fell to the earth with a keening screech that bothered even Pandor's hearing.

The bronze felt satisfaction warm him. He stretched his serpentine neck and returned his attention to what he was doing, and saw, too late, the majestic purple bulk of Baalan rearing in front of him.

Mylo found one of his guard working a fire line outside the pallans' ghetto. With a wry smile, the man shouldered aside to let his duke fall in. The two men said little, but grimly passed hand over hand the inadequate wooden buckets. The pallans scurried back and forth, their heavily shrouded forms no more human than before, their distress evident as they carried forth what they could from their shacks. Cinders and ashes flew as the clay hovels grew red-hot. The very air threatened to burn.

A pallan staggered to a halt in front of Mylo. As he reached for the being, the gauze mask burst into flames. With a screech, the pallan clawed it off, and for a second, the duke and the being stared face to face—the duke the only man in recent history to see a naked pallan face and live beyond the seeing.

Then a dragon swooped down. A bolt of orange issued from its jaws and exploded just behind the fire line. The pallan turned and ran. Duke Mylo, too shocked to do anything else, stayed in line and reached for the next bucket. His mind didn't seem to realize what he'd seen.

With a scream of pain, the burning Pandor crashed to the ground. Sweet grass crushed below him. He rolled in his agony, quenching the flames, and lay, his muzzle between his taloned paws, his torn wings in rags about him. Yet his ears trembled, and he looked back to the evening sky, toward the mountains. Beyond the sound of the humans shouting and the seaport burning, and the trumpeting of Baalan's victorious troops, he sensed another sound. This time, he prayed he could not be wrong. Turiana returned!

Baalan sculled to a stop. Valorek held on to the harnessing and cursed the dragon for pulling up.

"Turiana's coming," the purple beast said. He shook his head, spines rattling vigorously, threatening Valorek's purchase on his neck.

"I want them!"

"Not now. Besides, our man is below, working in the town. I'm not ready to meet Turiana yet," Baalan said. The dragon called to his wing. They dove one last time.

Dragonfire and acid raked viciously across what was left of the pallan ghetto and over Pandor's broken form. Then they wheeled in the sky and disappeared over the sea, as Turiana's golden form lit the darkness.

The last of the Baalan's forces had disappeared. In confusion, two of the dragons attacked Turiana as she appeared, but she batted them down, her talons sheathed. Orange flames lit the sky, and the stench of burning flesh and wood filled their nostrils.

Sharlin slid off her neck and held tightly. Dar jumped

and took her in his arms to steady her. Turiana perched next to Pandor and keened softly.

The bronze dragon's eyes flickered open.

Hapwith joined Dar and Sharlin, and the three looked at the wounded beast. Turiana nuzzled him a moment. She lifted her head and said, in a cold voice, "He will live. But it remains to be seen if he will ever fly again."

Shaken, the girl shrugged out of Dar's hold. She walked toward the pallan ghetto. Ashes flurried in the hot wind of its burning, funneling up to the sky. A man staggered toward her, his clothes torn and sullied, his face blackened.

"Lady Sharlin," he gasped, holding out his hands.

"Duke Mylo!" she responded. She caught him just as he went to his knees. The whites of his eyes showed. The man was hysterical, at the edge of his reason. Dar shouldered her aside and helped the duke to his feet.

"What happened?"

"I don't—I saw—burning. The dragons came. I saw—" The man's face went slack.

Sharlin put her arm about his shoulders. She looked to Dar. The south end of the Nettings overlooked most of the rest of the seaport. The stench of burning carcasses in the field, dragon and pallan alike, threatened to gag her. She forced out, "Is anything saved?"

"I see fire lines," the swordsman said. "There must have been one up here, too."

"There . . . was," said the duke. "But the last sweep . . . it rained fire and acid . . . the men next to me . . . the flesh just melted off them, and they ran, screaming . . . horribly. And I saw—I saw—"

Sharlin put her fingers to his lips. "That's enough now. Come with me." She put his arm over her and walked him across the trampled meadows to the manor. They skirted the blackened and roasted form of another dragon. Tears came to her eyes, making the last of the journey difficult.

Turiana launched. The rush of air nearly took Dar and Hapwith to their knees, and Sharlin staggered under the blast. But as the dragon swept the city, the fires flickered and died down. She laid a fog, cold and gray, over the raging embers. Sharlin bolstered the duke a second time and brought him to his home.

Missed by fire, on purpose or by accident, a servant peeked timidly out of the building, her lamp in her hand.

"Duke Mylo!" The girl gasped and reached for her master, and helped Sharlin bring him into the manor.

Dar turned to Hapwith. "Let's see what's left."

The youth shrugged. "Ah . . . why don't I stay with the wounded. They might need water or something."

Dar looked about the field. The grass was awash with blood and ichor. The dragons that could fly accompanied Turiana, and only Pandor was left behind. The bronze beast rested. Turiana had covered him with a kind of spittle that enveloped him like a poultice, and Dar doubted that Hapwith could do anything for the grievous wounds.

As for the pallans . . . their withered forms littered the grounds like autumn leaves. Dar clenched his jaw. What few were left began to appear from the shadows. They shrank from the two humans.

"I don't think there's much we can do here," the swordsman said. "And I think you'd better stay with me."

"Right," said Hapwith. Hooking his thumbs in his belt, conveniently next to his dagger, he followed after Dar.

Not since the goblin wars had Dar waded through such destruction. He'd thought he'd forgotten the stench of burning flesh and hair. The smell awoke fresh memories in him. Cinders and ashes stung his eyes, and he wiped them on the back of a sleeve. And as he looked over the destruction, he thought of Baalan and Valorek.

Valorek had conquered a kingdom once, village by village. The destruction he had wrought over three decades stood as nothing to this one night. Baalan had put a weapon into the witch king's hand that he would have had to be insane to resist.

Sickened, Dar turned aside from the pallan ghetto and walked through the muddy streets of the Nettings.

Hapwith followed after, a scented handkerchief to his nose. He'd pinched some of Sharlin's herbs, though none of the lyrith—he hadn't been able to get close to that—and was trying to ignore the pitching of his stomach. The swordsman made no noise. Hapwith decided that he was blind to the ravaged scene about them, or being a soldier, maybe he was immune to it. Shops and homes alike had been hit. There was no pattern to the attack, except one of destruction.

There was a snick as Dar drew his sword. Looters already picked over some of the shops that had been cracked open like eggs. The swordsman went after a trio, and they stopped. Expressions passed over their faces. It struck Hapwith with shock that they were trying to decide if they were brave enough to attack Dar. Hapwith drew his dagger and set his jaw, imitating the swordsman's stance.

"Get back to your homes," Dar said. "And help put out the last of the fires!"

"Yes, sir," a tall boy said. He ducked his head and loped out of the ruins, and the two stockier boys broke and followed after.

Dar tightened the grip on his sword. "Just kids," he muttered and continued down the street.

Hapwith found his hand had gone icy-cold, instead of the dagger warming to his touch. With a shudder, he followed. Fear prickled the back of his neck. He couldn't help it that he was not as brave as Dar. Cold terror had long lived inside his gut.

He twitched, thinking he saw a man-shadow that moved out of other shadows, pacing them. "Dar—"

But when the man turned to him, and he tried to pinpoint the movement, there was nothing.

"What is it?"

"I—ah—thought I saw something."

Dar stood still, listening. He shook his head.

Hapwith cleared his throat, embarrassed. "I—ah—nerves, I guess." He looked around. "I could swear that I—well, never mind."

"We need to keep moving."

"Right." The lanky youth nodded.

Dar couldn't put his finger on what he searched for, or what compulsion moved him through the wreckage of the Nettings, he only knew that he looked for something. Perhaps he looked for a reason behind the dragons' brutal attack. It bothered him that the pallan ghetto seemed to have drawn the most destruction. Was it because the dragons quartered close to there—or because Baalan intended to hit the pallans as well?

He kicked aside a burning beam. Orange sparks swirled into the night. Fog cloaked the streets now, a gift from Turiana to dampen the fire. It grew close and thick. Even Hapwith at his elbow became difficult to see.

A rushing form knocked Hapwith aside, but he blurted out, "Dar!" in warning even as he went down.

Dar whirled. His sword blocked with a *clang!* the rush of the man. He fell back as the other's momentum carried the attack. He saw only a blur of movement. The other was swathed from head to toe like a pallan. But he saw the human face in the dark hood. An assassin!

Dar gathered himself just barely in time as the other charged again. Metal gleamed in both hands. Dar parried the sword and kicked to deflect the small dagger.

His boot missed its mark, but then so did the dagger. Dar staggered back, breathing hard, afraid.

Assassins worked quickly. A whirl of weapons, and then it was over. Dar flexed his shoulders and waited for the next assault. It was no good thinking about it.

The man attacked again in a quick blur. Dar's years of training under Valorek and in the army allowed him to react automatically. The man died in the dust, his fingernails scratching into the streets of the Nettings.

Dar would have wondered if he was the assassin's target except that the man had time enough to cry his name before he died.

Hapwith got to his feet shakily, then turned to throw up in the shadows. He came back to Dar, face pale. He reached for Dar's elbow. "Who was that?"

"I don't know. But he was a paid killer."

"I think—" said Hapwith, and he paused to gulp. "I think I'd better get you back to Sharlin," the magician finished.

Dar decided that he'd found what he was looking for in the night-shrouded ruins of the city, and they returned.

Chapter 10

Sharlin held the ragged sail of Pandor's wing over her knees, examining the tears. Between her fingers she gripped a fine sewing needle. Its thread trailed over the injured dragon's skin like a spidery vein.

"I can stitch it," she said finally, aware of the great bronze dragon's labored breathing, "but there are holes . . . great holes where the saliva just ate through. There's nothing I can do about that."

Turiana had paused in her vigorous chores, but her tail pulsed on the ground like a nervous cat's, and Sharlin knew she had her attention only momentarily. The golden dragon had already done all she could for Pandor. "He'll not fly again," Turiana said. Her words were clipped and short. "Do what you can."

"What about patching them?" Dar interrupted. He squatted not far from Sharlin, the tip end of Pandor's wing balanced across his thighs.

"With what? Do you think a dragon is like a quilt?" Turiana's voice scorched across them, and she launched angrily into the sky, taking a green dragon with her.

Dar gently folded Pandor's wing up to meet Sharlin's lap. The bronze turned his head. He could see in the beast's eye that Pandor was grateful for the gentleness.

"It's grievous," Dar said, "but I'm not giving up. Sharlin, mend what you can, but don't touch the holes.

110

I want the edges raw. Don't put anything on them to heal them over—if you can stand the pain, Pandor."

The great lantern eyes, dimmed with agony, blinked. "I can stand it, cubling, if you think you can help."

"Dar," Sharlin said as he turned heel. "What are you going to do?"

"We'll patch him with the strongest hide I can think of—next to dragon hide. There's got to be a trader in town with fresh falroth skins. If they're fresh, not tanned, we might be able to use them. It's worth a try." He strode away from the meadow.

Hapwith straightened from the wreckage of the pallans' homes and gave him a wave. Dar returned it. Sharlin had instructed the young magician to work with the historians and see if anything further could be salvaged.

The prickle between Dar's shoulders was a familiar one. He'd not walked long without one for the past five or so years, and yet, just a few short weeks ago, he thought he'd laid that demon to rest for good. The irony of it quirked a corner of his mouth. Aptly said, that. Valorek and his demon Mnak.

He had no way of knowing if Valorek had sent the assassin last night. But there was no doubt in his mind that he'd been the target, and the man had been well paid and chosen for his work. Someone wanted Dar out of the way. Once again, he cursed himself for having been tired, slow, and out of practice. A little faster and the assassin would be alive this morning, telling Dar who'd hired him, though he couldn't really be sure of that. There was a moment when Dar thought Hapwith and his dagger would have made short work of the assassin if Dar had gone down.

That thought tugged at his mind as he traversed the ruined streets of the Nettings. Yes, the magician had more in him than Dar had figured. There were surprises there yet to be had, if the three of them lived long enough to go looking.

Duke Mylo had emerged in the morning light, tired and haggard and somewhat recovered from his ordeal of the evening. He had also emerged convinced that dragons were not gods or even godlike. The duke had the great creatures labeled somewhere between squabbling alley cats and wild dogs, at the moment. And Mylo had manifested his conviction that the Nettings was no longer a fit sanctuary for dragons. Never mind that Turiana disagreed with him. Mylo had ruled long and prosperously in the Nettings. If the duke chose to, it would not take him long to raise the population against them. And Dar had no wish to see another massacre.

The stench of tannery row roused him from his thoughts. He paused at the tradesmen's booths, working his way down the street. None had what he wanted. Falroth hides, yes, but not fresh and untreated. Dar scratched his head, then made his way back up the hill to the manor.

Duke Mylo looked at him. His eyes still held a slightly unfocused look, as though he hadn't yet quite assimilated all that had happened during the night. "One horse?"

"Just for myself. And I'll be back before this evening."

The duke sighed. Dar felt the overflow of his thoughts, and for a second he gripped the man's wrist.

"We'll be gone as soon as we can, your highness. But not all of our wounded can be moved yet."

Mylo's gaunt face brightened. "That's true," he said. "Well, then, I'll help as I can. Ask my stableman to give you Gingerbread. She's a plain brown mare, but she has the stamina of a gunter, and she's the fastest horse I own."

Dar expected a small, round, dainty beast, but Gingerbread when led out into the stableyard, all saddled and ready to go, was a great rawboned mare. She threw her head up and looked wildly from her eye as he reached for the reins.

Dar rubbed her forehead with his knuckles, and the mare settled. He swung up into the saddle and headed for the mountains, knowing falroth to be found there. He reflected a moment that no man willingly went after falroth, unless he was a trapper and cared little about what died in his traps. But Dar was going to face one alive, and hope he survived the encounter.

"He what?"

"Went up after falroth," Hapwith replied ingenuously. Ashes stained his face, but he looked enormously proud of himself. Scrolls and charred book bindings filled his arms. "Aren't those big lizards?"

"Those," Sharlin snapped, "are known as death machines in the wild. Why didn't you come tell me sooner?"

"I didn't know." Remorse filled the blue eyes. "Milady, let me stay with you. Perhaps I can soothe you somehow."

"Forget it." Sharlin carefully put Pandor's wing down. "My stitching here isn't finished, and you seem to be doing well with the pallans."

"But your vigil—"

She gave Hapwith a tiny shove in the opposite direction. "I can take care of myself, Hapwith, thank you."

Pandor rumbled with dragonish humor as the youth left. Sharlin looked him in the eye. "And what are you laughing about?"

"Nothing," the dragon said. "But it is good to be around you cublings. Dragons have but one spring, and it is likely to be a spiteful and ill-humored one, because the urge to spawn does not rise until death is close. Still, a dragon appreciates love and the mating urges in others. It is amusing."

Sharlin relented her sharpness. She leaned over and scratched the big male's face. "Brave Pandor," she murmured.

He sighed.

"I've got to get some fresh needles and thread. Can you stand any more sewing?"

"I must. To take away my wings—" The dragon paused.

Sharlin gently closed the eyelid over the luminous orb and patted his brow. "We'll do the best we can, Pandor."

Hapwith spotted the horseman first, in the fading light. He let out a yell and sprinted across the meadow, pallans running to stay out of his way. The rawboned mare was lathered and muddy. Flayed skin lay over her rump, and it looked as though her rider wasn't in much better shape.

Sharlin looked up from her sewing. Lanternlight dazzled her eyesight a moment. The bronze dragon voluntarily pulled his wing from her lap. "The swordsman is back," he said.

She got up, her legs gone stiff and numb from her position all day. "He isn't—" She paused, her voice choked in her throat. "I'll be back, Pandor!"

The bronze dragon watched the girl run across the meadow, stumbling at first, then faster and faster, so that she was the first to reach Dar's side, as Hapwith dealt with the fractious horse. The dragon felt a strange warmth in his chest. He'd grown quite fond of the humans Turiana dealt with. Yes. They'd brought a new and unexpected dimension into his life. He hoped that all had gone well.

"Dar!" Sharlin's voice broke as she reached up for him. The man was splattered head to toe with mud and blood, so that she didn't know if he was injured or bloodied by the skins.

Dar sagged into her arms and half fell off the horse, but she caught him. Gingerbread rolled her eyes and whickered. The falroth scent spooked her, but Hapwith had a firm grip on her headstall.

The swordsman took a deep and obviously painful breath. "When you're through with Pandor," he husked, "d'you think you can tape my ribs?"

Sharlin lost her grip, and he went to his knees and stayed there, swaying. He held his hands up.

"I'll be all right. I got—three skins for Pandor. I hope they'll be enough."

"Three?" Sharlin reached out. He wore one on his back, and the other two were draped across the mare's hindquarters. Sharlin retrieved all three gingerly. They were more than fresh—they were gruesome. Ichor and blood and muscle and fat still hung from the hides. She shuddered.

"I stumbled into a nest," Dar said. "I didn't have much choice—or much time."

"A nest?" Both Sharlin and Hapwith watched the swordsman with horrified fascination. Hapwith let go of the mare, and she trotted off to her stables.

"Seven or eight," Dar said dryly. He reached up. "Get me to my feet."

Hapwith's face shone with idolatry. "And you got out alive?"

"What do you mean, a nest? I've never heard of any such thing. Falroths in packs?" And Sharlin gave another shudder. As Hapwith helped him to his feet, she grabbed Dar and hugged him fiercely, ignoring his yelps of pain. "You idiot," she said when she let him go. "And if this works, I'll love you forever."

Lanterns on poles bobbed and swayed with the gentle evening breeze. Sharlin had to forgo taping Dar's ribs and had ordered Hapwith to do it, and so the two men sat out in the meadow, watching as she cut and sewed and patched the great dragon's wings. The falroth hide carried an iridescent pattern, faintly reminiscent of Pandor's own. Dar shivered in the evening breeze and shrugged his cloak over his torn leathers—yet another set ruined—and watched his love work on the dragon.

The thought nagged at his mind that little was known about dragons and littler still about falroths. Had he butchered a cousin so that Pandor might fly? Yet there was no relation between the intelligence of the bronze and the mindless killers that he could see, other than their scaled hides. Falroths were much smaller, of course.

"And so you had to wear the hide of one of them to sneak past the sleeping guards," Hapwith said, as he tugged the last bandage into place. "Remarkable."

"Smelly," Dar said. "I could go for a bath tonight."

"Then you'll have to be wrapped again!"

"Yes, but"—and a smile spread over Dar's tired face—"Sharlin will have to do it then."

Hapwith gave him a comradely slap on the shoulder and snugged the cloak a little closer. He'd not missed the scars on the other's torso, welts and knobs here and there. Most fresh, but one or two quite old. Dar was a soldier who wore his life's history of survival etched into his skin. He cleared his throat. "What is Sharlin to you?"

Dar was immersed in the fascination of watching Sharlin patch the falroth hide into the dragon wing, but he looked at Hapwith. His warm brown eyes reflected some of the lanternlight. "I met her," he said, "over a treasure map."

"A treasure map?"

"Yes." Dar settled into the bruised grass. It smelled still of char and cinder from the previous night's disaster. "Yes. She was disguised as a pallan and worked at a borderland inn, in lower Kalmar. I'd come there seeking the advice of the local oracle for some problems of my own. We came to the aid of a peddler named Chappie. Ever hear of him?"

Hapwith squinted in thought. "No."

"Mmmm. I thought he might have sailed to the Upper Reaches. Well, never mind. He'd told wild tales of a dragon graveyard, shrouded in magic and wonder."

Dar shook his head in wonderment, even as he remembered their meeting. "He'd carried that discovery around in him until his hair turned silver, then one night he drank too much and lost it all, including his life."

"What happened?"

"We were in the wilds. Hazers overheard and rolled him, hoping he'd tell them his story. Sharlin and I interrupted them. But we didn't get there in time to save his life. He gave us the map, told us that he hadn't been dreaming. He charged us to go find it."

"And you did."

"Sort of. Sharlin rescued me from the hazers the next day, and then I found out she was a girl, not a pallan. I tried to lift the map, figuring I'd pay her a fair share for it later. A journey like that was too hard for a girl, right?"

Hapwith looked over. "She's royalty, isn't she?"

"Yes. And that's another story, one connected with you, Hapwith." Dar shifted. "She'll have to tell you that one."

"What did she do? Did you steal the map and did she catch up with you?"

Dar's thoughtful smile spread. "Not exactly. She caught me first. Took out her knife and slit the map in two, and said we were partners."

"And you were the two who brought the dragons back to life."

"Mmmm." Dar wasn't sure if he wished to take responsibility for that or not, considering the damage the resurrection seemed to be doing to Rangard. "We only wanted to wake Turiana. But the spell was powerful."

"Is she yours?"

"Sharlin is not chattel. There's no bride price high enough to buy the likes of her. But for the moment, she loves me."

"I see," said Hapwith, moving away.

Dar watched him approach the girl and the dragon,

and wondered if Hapwith did indeed see. He got to his feet and followed.

The turquoise dragon also watched over Pandor. He lifted his shapely head as the two men approached, but said nothing. Sharlin rubbed her eyes and flexed her shoulders. She knotted the thread and clipped it off.

"There, Pandor. You look like a mad cobbler's been at you, but you're done."

The dragon lifted his head. He'd been lying quietly, doglike, on his stomach. Now he craned his neck. "Thank you, cubling."

Sharlin scratched behind his ear. "Not too painful, I hope."

The blue dragon spoke up. "I will lick the wounds."

Pandor brightened a little. His spines rattled as he shook himself. "The new skin sings. I can feel the life. Perhaps it will bond to me. Yes. Perhaps there is much hope in this." He nuzzled Sharlin. "You have my gratitude." He looked to Aarondar. "You also, swordsman. The falroth was a mighty foe to have faced for me. I will sing you a song for that."

Dar found himself swaying a little on his feet. "You're welcome, Pandor. And now I think I'd better recuperate myself." Sharlin came to his side, and they walked together to the manor. With a sigh, Hapwith followed after.

Chapter 11

Turiana reared in the morning light, her head snaked back, and her fangs bared with every word she hissed at the duke of the Nettings. "Make up your mind, little worm. First you want us, then you do not. Now you beg for us to stay."

"But just to leave, to pull out, like that." Duke Mylo licked his thin lips nervously. He did not like dealing with the dragon queen directly, but hadn't been able to find Sharlin or Aarondar that morning.

"Do you think your paltry civilization here drew Baalan and his might? Don't flatter yourself. Baalan came because of me and my followers. If we leave, you will be that much safer."

The duke stepped back involuntarily as her large head came butting down toward him, spite flashing in her eyes. He relaxed a little as he looked across the field and saw both Sharlin and Dar crouched under the wounded dragon's spread wings. He pointed to them.

"They made promises."

Turiana serpentined her neck to view the two watching her from Pandor's protection. She hissed as though the sight displeased her. "I am not bound by their vows," she answered, and shook her golden hide, scales ringing like coins.

Sharlin came out from under Pandor's sail and

straightened. She capped the jar of ointment she'd been anointing his wounds with and tucked it in her vest pocket. "And what about vows you've made?"

The dragon turned around, lightning-quick, as though to make a strike. Pandor threw up his broad head and spat, but Sharlin stood her ground. Dar quickly shrugged out from under the other wing. He did not pull his sword, but his hand cradled the guard.

Sharlin felt her booted feet root to the ground. The golden lamp of Turiana's eyes had narrowed to malevolent yellow slits, and she feared to be the object of their focus. But she had no choice but to stand, for she couldn't have run if she'd wanted to.

"Words can be difficult to remember," the dragon said. She scratched a talon into the dirt and grass, raking up a furrow. "Words are more difficult than deeds."

"There is one deed I performed that I would expect you never to forget," Sharlin answered casually. "Bones to flesh and blood."

Turiana's tail swished. "It is good to live again," the firedrake said. Her eyes widened. The yellow faded, then warmed and glowed again, and the golden glow Sharlin remembered returned. "And it is better for the creatures here if we leave."

"But, but . . ." the duke said. He rounded her and joined Sharlin.

Turiana lowered her head and butted Sharlin gently in the chest, her nostrils cupped. Sharlin rocked back on her heels from the blow and tried not to show the fear which refused to ebb away entirely. "I will not leave you easy prey to enemies. Pandor must stay until he heals, and I will give you wards."

"Wards?"

"Magical means by which to guard the Nettings. They will guard against all but the sea," and Turiana swept her paw out. "The sea, after all, was here thousands of years before I was. Even a dragon can hardly take credit for the banes of the sea. Is that fair?"

The poor color of the man had faded entirely, and his jaws worked, but he seemed unable to make a sound. Sharlin took his arm.

"There will be no more sorcerous attacks from the air."

He finally shook himself. "There is scarcely anything left to damage," he said dryly. "I think perhaps I preferred the old days, when we sent offerings for protection."

"You see?" Turiana said triumphantly. "Our going will benefit you."

"But will it benefit us?" Dar said then. He'd been listening quietly and alertly, off to the side. "You and Hapwith haven't even begun to experiment."

"There is no time for that now."

Turiana looked to him, but his gaze did not meet hers. Instead, he was eying her flanks, and the starburst rays of darkness that flared across them. "You warned us once that you had other duties pressing. Tell me now, Turiana—what are they?"

The great dragon raised her head and looked down on them, and her emotions shone from the luminous lanterns of her eyes, blazing. "I will nest," she answered. "I will return to the walls of stone that protected me long ago—protected my back and my flanks from old enemies."

"What of Sharlin?"

"That lifedebt I must put aside now. I will be queen again, or else I will live again only to see the others slaughtered, as they were once before. Is that what you want, man? Do you want to see rivers of blood washing through your cities?"

"What I want is the truth."

"Then ask me."

Dar's hair was caught by the morning breeze and played back from his brow. He looked up at the queen of dragon legend, and asked, "Do you carry eggs, Turiana? Is it your time to lay?"

Sharlin sucked in her breath. The meadow became deadly silent. Even Pandor's bellows breathing quieted.

Then Turiana stirred. She looked from Dar to Sharlin. Her nostrils flared. "Yes. The time I warned you about has come. I must forsake you now, Sharlin, and look to my own. My time is limited."

"Turiana!"

"Don't cry, fair daughter. There are still a handful of days left that I can give to you." The dragon laid her head on Sharlin's shoulder as the girl rushed forward and hugged her neck. "I'm not ready to give up yet, but we must retreat to the mountains, where Baalan cannot harry us. Every day now will be precious. We can't afford to waste a moment. I will help you as much as I can, and I must gather my dragons."

Pandor spoke. "Take Alzo with you."

"The blue?"

"Yes."

Turiana blinked. "I thought to leave him with you."

The bronze dragon snorted. "I can take care of myself. But the blue has never been to the Gates, and you must do it soon. He chafes, Turiana. He is ready."

"What is he talking about?" Sharlin loosened her hold about the dragon's neck, but did not step away.

"It is a ritual of adulthood," Turiana said shortly.

"Yes." Now Turiana trembled, and she hunkered down on all fours. "Run. Get ready to leave quickly. Time is running out!"

Duke Mylo helped Sharlin onto Turiana's back and lashed down her pack behind her. He paused. "It is said to beware of what you ask the gods for—you might be cursed enough to receive it."

"I'm sorry you view our visit here as a curse."

The gaunt man smiled. "Not that. No. I have toured

the city. Your queen dragon has made it possible for much rebuilding. And if not Baalan's attack, well, it might have been that we would have attacked each other. No, I don't regret your having come here. And I've done as you wished. I opened up my sister's wing of the manor, and we're housing children there." A wry expression twisted his smile. "Noisy. My life is going to be filled with more than I bargained for."

Sharlin felt a warmth curling inside of her. "I'm glad."

"So am I. Yet all I asked for was you." The older man took his hand from the dragon's back. "Are they gods indeed, milady?"

She shook her head. "No. But the return of dragonkind has brought back power, for good and evil. We'll be a long time learning to deal with them and with ourselves. Take care, Duke Mylo. Once that crusty old heart of yours is opened, you're going to find room for all sorts of occupants, I think." She gave him a soft kiss, and he leaned back in surprise as Turiana straightened up, taking herself from his reach.

Then a strange expression shadowed him. "Wait. There is something I need to tell you, something that I saw that night." He shuddered in memory. "But I can never seem to remember what it was."

"Tell Pandor when you remember. He'll tell Turiana and she'll tell me."

He squeezed the toe of her boot in final farewell. "Goodbye, then." He stepped back, away from the spread of Turiana's wings.

Dar watched from his seat atop the brown dragon. Hapwith flew alone on Alzo and looked miserable. Dar caught a glimpse of his pale face with hands clutched desperately to the harness leathers. The youth had been unconscious most of the time his last trip on dragonback.

Hapwith caught Dar watching him and forced a meager smile. "It—it'll be a long way down."

"Don't worry about it," Dar said. "If you fall, you'll never hit the ground."

"I—I won't?"

"No. Turiana will flame you first." The swordsman laughed then, and saw Hapwith struggle to do the same. Dar felt comfortable on the brown's neck. The brown, still of indeterminable sex to Turiana and Pandor, as well as the humans, called itself Chey. The beast was already Turiana's size, and the man gathered from dragon comments that Chey would grow bigger.

He watched as Turiana and Pandor consulted muzzle to muzzle. The bronze was being left on his own in the Nettings. The duke had promised to keep him well fed. Already the dragon had been down to the harbor once, swimming. He claimed it was excellent exercise for his wings. The falroth hides seemed to be taking hold, but even if they grew into the skin, it was a long way from knowing if the bronze would ever fly again.

The pack behind Hapwith bulged with histories, most of them dealing with the oracular ability of seeing events, both past and future. Turiana had had Hapwith ask the pallans for them, and although given reluctantly, still, they had been handed over.

Turiana gave a short trumpet and stretched her wings, the conference with Pandor over. Dar gathered in his reins for balance and awaited the massive bunching of muscle power that launched a dragon into the sky. They would glide over the harbor again, and for a moment he felt his skin stretch pale and clammy over his face and heard Hapwith laugh. Then Dar laughed at himself as Chey gathered and flew into the face of the wind.

"I think it's time you told me what I'm along for," Hapwith said. He shivered, in spite of the dragon-lit warmth of the cave, and beads of nervous sweat still dotted the peachfuzz blond-white mustache on his upper lip. His hands were wrapped solidly about a mug of hot drink, but his knuckles were white. "I've nearly been tarred and feathered, roasted alive by enemy dragons, and that—that fiend did two loops with me on board, for some sadistic reason of its own—"

Even as Sharlin said, "You can't blame us for the tarring and feathering," her voice was overridden by the soft chuckle of Alzo to the rear of the immense caverns, where the dragons lay huddled close to one another.

Hapwith gulped at his drink, then lowered it. "All right. But the other stuff—who are the two of you, really? What's going on here?"

"Dar's told you some of the story."

"But not where I fit in. I'm not a farmer's lad, Lady Sharlin. You didn't just wander into Bywater—you were looking for someone like me. And I can't say as I minded. The two of you had . . . possibilities—"

"Lyrith is more like it," Dar said, his voice dry.

"All right, then. Lyrith is a very potent herb. I thought if I hung around with you for a few days, I could borrow some, and then just sort of leave."

"Steal it and run away, you mean." Shadows darkened Sharlin's gray-blue eyes. "And what about all the help you gave the pallans at the Nettings?"

"I'd been a fool not to. All that knowledge, stored up there for anyone to look at, absorb, *use*. I may look the fop to you, but I have hopes. Someday I'd like to be able to point my hand, and *phfum!*—magic happens."

Dar straightened his crossed legs, bringing the circulation to life. He poured himself another drink from the kettle hanging over the small fire. It gave Hapwith a moment to compose himself, for his face had suddenly crumpled with a hunger and humanness the youth had not shown before. Dar knew something of the yearning, though he'd never had it for magic. "And so you got more than you bargained for."

"But that's just it. You haven't given me a damn chance to bargain for anything. Suddenly I find myself up to the neck, buried in dragons and a dragon war."

"Don't like the odds, eh?" Dar chuckled and blew across the brim of the mug, cooling his drink.

"What odds? And what do the dragons want with you?"

Sharlin leaned back against the pillow she'd made of her thick cloak. "Actually, Hapwith, it's more of what we want with the dragons. And it's tied in with your talent. What can you tell us about your fortune-telling?"

"You want me to give away my secrets?" A moment of greed shot across his face. Dar did not miss the expression.

The swordsman waved his free hand, taking in all of the immense cavern and its darkened caves beyond. "We're in the middle of lower Kalmar, where men haven't lived for generations. It took a dragon to get us here, and in all likelihood it will take a dragon to get us out. Don't be coy, Hapwith."

Hapwith sighed, and the puffed-up ego of the charlatan ebbed outward with that breath. "All right," he said. "I don't know what I do, exactly. But I can focus in on a past experience when I trance myself."

"But why?"

"Someone comes to me to have his fortune told. Of course, that's a common way to steal a person blind. So people are naturally skeptics and cautious, but they come anyway. I had to compete with the others. I discovered I could focus these experiences and use them to convince the subject I could authentically predict the future as well. It worked with you, didn't it?" he said to Sharlin.

The corner of her mouth curved a little. "Actually," she said, "I was looking for you before that."

"Oh."

"But what we have to know is how you do it."

"I wish I could tell you," Hapwith said and looked glumly into his mug. "It's the only genuine magic I've got, and I was born with it."

"Then," Sharlin said, and looked across to the dragons sleeping in the great rock hall, "we'll have to find out, won't we?"

"And what about you two?"

"Well, Dar told you his side of the story, but not mine."

Hapwith lay back, his lanky body finding comfort on a rounded boulder. "You're a lady of mystery."

The curve of her mouth dissolved into a full-fledged grin. "Not really. Have you heard of the house of Dhamon?" As Hapwith shook his head, she pressed. "War griffins?"

"Those half-bird, half-cat things? Legends, from long ago."

"Don't dismiss them so lightly." Dar's voice deepened, a subtle warning. "I've fought wild griffins."

Hapwith shrugged. "Maybe they existed. What's that got to do with you?"

"Because one brought me to Kalmar."

He didn't move, but his blue eyes widened a little. Sharlin crossed her booted ankles and smoothed out her riding skirt. "My father is a king, King Balforth of Dhamon. We were under siege by a sorceress named Rodeka and her armies—"

"Wait a minute," Hapwith mumbled, but she ignored him.

"In the plateau country of Dhamon, magic is a rare commodity. I knew we needed to fight Rodeka on her own terms. I decided to find Turiana and raise her from the dead, if I could, and bring her home with me to stop Rodeka's black arts."

Hapwith sat up and wagged a finger at her, his hand shaking. "I know that name. By all the gods, she's been dead for—"

"Centuries."

In the silence that followed, only the stentorian snoring of the dragons could be heard.

Then Hapwith shook his head. "I don't understand."

"Neither did I, at first. I escaped Dhamon on my war griffin, Gabriel. As we passed over Rodeka's siege encampment, a massive bolt of energy hit us. It mortally wounded Gabriel. I think I must have passed out for a moment, too, and then we were falling. He managed to right himself and bring us in for a landing here on Kalmar, near the borderlands. Then he died and I . . . I burned his body. But before he died, he told me that I would find my way to Turiana and not to give up, and I didn't. Pallans found me on the desert and took me in. Then I went to the borderlands inn and became a pallan servant, and waited. When Dar and Chappie showed up, I'd nearly given up hope, and then we were willed the map—"

"The treasure map."

Sharlin tucked a strand of amber hair behind her ear. "A map to the graveyard of dragons. I knew then I would find Turiana there, and I did. And I also found out the awesome truth. Rodeka's bolt had thrown us halfway around the world—and through time, as well. The kingdom I fight to save was conquered two or three hundred years ago. Win or lose, my family was dust long ago."

With a nervous clearing of his throat, Hapwith reached for his empty mug and filled it again. "I don't . . . I don't understand."

"You don't have to. But it happened, and that's why I need Turiana, and we both need you."

"But—why bother?"

Sharlin sat bolt upright. Color flashed across her cheeks. "Because I intended to save them, and I still do! The pallan writings that can tell me of what happened to my family have been destroyed. My family might have been ground under Rodeka's heel, or maybe I came back to save them. I love them! I want them to live full, happy lives! I want my lands to be free!"

"But Rodeka . . ." Hapwith stirred his drink with a finger, testing its coolness. "Well, her name is known. But I don't know when or how she died. Or even where, for that matter."

"So she might have left Dhamon and gone somewhere else, don't you see?"

"Look, if all you're worried about is your family, let me try to read your past. I don't know if I can go back that far, but— "

"You don't see! I wasn't there! My family's history is not part of my past now. I'm here and now."

Dar stirred. "Turiana is not all-powerful. She might be able to essay time, and might not. She took Sharlin on a spirit walk. There they met Rodeka, who was summoning ghosts who might stop her in her conquests. Yours was one of those ghosts, Hapwith. So we don't know how you fit in, or what has happened, but where there's life, there's hope. So we found you."

The youth sat hunched now. He said flatly, "Who else appeared?"

"Myself. Turiana locked in battle with Baalan. And Dar."

He ran a hand through his thatch of hair. "I met a woman in my dreams. She had everything that I wanted, and not just fleshly charms. I knew the moment I saw her that she held magic in her hands."

"Then you remember her and the summoning."

"Only a moment. She asked my name, and I gave it, then the silver cord wrenched me away."

"Silver cord?" asked Dar.

"A term of those of us who believe our spirits travel when the body sleeps. It's the tie that binds us to our flesh." Hapwith gulped down his drink. "I lied to myself. I thought she was an omen that I would gain what

I wanted. A goddess or something. But Rodeka . . . are you sure?"

"Fair-skinned, dark hair, bound in copper and leather—"

Hapwith waved his hand silently, and Sharlin stopped describing the sorceress. She saw with astonishment the tear that welled at the corner of his eye.

"What's wrong?"

"Don't you see! I thought I was going to be somebody! Not just a doorway or a window."

Sharlin reached across to him, after first looking briefly at Dar. "You are somebody, Hapwith. You don't have the full realization of your abilities yet. We need to find out how you do what you do—what no one has ever been able to do before. Then the rest is up to you."

Dar stood.

"Where are you going?"

"Chey's standing watch. I think I'll keep watch with it for a while. My soldier's reflexes are going flat."

"But Hapwith—"

"That's for you to deal with. I have other matters to take care of." He smiled, softening his tone.

"In the morning then," Sharlin blessed him, as he walked from the caverns. She sighed and looked back to Hapwith. "And you'd better sleep, too. Turiana and I have a full day planned for you."

The youth rolled his eyes. "Do I have to ride dragonback?"

"No." Then Sharlin added mischievously, "But if I think you're not cooperating, I can arrange it."

"Please, milady," he groaned, then caught the twinkle in her eye and they laughed softly together.

Chapter 12

For the first time in weeks—no, for the first time since he had died and awakened again—Dar felt comfortable in the night. He sought out the warm bulk of the guard dragon, a comforting sable figure in the darkness.

Chey lifted its head. "Man," it said, and its voice rumbled. Dar was reminded for a moment of the basso profundo tones of the dwarves.

"Chey," Dar returned. "I'll stand watch with you."

"It is not necessary."

"No. Not for you, perhaps."

They both relaxed a bit. Dar looked out over the mountains. As his eyes adjusted to the night, he could make out the deep shadows of the peaks against the lighter velvet of the sky. Neither the Shield nor the Little Warrior shone in the heavens that night, so he could see little else. The dragons had some nightsight, like cats, he knew, but he wondered if Chey could see other things.

"It reminds me of goblin country."

"Oh? I, too, have fought goblins," Chey said, its ears pricking in interest. "They are good, roasted."

"About the only thing they are good for," Dar murmured. "I haven't seen any in Kalmar."

"There are eight main continents, or bodies of land,

131

on Rangard. Goblins are the scourge of five of those lands."

For a moment, Dar envied the dragon its sense of the world. If it were not for ancient dragonkind, man would still be ignorant, thinking that the ground he stood on was all there was of the world. But he'd seen maps and even globes that told the wonder of his world. "Even to dragons?"

"Yes. They search out and clean out our hordes. That is most distressing."

"They clean out our farms and people."

"They must distress you, too."

"You could say that."

"Is that how you became a soldier?"

Dar scratched his temple. "One of the ways. My father was a soldier, and I was later . . . trained to follow in the footsteps of a conqueror."

The dragon looked down at him. "Footsteps you have left."

"I don't like conquerors."

"But there is chaos without order."

"Even chaos is better than living without choice."

The beast moved slightly. The warmth of its body flickered over Dar, protecting him from the wind off the mountaintops. "I will think on that." After a long time, it said, "That is profound."

"Thanks," answered Dar. "But I think of it as common sense. Any man works better if he has something to gain for it." They stood quietly again, then Chey said, "Tell me of the goblin battles you have fought."

And so Dar did, though he thought he'd forgotten most of them. Then Chey regaled him with a tale of a dragon who saw his horde slip away from under him literally coin by coin and jewel by jewel and how he caught the goblin thief who'd done it.

After that, they watched some shooting stars.

"Man," said Chey, finally, "I have picked my sex. I will be male."

Dar sensed that congratulations were in order, and so he slapped the big beast on its—his—scaled shoulder, under the wing. "A good choice. Do the others know yet?"

"Not yet. Turiana will know in the morning." A pause. "It is the custom to pattern oneself after another one admires. I have done a thing unknown to dragons. I am patterned after you."

"What?"

"You are insulted?" The dragon's eyes glowed like pumpkins in the night, and Dar surprised himself by reading hurt in them.

"No, I—I'm honored and surprised."

"Ahhh." Chey hunkered down a little. His cupped nostrils exhaled his warm scent over Dar, a scent like newly mown summer grass. "I am surprised myself. But I have sensed that in you which tells me the choice is a proper one."

Dar mulled that over. "Thank you, Chey."

"You are welcome, man. May I call you Aarondar, as Turiana does?"

"Yes. Or Dar, as Sharlin does." He paused. Chey had no magic powers such as Turiana and Pandor had. In that respect, he was like Alzo. "Does that mean you'll get your powers now?" They could use all the powered dragons they could find.

"Perhaps. That is a different thing. If Turiana wishes to take me beyond the Gate."

"The Gate?"

Chey moved uneasily. "I cannot tell you more, Aarondar."

"I see. It's all right." Dar did not press, but he knew the dragon didn't wish to withhold from him either. Another time, he might get the answers he sought. He put aside his feelings of unease. A dragon was not something to be pushed. His hand curled about the wrappings of his swordhilt. Not that Valorek left him much choice or time to be delicate. No, the man had been introduced to the vast opportunities of dragon power, and the witch king would not hesitate to exploit it.

Mentally Dar toasted his former mentor. If not for the most recent attack on his life, he would still be stumbling around, half a man, without even knowing it. Sharlin had noticed, but said little. Perhaps she had not even known enough about the wrongness to tell him, for if she could have put her finger on it, he thought Sharlin would have told him. Now Valorek had him to fear.

But even as he settled his shoulder against that of Chey and they stood, silent comrades, watching for enemies in the night, he thought uneasily of Turiana. Her temperament changed from moment to moment. If all dragons, benevolent or not, were so capricious, where was man's safety in siding with them?

In the past, he'd held contempt for the dragongods. Now he knew they were not gods, but beasts. Beasts of great intelligence and magic, beasts that were undoubtedly greater than he was, but beasts nonetheless. Could he trust the humankind of Rangard to their guardianship? He didn't think so, and though that thought rankled at him, he didn't wish it away.

The only hope for Rangard was a partnership of power, man shoulder to shoulder with dragons, even as he stood with Chey. But to obtain that partnership, when man fought with man from township to township even as the dragons fought among themselves, seemed an insurmountable problem. Yet if he did not try, he would never forgive himself.

As he looked out over the nightscape of jagged peaks and valley washes, he thought of the swamp witch who'd trailed him across country because she sensed a destiny in him. Her feelings had been echoed in the old fortune-teller by Bywater. It wasn't destiny he felt, at

last. It was life. Living, with a purpose other than to
shadow Sharlin and answer her love with love of his
own. He was a man, himself, beyond that relationship,
and tonight was the first time he had felt it in weeks.

Hapwith woke, stiff and cold, on the rocky floor.
Sharlin lay curled on her cloak, one hand bent back
under her cheek. She looked for a moment like an
exquisite child. He cleared his throat and broke his
stare. Dar hadn't come in during the night.

Hapwith rubbed his eyes. They'd told strange tales in
the evening, and he wasn't sure how many of them he'd
believed. Across time? There was no one he knew who
could travel through time. But the woman was beautiful, no doubting that, and he found himself thinking
about her more and more. He couldn't do much with
Dar at her side constantly, but get the swordsman away
and pepper her tea with a little lyrith, just to open the
senses and send the heart pounding a little . . . yes.
She might then look at him for once instead of the
swordsman. And Hapwith wouldn't mind that at all.

He stood up and stretched, unwilling to wake her,
feeling guilty as if she could sense his thoughts. It was
not as if he had much control over it. His body had a
mind of its own, had for years, and truthfully, Hapwith
had enjoyed following its lead. He could no more imagine impotency than he could imagine having been born
a flower.

But the feeling faded as he stared off across the
caverns. The dragons were all gone. How could anything of that bulk leave so silently? Hapwith ran his
fingers through his hair. He could do with a comb. And
he missed his bag of tricks left behind in Bywater.
Cards and dice would help the monotony. Yet he stared
across that cavern and found himself following that stare,
soft-footed and cautious.

Beyond the end caverns, in the darkness that Turiana

had not magically luminated, but a torch could, lay her caves. Caves that must be filled with the stored treasure of centuries. He might find a comb in there. Or a lute. Or a bag of golden crowns, enough to purchase him comfort for the rest of his life. To hell with lyrith, if he had enough gold.

Hapwith licked his lips and paused. He found his heart pounding and his pulse drumming in his ears. Dragongold was said to be cursed—not to mention what the queen would do to him if she found him wandering in there.

Still, he did not turn back. He quietly went to the edge of the illumination and paused, the darkness enfolding the caves beyond, their imaginings a siren song that brought him to the brink of destruction.

"I wouldn't go any farther if I were you."

Hapwith jumped. His heart stopped, then began palpitating in his chest. Dar stood, the heel of his left hand resting on his sword's hilt, but Hapwith had no doubt he could draw it fast enough if he wished.

"I—ah—was just looking."

"No doubt. It has a certain lure, doesn't it? But we're guests here, and chancy ones at that. Turiana could wither you with a glance, and I suggest you don't forget it."

Hapwith wiped his damp palms on his breeches. "I really don't know what came over me."

Dar sighed. "Come outside. Get some fresh air. I've killed and grilled a couple of softfoot for breakfast."

More than softfoot waited. A pile of fresh roots and four sweetfruit lay on a broad, shiny green leaf. Hapwith went around the foot of the caves to relieve himself and came back to find Sharlin had come out of the cave as well.

She sat cross-legged, pinning her hair back with her shell comb. She laughed at Hapwith and said, "Remind me later to fix your hair. It's sticking up all over."

He found himself blushing as he sat down and reached for a chunk of softfoot.

The wing of dragons returned as they finished their breakfast. They landed in a flurry of colors and sound, their wings rifling the morning air of the mountainside. Dar watched and wondered, thinking of how many dragons a country could hold. They all crouched behind Turiana, with the exception of Chey, who sidled over and backed up Dar. Turiana looked to him, but he couldn't read any meaning in her glance. What would she be like this morning? Benign or nasty? And would the nearness of humans to her nest unsettle her further?

Dar stirred uneasily. The darkness that crept from her stomach stood out. It had gone from sable to black, obsidian black, the black of the dragon that had raped her.

He stood. "I think it's time, Turiana, to talk of your plans."

"Dar . . ." murmured Sharlin, and he recognized the fear in her voice. She'd hoped to dissuade Turiana, but this morning, he disagreed.

"We can't afford to waste time on the past," he said.

She took a shocked breath, then stood as well. "It's my time and my past."

He wouldn't, couldn't, look at her. "Your past, perhaps, but the time belongs to all of us. None of you knows Valorek the way I do. You don't know his gall, his spite—or his military genius. Baalan's dragons have given him a weapon that he won't put down easily."

Hapwith looked up and licked a finger clean. He said nothing.

Aarondar felt the soft hand upon his arm, and the wash of scent from her fragrant hair and body, subtle chains upon all his actions and thoughts. "You know what this means to me," she said.

"Yes. But Turiana can't afford to remain idle. We

don't even know how many dragons range across Rangard
now. We don't know, but I'll wager our lives that Valorek
and Baalan have a fairly good idea. We've found dead
beasts, slaughtered, in the far reaches. We've been
attacked in an area where we should have been safe.
No, Valorek wouldn't wait for you to resolve your problems, Sharlin. The time to act is now, not a faraway
yesterday."

"What do you suggest?" Turiana said. She settled
down onto her stomach and put her chin on her paws.

"A census. You've dragons here, and Pandor. You've
got to sweep Kalmar and the Upper Reaches, then the
other lands. If you're to be queen again, you've got to
know your subjects and allies. Baalan is massing for a
war. We can't stand the first assault."

"That is true. But there is no one here who has been
beyond the Gates but myself. The sort of survey you
suggest is difficult."

The turquoise dragon behind Turiana shifted. Even
in the morning light, the sky seemed to play upon his
scales, blue to aqua to bluer. He dazzled with a kind of
blue fire that is seen in flames. "I'm ready," the beast
said.

Turiana quivered. "As is Chey, now. But I don't want
to chance the Gates without backing, and I cannot get
the backing I need without doing what Aarondar suggests, unless I use the Gates. It is a paradox."

"Can't you send?" Sharlin said quietly, her voice
muffled.

"I can. Would you risk Baalan answering?" Turiana
got to her haunches. She put her muzzle to the sky.
"Tonight, Alzo, you'll come with me. We will chance it.
Then, if you succeed, you will begin to do what Dar
suggests. Find our brothers and sisters, even those who
have not their powers. You will begin a gathering for
me."

Dar looked then at the woman beside him. She did
not look back.

Turiana intoned, "In the meantime, I have promised Sharlin to see what Hapwith is made of."

The youth squeaked. "Me?"

"Yes. But don't worry. I don't intend to tear you limb from limb to find out—though you may wish later you have been." Turiana gave that dragonish chuckle.

Hapwith followed the waddling dragon queen into the caverns, a resigned slope to the set of his shoulders. Sharlin made as if to go after them, then stopped. She looked at Dar.

"Why?"

"Because it is necessary. Because, as much as I love you, there may not be a way back to Dhamon. I know Valorek. Here and now is what I have to be thinking of."

An unreadable expression flickered across her face, then she nodded, tucking in her small chin. "I think I understand." She turned to follow, and stopped again. "You didn't come in last night."

"No. Chey and I stood watch out here."

"All night?"

"No. Alzo relieved us. But the sky was so beautiful, we decided to sleep outdoors."

"And did you?"

"Did I what?"

"Sleep."

And her gaze locked with his. He smiled. "Yes. I slept well."

"Good." This time she followed Turiana and Hapwith, leaving him looking after her for the longest time.

"Try it again."

"My head hurts."

The dragon opened her jaws, grinning, her forked tongue lolling out. "I have a charm for that."

"Never mind," Hapwith said hastily. He took a deep breath, looked at Sharlin, and tried the trance again.

This time he felt himself drifting. Involuntarily, he reached for Sharlin's hand, grabbing it tightly.

Turiana murmured, "I'm following."

The vision moved across Hapwith, burning his eyes, stinging his thoughts. Dwarves, on ponies. The vision blurred, however, for the dwarves did not all seem to be dwarves. The youngest one wore no beard, and he had the oddest sensation of Sharlin's face behind it, as they sang rude songs and rode across the badland countryside.

Hapwith broke away suddenly, leaned over, and threw up into the sand. It was dry heaves that racked him until his spittle brought up yellow bile. Sharlin handed him a damp rag. He wiped his mouth apologetically and buried the bile in the sand.

"I'm sorry."

Sharlin sat back, sighing. "It's disorienting."

"I keep failing."

"That was no failure."

The youth looked at her. "What? What do dwarves have to do with you?"

She gave a nonchalant shrug. "I traveled disguised as one for a while." She looked to Turiana. "What do you think?"

"I think I have it. Let me ponder for a moment." And Turiana closed her eyes.

"Here we go," Sharlin whispered. "She'll be asleep an hour or so."

Hapwith followed her lead and stood up. Beyond the cave's mouth, he could see that day had given way to late afternoon. His stomach rumbled. "I wonder if there's any more of that grilled softfoot."

"I'm sure. And I smelled journeycakes a while ago."

"What?" How could he have missed that?

"You were in a trance," Sharlin said. "Dar poked his head in, gave me a wink, and was gone again."

"My head feels like an overripe melon." He stumbled outdoors and blinked. A leaf-wrapped bundle awaited them on the flat rock used for cooking. A few gnats buzzed around lazily, and he slapped them aside. "Not warm, but still good."

Sharlin paused beside him. Her cool hands slipped about his neck and began to rub gently.

He froze, the sensations washing through him. A crumb of journeycake dropped from his lips.

"There. That should help." She passed him by then and grabbed a cake for herself, its golden flakiness breaking apart in her fingers.

It took a moment for Hapwith to compose himself. He swallowed his mouthful and absorbed himself in devouring a second, unwilling to look at the princess. At the back of his thoughts, he wondered where Dar was.

"What are you thinking?"

He choked. Sharlin handed him a mug of fresh water. "Dar's cooking isn't that bad," she chided.

"No. I guess a soldier learns how to take care of himself."

"Usually. How do you feel now?"

"Better. How did you know she"—Hapwith gave a shrug to the cave—"was going to sleep?"

"Almost all mothers-to-be I know of like a nap now and then," Sharlin said. She licked her lips. "These would be better with honey."

"I'll find you some tomorrow."

"No." Sharlin laughed. "You have other work to do, if your head stays in one piece."

Hapwith sighed. "I'm afraid I'm not much help. What can Turiana do with me?"

"I don't know, yet. What's that?"

Hapwith kicked a rolled-up skin by his foot, picked it up, and handed it to her. She unrolled it. He could see charcoal scribblings across the surface. She frowned.

"What is it?"

"Dar's taken Chey and gone off on his own. He'll not be back tonight, he says." She looked off over the mountain valley, her blue-gray eyes gone far away, as if to follow him.

"Why?"

"He doesn't say. But I can guess. He's gone in search of dragons."

"But Turiana said it should be done with power—"

"He always was the impatient one." She rolled up the skin and let it drop among the cool ashes of the fire.

Hapwith ate the last journeycake viciously, saying, "He has no business leaving you."

"On the contrary." Sharlin stood up. "I think perhaps I had no business bringing him along."

The dragon snore from the cave stopped abruptly, snorted, and then a voice said querulously, "Where have you gone?"

Sharlin smiled. "Our dragon queen awaits." With a sweep of her skirt, she turned and answered the call.

Hapwith took a moment to wipe his mouth. He looked around the camp nervously, and saw Sharlin's pack to one side. Quickly, he went to and opened the flap.

Packets of herbs lay on the top. With deft fingers, he plucked out the yellow parchment of lyrith and slipped it into his breeches pocket, then refastened the pouch.

Chapter 13

Even winter rains didn't slow the prosperity of a town like Murch's Flats. The hazers came and went with their herds of wild gunter, and the thieves' trade did briskly, and, of course, there was always a demand for the likes of Whores' Street. All in all, Trader Joe felt quite good about the coming season. A den of iniquity such as he bossed was not likely to feel an economic pinch in bad times.

He slapped the lean hardness of his stomach. Gray flecked his dark hair, but age stopped there. He was short, compact, all muscle, with a neck as thick as a gunter's. His guards often topped him by head and shoulders, but the tools of his trade and the quick fitness of his body kept them in line. They respected his abilities.

He marched through the alley to his offices, ignoring the muddy slop that churned under his boots. Dark clouds roofed the skies over Murch's Flat, making it difficult to see beyond the next building or so. Let it rain. It kept them indoors longer on Whores' Street. And, with pleasure, he felt himself grow hard at the thought. Perhaps he himself would visit there later.

It was a luxury he had been able to give back to himself only about two months ago. Before then, that accursed wizard Thurgood had taken away his potency.

Trader Joe had tried to have the man killed, but failed. Joe's lip curled. The miserable, pitiful slip of a wizard, his face slack and arm and leg failing, the sign of a weak heart. Yet Thurgood hadn't been too weak to steal away what Joe had prized most, and keep it.

No, Trader Joe didn't regret the ensuing bargain he'd made with the stranger, though it had cost him no end of trouble with Nabor and his hazers. The man coming through town had not been of the usual cut of cloth of Murch's Flats inhabitants. Joe was pleased he'd read the man right, even though he threw in with Thurgood and rode out of town with him. Fifty crowns it had cost him, but word filtered back. The black dragon Jet was dead. With him, the wizard Thurgood. No gossip had to bring him that news! His manhood knew the second it had happened.

Joe paused on the stairs outside his office and impatiently shouldered aside one of his bodyguards.

"Let me at the lock, dammit. Keep a sharp eye out for stingers!"

"Yessir." The guard turned, his keen eyes sweeping the alleyway for trouble.

Trader Joe didn't worry about stingers, but it was right his men should. That's what he employed them for. That, and to keep a certain amount of respect among the unruly residents of Murch's Flats. He left his men outside and settled into the massive chair behind his desk. He took a deep breath, immensely pleased with life.

"Comfortable?"

Joe's feet dropped to the floor. Before he could shout, the shadow moved away from the wall, and he saw the glint of a sword in his hand.

"I wouldn't do that if I were you."

Joe's eyes widened. "What are you doing here? I paid you. Why did you come back?"

A grim smile creased the swordsman's face. "What's the matter, Joe? Didn't you like the job? Wasn't it worth it to you?"

The town boss looked to the door. Beyond it lay his protection. His wrist sheaths chafed. He carried a spring-loaded dagger in each. One tiny movement, and he had a well-balanced throwing blade ready to go. He licked his lips. There was something about the swordsman that nicked his confidence. The other had come from another place . . . a place with different rules. Joe feared him without quite knowing why.

"If you were going to kill me, I think you'd have done it." The town boss got a grip on himself and leaned back in his chair, feigning relaxation.

"Possibly. Maybe I wanted to hear you beg me first." The swordsman moved a step closer.

"Then you'll die waiting." Joe flexed his wrist, and with a snick, the blade was in his hand.

The man outguessed him. With a fluid movement, he'd crossed the floor and leaned over the desk and had the point of his sword at the hollow of Joe's throat. "I don't think you want to do that," the swordsman said.

"Right." Joe replaced the blade. "What do you want?"

"Talk."

He placed the flat of his square hands palms down on the desktop. "All right then. What brings you back to Murch's Flats?"

"You do." The swordsman brought his sword away, but kept it on the ready. His gaze flickered toward the door, and Joe knew that he knew men waited outside it. The town boss felt a little confidence eking back. "You asked me to kill a wizard for you. You gave me the silver bolt that would totally destroy him, even his soul, to do it with. How do you know I did the job?"

Joe laughed then, a nervous laugh that rumbled. "Oh, I know. Believe me, I know."

The swordsman tilted his head, then smiled. "Thurgood had you by the balls, did he?"

Heat flooded the town boss's face, though he did not answer.

The swordsman lowered his sword and leaned on it, digging the tip into the wood floor. It was an expensive wood floor. Joe looked at the notch being dug into it.

"I've a proposition for you, then."

"If it's more money you want, it's worth it to me." Joe slid a hand to his desk drawer, where he kept a stinger, loaded with a red-fletched stun dart.

"No. I offer you something worth even more to you, Trader joe. I'm going to offer you the chance to remain town boss of Murch's Flats."

The square man's eyes narrowed. "Do you know someone who wants my job?"

The swordsman laughed. "Not I. But you have more to fear than another man. Dragons, Joe. Dragons everywhere, hungry for power and to rule."

Joe grunted. He eased his hand away from the drawer. "Don't I know it," he said. "They've been decimating the wild gunter herds. No dragons here for two generations, and then we're up to our asses in them. Only beast I ever heard of before was the god Jet, in the Upper Reaches. Now he's gone, and these others are around. Buzzing like bees around honey."

"Pesky critters."

"What's your point?"

"The mature dragons, the ones with magical powers, intend to be more than pesky. They like the idea of being gods, Joe. They've come back."

Joe liked to think he could stay one step ahead of the swordsman. He smiled shrewdly. "And you're going to get rid of them for me. Well, now. I'll have to think on that. What's a dragonslayer worth to Murch's Flats, eh?"

But the swordsman shook his head. "No. You're going to have to learn to live with 'em. They're back to stay. But first there's going to be a power struggle, and I'm here to tell you which side you want to pick."

"Let them kill each other off. Murch's Flats is a hole in the mud. Don't kid yourself. Ain't nobody going to be fighting over us."

"It's almost begun. Don't kid yourself, Joe. I'm going to give you some advice, and I want you to take it . . . and I want you to take it because I didn't kill Thurgood. He was a friend. Jet killed him. But before he died, he told me some of his . . . secrets. And if you value what you've gained by his death, you'll remember my advice. Murch's Flats wants to be on the side of the golden dragon, Turiana. Remember that, Joe."

"T-Turiana?"

"That's right. And if you hold steadfast, I can guarantee you'll still be town boss and Murch's Flats will still be the same mudhole it's always been. But if the purple dragon Baalan wins, then you'd better dig yourself a deep grave and hide in it, because there's no room in his plans for any other rulers, not even a petty man like you."

"Now wait a minute," Joe said, straightening. "Who the hell you calling petty?"

But the swordsman was gone. He had reached overhead and disappeared through a hole in the ceiling, a hole that Joe hadn't seen before. He kicked himself out of his chair and went to look in the shadowy corner.

A dark cloud billowed overhead, a dark threatening cloud that looked almost like a winged dragon. But the man was gone, and Joe shouted aloud in anger. His door splintered open almost immediately before he'd even caught his breath.

"What is it, boss?"

"I want this goddam ceiling fixed, and quick. And this time make sure no son of a bitch can saw his way through again." And Joe rubbed his throat, tight with his anger, his fingers trembling. But he knew that the swordsman had, in his way, offered him a choice, and even a villain preferred a choice to none. He'd remember the name Turiana.

The golden dragon's eyelids drooped slyly. "I think," she said finally, "I know what we have in Hapwith."

The youth sat on the cave floor in abject fatigue, cradling his head between his hands.

"What is it?"

"He sees the past."

Sharlin reined in her exasperation. "I know that."

"Ah, but not all that. I have been trying to determine how he sees the past."

"He reads it through the person he's working with, doesn't he?"

"So it would appear. But I have been following, and I have been wondering what Rodeka fears in him, and I think I have found the key." Turiana twitched her nostrils. "He's been a tough lock, I admit."

Hapwith groaned. "Mercy on me," he said. "I've been trying."

Sharlin patted his shoulder comfortingly. "There's no doubt of that," she told him.

Turiana made a rumble. They looked to her. "Have I your attention again?" she said.

"Yes, great one," Sharlin answered, and kept her eyes wide and innocent.

"Good. Then this is what I perceive. If Hapwith is reading past experiences, it is logical that he would read it through your eyes as you lived it."

"Of course."

"But he doesn't."

"He doesn't?"

Hapwith looked up, a dawning in his face. "No, I don't! I saw you, Sharlin, disguised as a dwarf boy! But if I was you, then I would only have seen the others—don't you see?"

"Yes, and no. If he doesn't read my experiences, then what does he do?"

"He travels there himself," concluded Turiana smugly.

Sharlin shook her head. The amber strands of her hair swung about freely as the shell comb tumbled to the cave floor. Hapwith snatched it up to return it to her before she could move. Sharlin took it absently, not noticing the effect the touch of her hand had on the magician. He swallowed and stood up, back to the cave wall.

"That can't be, Turiana. At least, not in the flesh."

"No, but he's untrained. If he can open those doorways to the flesh, then we have your Rodeka in the palm of our hand."

"But you did that with me already. When we walked at Lyrith. You saw my home, the griffin eyrie, the fortress, Rodeka."

The dragon shook her head. "No, daughter. Only you saw that. I but followed. But if Hapwith here can look within and unravel his powers, then he can open a door and a vision that I can transport to . . . transport flesh and blood. And Rodeka will have me to answer to!" The dragon threw back her head and trumpeted.

For the first time, Sharlin felt afraid of Turiana. She took a step backward and found herself stopped by Hapwith. His awkward hands braced her shoulders. The two of them waited in silence for the dragon to compose herself once more. Sharlin feared to see her eyes narrow and become malevolent again, but they did not.

Turiana looked down to them. "I can do no more today. I must eat, then rest, for I take Alzo to the Gates when the moons are high."

"I know."

"Aarondar has Chey, so you will be unguarded tonight."

"No one knows where we are," Sharlin answered. "I'm as safe in your nest as I can be."

"Fare thee well then," the dragon returned, and nuzzled her gently. "I will see you in the morning." She lumbered from the cavern, and with an imperious sound summoned the dragons waiting outside. With a great rush, they took to the air and were gone.

"Where do you suppose this Gate is?"

Sharlin moved away from Hapwith. She felt uneasy. "I don't know." She flexed her neck, easing tense muscles. "What do you say I cook dinner?"

"And I'll wash," the youth returned, with an easy grin.

After dinner, they sat in easy, companionable silence. Hapwith was true to his word and cleaned the trenchers, then stoked the fire.

"Another cup of tea?" he asked.

"Yes," said Sharlin wearily. She looked to the darkness overhead, and the banners of stars white-hot in the sky. She looked for Dar, even as she knew she wouldn't see him. Hapwith pressed the mug into her hand. "Drink and sleep," he said softly. "We've all had a rough day."

It sounded like a good idea.

Sharlin slept restlessly. She dreamed of flying again, without dragon wings this time, and as though she knew she did not have the magic, she skimmed the ground dangerously low, whipping through treetops and across fields. Her hair streamed out behind her. She wore a gown of softest white, beribboned at the neck. A wedding gown, she thought in surprise, and it didn't keep her warm at all from the icy winds that tore at her as she flew.

Something jerked at her. Her hands grasped at her stomach as it tore. The silver cord, she thought, remembering what someone had said once. Now I must go.

But she continued to rush over the ground. I must hurry, she thought to herself. Dhamon hasn't much time.

Time.

The silver cord pulled again. She looked down and saw it threading below her, a strand billowing through the sapphire sky. It was then she recognized the hills under her.

Home! Something drew her home again. Sharlin made a tiny noise in her throat, half of joy and half of fear. As she licked her wind-chapped lips, she recognized the taste of lyrith. What was happening to her?

The stomach pains ended. Her speed slowed, and she glided in over the plateau that housed the fortress of Dhamon, its stables and lands, and griffin eyrie. The grass sparkled like a green gem. She felt a tear at the corner of her eye and brushed it away.

She thought of swerving away and forsaking it. Like a bird on the wing, she drifted on the winds, and almost circled about, but the cord jerked at her, savagely this time, and Sharlin cried out in fear.

Was this her dream, or Rodeka's summoning?

Lyrith. The taste and smell of it about her, like rain. Some fool had given her lyrith, and now what was she to do? Where were Dar and Turiana?"

"Dar!" She strangled on the word and the need to wake and cry it out. "Dar!"

Snared, the power pulled her down crashing onto the flagstones of the courtyard. She lay for a moment. Now she knew what it was like to be a bird arrowed down from the sky. Sharlin rolled to her flank and lay a moment, then raised her head and stood. She was wanted within the fortress, and she could not deny the geas laid upon her.

A small, warm hand forced itself into hers as she stood. Sharlin looked down in shock. A child stood there. Not even a child, but a sturdy babe, a toddler, in homespun shirt and trousers, with tiny fur boots upon his feet. His legs bowed out a little, and she was reminded of her brother, Erban, at two years. He looked up and said nothing, but chewed fretfully on the fingers of his other hand. Fear caught in her throat. Was it Erban's blood that summoned her?

For lack of anything else to do with him, Sharlin brought him along. The great wooden doors of the hall swung open before her fingers even touched them. She felt the wrenching of soul that pulled her in, and the child beside her came, too.

"Come in, spirit of the night. You are welcome here," the sorceress said. She stood in the center of her diagrams again, and the brazier blazed. The hall was bare this time. The treasures and furniture had been stripped. The tremendous stone fireplace was piled with ashes. Sharlin hesitated to look there, for fear of seeing what had been burned.

Rodeka capped the vial in her hands. "I sense your presence, spirit. Make yourself seen to me."

That gut-wrenching tore at her. Sharlin nearly went to her knees, but the presence of the toddler seemed to uphold her. Her hands were icy, but his was warm. And he looked at her with soft and trusting brown eyes.

It was a dream, she told herself. A lyrith dream, and even though Rodeka had caught her up, she could still escape. She could still get back. She had to!

"Dar," she said, and was surprised to hear her voice. The sorceress looked keenly in her direction. Her blue-black hair hung unbound this night, but feathers adorned it. She looked like a wild, savage bird of prey. "You speak. Now show yourself!"

She felt hands upon her waist and a soft voice at her ear. "It's all right," he said. "I'm here."

"Dar," Sharlin repeated, drawing strength from the name of her beloved. "Let me go, Rodeka! We'll meet soon enough!"

The child whimpered then, and pulled on her hand. The warmth of his need was different from the insistent pull of the other's hands on her. She felt chilled, as though she were naked.

Rodeka stepped forward. "If you are Dhamon, then I have you," she said triumphantly. "I called you, and I have you, and with you, if you are the daughter, I will break them!"

"No!" screamed Sharlin. She twisted away, picked up the child, and ran, ran through the open doorway.

Hands raked over her. The fabric of her gown ripped from her shoulders. She dropped the child into the grass and went to her knees, sobbing, grasping for him.

A beast covered her and grasped her, rolling her over, a beast with a soft voice that said, "I'm here. It's a nightmare. Let me comfort you." And the beast pulled down the gown from her breasts and tried to suckle them.

Sharlin threw back her head and screamed. The child was being suffocated between them, and he struggled, and the only thing she knew was that she had to protect him, with her life if necessary.

Chey swooped down to the mountainside. Dar gripped the harness tightly, with knees so numbed that he wondered if he could walk again. He swung down as the creature halted, and held onto the harness for a second.

The dragon slowly collapsed to his stomach under

him. Chey gave out a wheeze. "The flight was long," he said.

"But good work," Dar answered. He took a deep breath and stood and flexed his legs. Pins and needles prickled at him. "What's that?"

He thought he heard a noise over the night wind.

Chey's sable ears flicked.

"Dar!"

Faint, but it was Sharlin's voice. He drew the sword and ran toward the caves.

Hapwith lay over her, clawing at her blouse. She struggled feebly under him, in a nest of the shreds of her clothing. Dar made a low sound in his throat and went for the youth.

He grabbed him by the shoulder and threw him off, then kicked him for good measure. The magician screamed in pain and scrabbled away, blue eyes wide with fear.

Dar went to one knee beside Sharlin, reaching for her. He touched her skin, found it icy-cold, and though she quivered at his touch, she did not open her eyes or seem to know who it was.

"You've drugged her. Drugged her so you could rape her! Turiana!" Dar raised his voice, and the caverns rang with anger.

"She—she's not here," croaked Hapwith. "Please don't kill me. I didn't—I didn't mean to. I never have before. It's just that she—she seemed to like me, and I . . . I knew you were going to be gone. I used the lyrith. And she dreamed, but it went bad and she reached for me. I—gods help me, Dar. I couldn't help it!"

Dar smoothed the tangled hair from her face. A lyrith dream, and this time, without Turiana, he had no idea how to wake her. He pulled what was left of her blouse over her breasts. The magician could be telling the truth. He seemed as appalled as Dar by what he'd tried to do.

He had two choices. He could kill Hapwith for what he'd done, or he could try to save Sharlin.

In the end, it was no choice at all. He dropped the sword in the dirt. "Go get fresh water," he ordered, and as Hapwith scrambled out of the cave, he took Sharlin in his arms.

Sharlin woke, wrapped in a heavy blanket, a fire sending orange bursts of light into the magical illumination of Turiana's caverns. Her lips felt thick and bruised, and she licked them. The hold of the nightmare still clutched at her, but she knew she'd awakened.

A figure sat beyond her, bowed over the fire. From the angle of his head, she knew he slept, but she smiled and did not hesitate to wake him.

"Dar?"

He jerked awake and twisted around, reaching for her, taking her in, blanket and all. "Are you all right?"

"I was dreaming. . . ."

"I know. Hapwith gave you lyrith."

She felt his jaw tighten, even as he hugged her close, and knew there was something beyond that, but he said nothing further.

"Rodeka summoned me again."

"What happened?"

"Nothing. I—I was able to get away. And there was this beast, clawing at me, smothering me . . . it was awful. I thought I was going to . . . going to . . ." She halted, unable to say it.

"I'm here now. It's been a bad dream, but you're going to be all right. I tried to help you, but we couldn't do much. You broke it yourself." He kissed the side of her face.

She pulled back then, and looked at him, and fear swept through her entire being. She ran her fingertips through the light brown waves of his hair and let herself be lost for a moment in the pools of his brown eyes, and knew then that she hadn't broken the power of the dream. Not she alone, but what she carried within her.

And she could not tell him, for if she did, Dar would never let her go back. Dar would bind her forever to this day and this time, to his destiny and not her own.

He would never let her leave him if he knew that she carried his son.

Chapter 14

"He was a fool to use lyrith in this place," said Turiana. The tip of her tail lashed the air, then she curled it about her left leg, though the tip continued to quiver irritably. "Magic is seeped into the very rocks. Things here are more powerful than they would be elsewhere."

Sharlin combed her thick hair back from her face with her fingers. "It's done. He'll be all right, really, Turiana. He seems more shocked than I am over what happened."

Dar said nothing. He studied the goblin-blood stains on his boots. He had not told either Sharlin or Turiana about the attempted rape and did not intend to. Hapwith could hardly be more contrite, at any rate.

"It is your justice," Turiana answered. The tone of her voice said that the matter was closed, as far as she was concerned.

Dar looked up. Her flanks bubbled. Her laying had to be close. A week, two at the most. And what would she be like then? How long would it take her to lay her clutch? How long to die?

The queen flexed a talon. It glittered dark amber gold. "Leave us, Sharlin. I wish to speak to Aarondar."

Outside, crows cawed raucously, and the screech of a vystra interrupted them. Sharlin's mouth opened and

157

then closed on a silent protest. With a flash in her eyes, more stormy gray than blue this morning, she looked at Dar, turned heel, and left.

Warily, Dar stood his ground.

"I will be taking Chey beyond the Gates tonight. It will be our last chance before the Shield and Little Warrior part. He told me of what happened yesterday in Murch's Flats."

"I hoped he might. What you must understand, Turiana, is that men are as fragmented as the dragons. This works to Baalan's advantage if we ignore it."

"We shall see. Alzo passed beyond the Gates successfully last night. I took advantage of the time to try a summoning."

"But Baalan—"

The dragon shrugged. Her mantle of spines shivered with the movement. "My time is limited. I took the risk. Do you know what it means to go beyond the Gates?"

"No."

Her eyelids came down slightly. It gave her a sleepy look. He shifted weight uneasily, aware that if her eyes narrowed down much more and that yellowish cast took over, he was in trouble. "Alzo will work with you and Chey. We'll have to contact all we can. There will be those too young to even think about taking beyond the Gate."

"And what can you do with them?"

"They're the dragons you men fear most. Rapacious, vicious. Dragonkind at its worst. We usually let them kill themselves off. Only the bravest, most resourceful, or shrewdest survive." Turiana looked into Dar's face. "Do you think Valorek will have ignored those dragons?"

"Not likely. If they can be brought in line, he'd find a use for them. Killers without conscience would suit him fine."

Turiana sighed. "That is my thought. Then I have no

choice. I'll have to find them and bully them first. They'll follow me then. Me or Pandor or whomever I leave in charge." She groaned then and half-rolled to her side, panting rapidly.

"What is it?" He went to her immediately.

She turned her head to him, and he saw the malicious cast to her luminous eyes, and his blood went cold. Then she shook her head, and the old familiar glow returned.

He put a hand on her flank and felt the jostling below it. Eggs. Eggs or dragonets stirring there. "Tell me what I can do to help."

She laughed, that hollow gusting sound she made when amused, and then returned to panting as she talked. "Stay with me. Talk to me. This is not any clutch of eggs I prepare to lay. Nightwing has poisoned me. He takes me over, bit by bit, scale by scale. I may not die when the clutch is laid, but I may not live either. I don't know what's happening."

"Poisoned you?"

"His hatred and fury burns in my veins. Sometimes I can control it; others, not."

He'd seen it. He'd begun to sense it. The fact that Turiana was as frightened and bewildered as he was didn't help. He stroked her. "I'll bring Sharlin back in."

"I'd rather not, just yet."

He stepped to her brow and rubbed the scales there lightly as he'd seen Sharlin do.

"When my time comes, man, I may have to depend on you to do what Sharlin could not."

He looked deep into her eyes, those burning pools of gold, with tiny lights of darkness in them. She said nothing more, and he was afraid to ask, so he simply stood there, stroking her, until she could breathe easily. And at the back of his mind, he wondered if the day would come when he would have to pull his sword on her—and use it.

* * *

Sharlin waited for him outside the cave. He could tell from the look on her face she'd heard most, if not all, of what they'd said.

"What are we going to do?"

"Wait. There's not much else we can do."

"I can't afford to wait. I'm running out of time, too." She turned away from him. She held her hands tightly, as if she could somehow anchor herself that way.

"I don't have any answers." He whistled for Chey.

"Where are you going?"

"There are a few villages within striking distance of us, and we're even not too far from that plateau city of the pallans where they turned us away, though I doubt if they'll do us any good. I had some small success in Murch's Flats yesterday. Turiana's only going to be as strong as her support. I'm doing what I can."

"What about Hapwith?" Chey's winging form shadowed Sharlin's face, and he saw a few lines there that he didn't remember. From the sun, perhaps.

"He's your project. I think he's learned his lesson, and if not, make sure Turiana is always near." As the dragon crouched near him so that Dar could put on the crude harness they'd made for dragon riding, he felt Sharlin's reluctance to see him go. He turned back and put a hand on her shoulder. "I can't stand around doing nothing but being ready for you to call me. Do you understand that?"

"Too well. Neither can I stop what I must do."

"I know that. I wouldn't expect you to." Chey moved near him. He took comfort from the dragon's presence and had a hint of the relationship between Turiana and Sharlin. More than the loyalty of a good dog or horse, more than a lover or a parent. He couldn't quite explain it. Through Chey, perhaps, he caught a touch of Sharlin's fear, and it went through him. She normally wasn't afraid, and that bothered him. What was she afraid of?

He almost told her his real plans, then hesitated. That would bother her more. It had taken him all day yesterday and most of the night to convince Chey.

Tonight, strapped and secured in hiding underneath the great brown's wing, he would go beyond the Gate with Chey and Turiana. Whatever secrets dragons kept hidden, he was determined to know.

He swung up on Chey's back and leaned down. His kiss passed across Sharlin's forehead, a slighting gesture, as the dragon moved when he did, but Sharlin laughed.

"I'll see you tonight, then."

"No. Tomorrow morning."

Disappointment clouded her eyes, then she nodded. Dar knew then that she had not heard of Chey's appointment with Turiana and with the Gate. She would not be able to stop or betray him.

He nudged Chey. "I'm ready."

Sharlin watched the two wing off and wondered why she felt so uneasy. Dar was more than able to take care of himself. Perhaps it was Turiana that worried at her. She turned, to find a nervous Hapwith approaching her. He was trying unsuccessfully to straighten his thatch of wild blond hair.

"Here, let me do it," she said and took her comb, letting her own heavy waves of hair tumble where they would, while she put some order into his. "Are you ready to work today?"

"If you'll let me."

"Let you? Turiana's been bellowing for you since sunup. Where have you been?"

"I—I slept down the mountain, with the green dragon. I needed to clear my head a little." He blinked rapidly as he looked at her.

Sharlin sighed. "Hapwith, you didn't understand the implications of what you did last night. It's over, done with. We have more important things to do now."

He nodded brusquely. Sharlin followed him in. At the back of the caverns, Alzo lay at the edge of the illumination and the natural darkness of the rear caves. What she'd overheard between Turiana and Dar cut her to the quick. The dragon ailed. She feared death or worse, and whatever worried at Turiana jeopardized Sharlin's plans to return to Dhamon. Time was against her. As she ducked her head in thought and approached Turiana, she thought of a plan. All she had to do was get the golden dragon and the magician so involved in each other that they didn't need her.

Alzo glided lazily over the plateau. The high noon sun warmed Sharlin's back, even as the high winds iced at her face. She shivered. Her movement touched the harness, and the dragon's face turned back toward her.

"Is everything all right?"

"Wonderful, Alzo. You are a magnificent flier." She had never known such smoothness of movement. The blue dragon moved through the skies as though it belonged to him alone. She thought then of Turiana's raggedness. First injuries and then pregnancy had hampered the gold, but Sharlin had never guessed how much until now.

The dragon-scarred plateau of the pallan city stretched below them. Alzo trumpeted in delight. When she'd talked him into taking her, he had said he knew of the place. As they swooped low, Sharlin wondered if he had landed here before, in his previous life, and if he remembered it now. How many years ago could it have been when all the dragons passed away, and why had so many of them gone to the graveyard, old, young, and in their prime, to do it? What could she do to stay Turiana's fate? Beyond the ruined walls of the pallan city might lie her answers, if she could convince them to help her.

Alzo touched down gently and ran until his speed diminished, then sat in front of the walls to let her down. Sharlin slid down his side, and he turned to nuzzle her.

"Take care, beloved of Turiana and Aarondar."

"I'll try. I need some answers, Alzo, but I don't know if they'll give them to me." As she turned, her voice died in her throat. The pallans awaited her.

They were veiled in silence and obscurity. She felt the wall of hostility before she even faced them completely. She was stupid to have come. Stupid to have hoped they might want to help her or the dragons.

Sharlin stepped away from Alzo's side.

"Return to whence you came. You are not wanted here."

Was it one voice or many? Sharlin scanned the veiled and masked faces. "I've tried to help you. . . ."

"You are not wanted." The whispery voice echoed in the ruins of the high mountain city.

"I can't leave," Sharlin said. "At least let me tell you what I need to know. Perhaps this much you'd be willing to tell me. I've come for all of us, pallans, dragons, men, dwarves, the whole world of Rangard. Please help me, unless you want Baalan to spread dragonfire and blood wherever he goes."

"It's of no concern to us." Several of the figures turned away, gliding with their grace that no woman could match.

Sharlin lifted her hand in entreaty, but Alzo raised his head. His jaws opened, his nostrils flared, and he issued forth blue lightnings. Rock powdered where they hit, the discharge thundering through the mountains. The girl jumped in shock and stared at the dragon, feeling her eyes wide in her face.

"Alzo! When did you start that?"

The dragon kept his jaws open, his lips pulling back in a grim parody of a human smile. "Yesterday," he said. "When I returned from beyond the Gate." He raised his voice and addressed the pallans. "It is Turiana's and my will that you talk to this human. We have come back to claim the respect that is due us."

"Or you will destroy us?" a pallan returned dryly.

"If that is what it takes, for your disobedience may mean the destruction of us all."

Sharlin hadn't told Alzo of her mission—the beast had taken up the importance of it from what she had said to the pallans. She patted him on the shoulder cautiously. A kind of static energy played over his scales. She was surprised she hadn't felt it before. Her hair crackled and stood out a little from her shoulder as she turned away.

"Very well then. She may ask, and we may answer, though she may not like what she has come to hear."

"And I will wait." Alzo curled at the front wall, his muzzle poking through the new breach, pointing down the main street.

She could have sworn that amusement danced in his deep blue eyes as he watched her walk away with the pallans.

They took her into the first building, among the shade and the dust. A lizard scurried up a wall and through a hole in the tiled ceiling. The lead pallan, dressed still in white robes that reflected all the colors of the rainbow, sat down in front of her and folded its hands.

"What is it you want?"

"Not what we wanted last time. I want something that I think only you will be willing to give me." Sharlin stretched out her hands to the impassive being. "I want to know about the dragons. Everything. I want to know how they mate, lay their eggs, how they mature, how they live and die. I want to know why some are magical and some are not. I want to know what it is they do when they go beyond the Gate. And I want to know how to save Turiana's life, if possible."

Her words fell into the oppressive silence of the ancient library. As she looked at the pallan and beyond, she knew that no one had been in here for at least a generation, perhaps longer. Did the other buildings also contain libraries—the pallans adding onto their city as their passion for recording dictated? If this was so, then perhaps she had the barest ghost of a chance.

The pallan sighed. "You ask for our heart, and think it isn't much. You're with child, Sharlin of Dhamon. Don't you think perhaps it is wiser to stay here, make a husband of your hero, and stop trying to fight that which was?"

"It might be easier," Sharlin answered, hiding the surprise she felt, "but I don't know if it would be wiser."

The pallan ignored her outstretched hands. Then, with a sigh, it moved its own hands up toward its face and veils. "Then look," it said, "and see the first of your answers."

Night fell and Turiana came out of the caverns, waddling, and mumbling to herself. She cast about until she caught sight of the two moons' rise in the sky over the horizon.

"Chey!"

The brown dragon lumbered from down the slope, his ears pricked alertly. "Yes, great and wonderful queen?"

Turiana looked closely at him. Was it her imagination, or did the brown look somewhat lopsided? He had grown since his resurrection and, like most gangly youths, had his awkwardness to overcome. Then again, it might be her sight. She had been staring into the pale blue eyes of the youth Hapwith until she thought she would be cross-eyed forever. She thought perhaps the magician had made some progress into understanding his talent; however, that had to be put aside now. Sharlin would be pleased when she roused from her napping. It was Chey's turn to go beyond the Gate.

"Are you ready?"

"Yes."

Though the brown's tones were even, his body fairly quivered. She could sense the rush of excitement through his blood. "Where is Alzo?"

"Hunting, most likely."

Turiana hesitated. She would have liked to have had an escort, but the green would be of little use if there was trouble. She was as good as alone. "Very well then. Stay close with me." She took a run off the mountain and plunged into the wind, spreading her sail to the wonders of flying. Chey followed after her like a sable arrow.

Sharlin stared at the face before her. It was human, and yet not. She put her hand up to touch the pallan. The flat nose and scaled skin felt remarkably like Turiana. A saurian people. She felt wonder as the pallan dropped the hood to her shoulders. She regarded the aspect of one of the greatest secrets of Rangard.

"I never guessed," she said finally.

"You do not shrink in revulsion? You do not revile us?"

"Why, no." Sharlin looked at the mane adorning the head, too coarse for hair, yet lovely in its colors, colors that matched the robe the pallan wore. She guessed that the pallan was female. "I think you're beautiful."

The pallan smiled. "Thank you. I am named M'reen. As you can see, we are not as you."

"And I can also see your affinity to the dragons." Sharlin sat back a little in her chair. "Or at least, at one time."

"Yes, at one time. When you look at me, you must remember how we guarded, then loved, then came to hate the dragons, and you will understand why we turned you away. Now listen.

"The dragon mates but once, generally, when its lifespan is near closing. Because of this, and the trials of birthing the hundreds of eggs laid, the dragon usually dies."

"Hundreds of eggs?"

"Yes. It is a wonder, is it not, that we are not up to our proverbial asses in dragons? But you will understand more as I finish. You're concerned about Turiana?"

"Yes."

"It is possible she can survive the ordeal." The pallan looked away, and the rainbow colors of her mane rippled in the slanted light that filtered into the dusty building. "However, she has other trials to face when her time of laying comes." M'reen paused. Another pallan slipped into the library. It stopped in absolute shock as it saw the bare face of M'reen. The pallan smiled. "Get down the drinks and pitcher and come back when the lamps need lighting."

The pallan bowed. "Yes, your grace."

"Your grace?"

M'reen shrugged. "An empty title, much as yours, princess."

Sharlin recognized the irony. She took the cool goblet and tasted the wine, the wine so smooth and gently sweet, that she remembered from her time of living among pallans in the badlands. "Tell me of the hundreds of eggs."

"First I must ask, is it true you went to the cradle, called Glymarach?"

"Yes."

"Then you must have seen for yourself, but I will try to explain what it was you saw. The dragon lays hundreds of eggs. A few, maybe ten or so, contain dragonets of considerable worth. Of the others, they hatch as fireworms. These are the food of the dragonets when they hatch. The fireworms themselves are worthy of respect and caution."

"I saw them," remembered Sharlin. "They covered the plains across Glymarach."

"They can. Then they go into the waters and live. From those river waters, they spill into the sea as eels."

Sharlin nodded and refilled her goblet from the pitcher. "We met the people who lived at the edge of Glymarach. They live on the eels."

"Yes. Those eels cross the ocean and grow and eventually seek out freshwater streams again, as adults. You know them as falroth in that stage."

Sharlin sat, stunned. "Good god," she said. "You mean all of these animals are one creature?"

"Yes, and no. The dragonets follow a similar life cycle. From mountain to water to ocean. Some of the adult dragons prefer to stay in the sea, even after they've grown their wings. Most stay in the sea, feeding themselves to immense size, then roam the lands, waiting for their wings to grow and to learn the use of them. It is in this last phase that dragons are most vicious and spiteful. And vulnerable."

"But these are beasts we're talking about, not intelligent beings. Not gods."

"We never revered them as gods," M'reen said quietly. "That fell to you and dwarves and goblins."

"But Turiana—she's got far more knowledge than any human. Her wisdom and her abilities . . ."

"Yes?"

Sharlin looked at the pallan. "What has this to do with you?"

M'reen nodded wisely. "The rest of the story is the story of our sorrow.

"Once, long ago, our people were the holders of much power and magic. We were fewer then than we are now, and stayed out of the affairs of goblins, men, dwarves, and others. The reasons for that you don't need to know now, nor do I think I remember them correctly. It was many generations ago. We enjoyed our

magic and were selfish with it. Then we began to sicken.
It took us a hundred years or so to discover that the
illness was linked with our powers. It became clear to
us then what we had to do. We had to put aside our
magic and hope to live among the others in peace, or
die out as a people.

"We found that the ability we carried was a tangible
asset. It could literally be carried from one pallan to
another. It was something that could be put aside like
an old veil or robe. We never questioned if it was
something that should be put aside. We created a place
where our magic could be stored, until we solved the
mystery of our illness, and then we could return and
pick it up again."

Perhaps it was the wine that tingled the edge of
Sharlin's mind, or perhaps it was the intuition that she
knew what would come next. Her attention riveted on
the pallan's story.

"So we created this storage place, and shed our magic,
and went away, hoping that we had also shed our
illness. And we had. But we feared to go back, for
several generations, and in that hesitation, we lost everything. The dragons discovered our hiding place.

"They had always been shrewd beasts. They coveted
gold and beautiful things, the adult ones did, and they
appreciated our abilities. But they did not hesitate to
step past the gates of our sacred temple and steal our
magic for themselves.

"At first, we feared they would be like children with
it, and even more vulnerable to the killing disease than
we had been. We guarded them for several hundred
years, watching, waiting, wondering. Then we tried to
dissuade them from what they did, and they locked us
out. Our blood ran as water. The dragons waged war on
us. They barred us from passing beyond the Gates of
Knowledge. We nearly became extinct. As a people,
the pallans were lost to history. It was death to be a

pallan in a dragon-ruled world. We were scattered across the face of the earth, homeless and useless."

"No wonder you hated them."

"Yes. After a thousand years, we learned to hate. Because our magic did not destroy them as it did us. At first we were resigned. Then some of us decided that it was fitting they had the powers and not we—it was obvious they were more fit for it. And they fought among themselves and misused their abilities, for, by the most part, dragons are still just beasts. We tried to help. We tried to school and counsel the younger ones. It worked, a little. We kept copious histories, guilty that we had interfered with the way of the world. But we could not stand against their prejudice and hatred. Eventually, we had to abandon Lyrith, though it was the best place to guard the young striders. We lost nearly everything we had gained. Then, one year, it began to happen. The dragons sickened. They made their way to the Pit, as they call it, and most died there."

Sharlin stood. She had heard enough, more than enough, and the pain in her body made it difficult to keep thinking. She tried to swallow the lump in her throat.

M'reen stood with her. "And have you the answers you need?"

"Most of them. As for helping Turiana—"

M'reen nodded. "She must be strong. Strong enough to birth, and strong enough to fight the poison that Nightwing surely injected into her system. By his magic, you see, he will try to overcome her."

"And all I can do is wait."

"Yes. She is either strong enough—or not."

Impulsively, Sharlin leaned over the dusty stone table and kissed the pallan. Her skin felt like Turiana's, soft, warm, almost feathery. "Thank you," she whispered.

Outside, the sun just tilted at the edge of the horizon. Alzo woke and looked up at her. She felt almost guilty.

"Have you finished?"

"Yes."

"And did they help you?"

"I think so." She climbed aboard and gripped the reins tightly. "I hope so."

They landed at Turiana's caves well after dark. Hapwith paced nervously by the campfire. He helped her down, his young face bruised purple with worry.

"Where have you been?"

"Learning history," she answered. She stretched gingerly. "Where's Dar?"

"I don't know. He's gone."

"Turiana?"

"Gone too. She took Chey to the Gates."

The Gates, Sharlin reflected ironically. To steal away more of the pallan magic. Then she turned sharply to Hapwith. "Chey's with Turiana?"

"Yeah."

"Then where is Dar?"

"I don't know. I thought you did. You talked to him this morning."

Her thoughts whirled. "Dar was supposed to be with Chey. Oh, gods, Hapwith. He still may be! He's gone with Chey to the Gates!"

Chapter 15

Dar clung, his eyes closed, the night air whistling through his hair, as he hung on to everything he knew. The bile rose in his throat, but he dared not vomit or even spit, for he clung upside down and it would just come back into his face. Never spit into the wind, he thought ruefully. The humor for a moment combated the dizzying effect of Chey's flight after Turiana.

It was more than a flight. It was a test, of sorts, of strength and intelligence and sheer brawn, as near as he could tell. Once begun, the golden dragon had done much to leave Chey behind. Only Chey's skill and determination kept him after her. They had climbed and dropped, plunged to the earth, skimmed across phosphorescent seas, then climbed again. Even once Dar was ready to swear Chey had been upside down, for the plunging in his stomach told the swordsman he had been righted at last—but the sensation fled rapidly. His ears rang and blood surged. At one point he considered letting go of the straps and unwrapping his legs from the harness and plunging to the earth. Even death would be better than going through this hell.

At that point, Turiana slowed, and Chey surged even with her.

Dar twisted his neck in an attempt to see forward.

He saw a jagged purple mountain range, wild and new, pointing at the velvet sky. The peaks were layered with white that reflected bluely in the night. The beauty took what was left of his breath away. In all the lands he'd traveled, he'd never seen a mountain range as majestic as this.

The dragons lowered in the air, and he realized they headed toward their final destiny. He would have shivered, but the warmth of Chey's body comforted him a little. He shrugged. Yes, his sword sheath was still secured across his back, though Dar had serious doubts if the blade could still be in it. He wanted the security of grasping that sword when he strode beyond the Gates after Chey.

Air shrieked at him as the dragons swooped to a breathtaking stop. He dug his fingers into the leather straps. It would be a fine line between landing and being smashed to death on the icy slopes of the mountain. Particles of snow and ice inundated him as Chey slowed to a halt, wings down, braking himself on the slope.

Turiana breathed heavily. He heard her imperious tones as she spoke to Chey in the voice that dragons used with one another. He could almost understand what she said. She was probably taunting him about his ability to stay with her.

Chey answered, a rumbling note to her fluting one. Dead silence followed, and the swordsman wondered if Chey had given in to her taunting or if he had made mention that he had managed the flight in better condition than she, for although his pulse pounded in Dar's ears like drums, the brown was not breathing hard.

Turiana moved. The snow gathered under her form, and Dar tilted his head. Were they already at the Gates? Or did it lie beyond in the passes? She trumpeted, and the mountain answered. Stone grated and growled. Chey moved and with a great twisting, Dar could see. The mountain literally broke apart. Its dark heart glowed at them in the night, a smoldering depth that could swallow them up.

A split second after Chey, Dar felt the dragon's fear and awe, and he understood Turiana's words as they echoed through the brown dragon's understanding.

"There is magic inside. I must leave you here, for you must seek and find for yourself. We all have different abilities. There is that in you, as it was in me, to find magic that will do good throughout the world. I pray that you seek it out and find it. What you face, I cannot tell you, for we each have faced something different. When you are done, I'll be back. Go forth, Chey, and receive the vaunted knowledge of your ancestors."

Abruptly, she was gone—magically gone. Thunder cracked at her leaving, and Dar's ears popped. He kicked his feet free of their binding and curled downward to the ground. Lastly he let go. Great bloody blisters rose across his palms. Dar stared at them a moment as Chey folded back his wing.

The silvery moons reflected whitely off the snow and ice. It was not as good as a torch, but he could see fairly well. Chey looked around at him, orange eyes embers in the night.

"Are you all right?"

"Fine. How about you?"

"You were a burden that nearly dragged the two of us to our death," the dragon said smugly. "I did well to keep up with the queen."

"Yes, you did." Dar stretched and reached to touch the hilt of his sword, still there after all. "I hope, going back, we have an easier trip."

"Going back, I shall use magic," Chey assured him.

"If that's one of your talents." Dar took a cautious step across the field of ice and snow, leaving behind a startled Chey, who evidently had not considered the possibility that his ability might not include transporting.

The night would be cold, but for the maw beckoning to them. A subtle heat washed over them, warm and musky and tantalizing. If magic had a scent, this would be it, carrying all the notes of the mysteries of the universe. Dar felt himself drawn forward.

Chey stopped him. "It is forbidden."

"But you brought me here. I want to see what's inside."

The sable nostrils, cupped wine-red as though lit by a fire banked inside him, flared a little. "My senses tell me that the Gates lie a short distance within. Come inside, and wait for me, if you will."

Dar unsheathed the sword. "I'll follow."

Chey moved forward, plowing up a wake of ice particles that bit and slapped at Dar's face as he trudged after in the dragon's footprints. He wondered how he was going to be able to see once inside the mountain.

At the touch of Chey's paws, the maw took on a golden glow, a magical illumination, muted as though for other eyes. Dar squinted. He still could not see well, but there were no torches ensconced on the cave walls and there had been no dead wood outside to use. He reminded himself that this was not a place built for him.

Chey let out a sound of awe, his breath gusting foglike into the immense cavern. The entire mountain must be hollow, its shell just a skin.

And in the depths, a red heart glowed and steamed.

The brown dragon pushed forward. Two dragon lengths inside, about fifty feet, stood two immense statues. Dar craned his head back to look at them. They dwarfed even Chey, their marble veins glittering with gold in the illumination. He had never seen their like, and could not possibly guess what gods or people they had been patterned after. Sinuous of limb and standing upright, they had manes of marble down to their shoulders, and faces that had something of the look of dragons about them. They held their hands up, palms outward, facing each other. He had a sense of an invisible barrier between them, generated by those palms.

"The Gates," Chey said, and added a sound of drag-onish after that. His ears pricked forward, cupping to the muffled echo of his voice.

Dar felt the hairs on the back of his neck raise. There was evil here, a biting evil that reached for his very soul. And, on the other hand, he felt the sorrowing warmth of a benevolence as well.

This was a place where man had never been intended to walk. He gripped the sword tighter and pushed forward.

"You have to take me."

Alzo stood his ground stubbornly. "It's forbidden," he said. "And Turiana would have my hide if I did."

"And if she finds Dar, she'll have his hide." Sharlin crossed her arms. After what she'd learned about drag-ons in the pallan stronghold, she wasn't about to let the beast cross her.

His eyelids dropped shrewdly. "I'm not sure I can find my way back."

"That is a journey no dragon would forget," Sharlin answered.

"Perhaps. Anyway, our earlier flight has exhausted me."

She approached angrily. "I think I can find the spur. If you won't help, I can summon Turiana. But that might endanger whatever she and Chey are doing beyond the Gates. Do you wish that?"

"She will not be there. Chey must find his way alone inside the mountain."

"Then you've nothing to worry about!"

Hapwith smothered a chuckle as the dragon flexed his wings and managed to look woebegone. "I am tired," he whined.

"I know that. But Dar is in danger, and perhaps Chey, too. You know how Turiana has been. I'd rather face her than have Dar face her, but I don't think any of us wants to face her when she's . . . turned."

Alzo looked at her. "No, princess," he said, finally. "Mount up."

"Come on, Hapwith."

"Me?"

"Yes, you. You have some talent, and we might need your aid."

"I don't think I can carry two of you," whimpered the blue beast.

"Oh, shut up," Sharlin said, and threw the leather harness over him and strapped it tight. He let out a squeak, then quieted, as though aware he faced a stronger will.

Chey paused, his nose at the barrier between the Gates. He shook, rattling his few spines, and lashed his tail uneasily.

"I'll come with you."

"No!" the brown roared. He subsided as the sound bellowed throughout the cavern. "No," he then repeated. "This is for me alone."

"Right." Dar wasn't going to argue with him. Once the dragon was through, he would follow. Though he feared it, the depth of the mountain beckoned to him.

The dragon pushed inward. He groaned and grunted, thrusting with all the brutish strength of his great frame, and Dar watched in awe, knowing that the barrier must be incredible indeed, forgetting his intention to follow. An aura of energy began to crackle about Chey, lighting his sable hide. It flickered and grew as Chey pushed through. Then, suddenly, he was in, and stood trembling, his tail whipping the air.

He looked back at Dar. The orange lanterns of his eyes were wide with wonder and shone brightly in the dim light of the mountain. "It's calling," he said.

"Then answer," Dar told him. "I'll wait for you." He stood uneasily, wondering if he could pass the Gates after what he had seen. A bright sheen of sweat stood on the brown, sparkling like diamonds.

Chey pivoted, his bulk moving much faster than Dar could have reckoned, giving him a terrible insight into what it would be like to face a dragon and try to slay it, and then the brown moved eagerly into the depths of the cavern. He faded from Dar's sight.

Dar gripped the handle of his sword ever tighter. The wrappings stayed warm and firm, despite the sweatiness of his palms. This was why he had come. Yet he feared to go past the statues and the gate they upheld.

Laughter echoed in the dark wings of the cave to his right. Dar whirled. He knew that cruel laughter well, and knew then that neither Chey nor he was intended to leave the Gates alive.

Baalan pushed forward out of the dimness, Valorek riding high on his neck, muffled by his black cloak.

"Can't you hurry?"

"I'm tired, and I'm not eager to meet with betrayers— or the betrayed," Alzo said into the wind, his voice tinged with bitterness. "Whatever happens to Aarondar, he probably deserves."

"Maybe." Sharlin gripped the dragon tighter. She knew the beast was undoubtedly right. But Turiana and Dar had had a tenuous friendship all along, and she did not want to risk either of them now, Dar because she loved him and Turiana because she needed her. She ran her hand along the drake's neck. "Please hurry."

The blue-white illumination of snowfields caught her eye, and Alzo did a lazy turn. "There," he said.

Hapwith gripped Sharlin's waist tighter. "I don't like the looks of this," he said.

The mountain broke open below them, and she could see bursts of fire dancing inside, and hear a muffled bellowing.

Hapwith shuddered. "Magic," he added, "and blacker than soulless nights, at that!"

Dar backed up to the statue rapidly. "Blast me, and destroy the Gates," he said, though his voice sounded a great deal more confident than he felt.

Valorek held a crossbow in his right hand. He leaned over Baalan's neck diffidently. "We needn't resort to that," he said. "You scarcely require measures that drastic."

Baalan made a pleased sound, a thrumming deep in his purple throat. "After all the plans and sorties," he said, "capturing Turiana off-guard is as easy as this. I should have guessed she'd resorted to taking potential followers beyond the Gates. Yes, I should have guessed."

"Turiana isn't here."

"She will return," Baalan told him, "when we have butchered the trespassers we've found here, you and the brother inside."

Dar moved. Valorek's eyes gave him away even as he raised the crossbow and aimed. Dar slipped to the far side of the statue, falling at its feet and rolling away as the bolt thunked past and clattered against the marble. Then Dar dove, as Baalan bellowed in disgust. His sword slid away from him.

Fire and thunder exploded at his heels. Dar thought of yelling for Chey, then decided against it. If the noise didn't bring him, a yell wouldn't. And if Chey did come, he would come forewarned.

Dar gathered himself and dove again, skinning hands and jolting a shoulder. The rock powdered next to him. Without another thought, he launched himself again, and felt the heat of Baalan's breath at his heels.

He hit, rolling. Then the cave walls shook and he looked up to see a blinding flash of light, and the stone dropped down on him.

*   *   *

"Stop!" Sharlin cried, the wind tearing her words from her throat, but Alzo heard her and reared against the currents which lofted him.

She saw the dragon rampant in the mountain's throat, with the aura of light behind it.

"That's not Turiana!"

Alzo growled deep in his throat as they spiraled slowly downward. "Baalan," he said.

Hapwith squeezed her tightly. "Let's go back," he begged. "Call Turiana! We can't do anything for them now."

"You fool."

"Not a fool, a coward," he returned in her ear.

Sharlin savagely dug her heels into Alzo. "After them! They need all the help they can get!"

Alzo spread his wings and dove at the peak, where the snowfields now glowed red with dragonfire. He landed precariously, slipping and sliding on the ice, losing Hapwith in the process.

Sharlin turned as she felt the magician go. Alzo shook, dismounting her as well, and she landed in a cold, wet snowdrift. The blue dragon trumpeted and reared, and charged into the open peak.

Hapwith waded up to her, dusting the snow and ice from his face, and helped her up. Sharlin put her hands to her temples and thought for a moment of Turiana, Turiana pure as the newly risen sun, as warm as molten gold.

"What are you doing?"

"Calling Turiana. I don't think there's much more damage she can do." Sharlin gripped his arm to right herself. "Dar!"

They ran through the trampled field and halted at the mouth of the mountain, to see Alzo and Baalan entwined in mortal combat, scratching at each other with their rear legs, necks serpentined, rolling about in the cavern. Baalan still bore his rider.

On the other side of two immense statues, Chey reared, his body afire with an orange glow, twisted in suspension as though time had stopped for him. A crimson gash opened his chest.

"Is he—is he dead?"

Hapwith trembled with the cold and his own fear. "I don't think so. I think he's caught. I can feel tremendous power in there."

Behind them, Turiana's voice coroneted against the bellows of the two male dragons. She landed, in an avalanche of snow and crystal, and brushed Sharlin and Hapwith aside as if they were feathers. Sharlin went tumbling, brought up against the cold stone of the mountain's interior. She reached to right herself and get up, and her hand brushed the still hand of another, his body half buried by a jumble of rock.

"Dar!" she screamed. She jumped back bumping into Hapwith, and then clutched at him. "Help me get him out!"

Turiana spat, and gold fire burst inside the cavern, flaming at the purple dragon's eyes. Baalan recoiled, letting go of Alzo. She grabbed the blue drake and thrust him aside.

"Get Chey!" she commanded.

Hissing, the blue did as she ordered. The invisible gate discharged wildly as he crashed into it, and the brown dragon slumped to the ground.

Baalan got to his feet. He roared with anger. The mountain reverberated with the sound. Turiana spat at him a second time. Golden chains of fire and sparks encircled the male's hind feet as he lumbered forward. He fell with a crash as the chains went taut.

Chey and Alzo lumbered out of the gates.

Turiana hissed. Then, "Fly! Leave us!" The two beasts took off, Alzo close by Chey's wobbly form.

The golden dragon pivoted. She swiped at Sharlin and Hapwith. "Leave him!"

Sharlin clawed at the rock and dirt. Her nails broke and her fingers were raw and streaked with blood. She cried as she dug.

The dragon struck at her again. "Leave him, I say. He's dead! If not, I would kill him myself!"

Sharlin whirled. She struck the dragon across the muzzle. "Then go! Get out of here! But I won't leave him!"

Turiana started back in amazement, her eyes wide. Then she twitched, nose wrinkling. "Baalan will not be down for long," she spat. "My magic is not greater than his."

"Then get out of here." Sharlin's voice dropped to a husk, and she returned to clawing at the rocks. "I won't leave him. I won't!"

Hapwith joined her. Rocks slid in a powder of dust. He coughed, she coughed, and a third voice, weak, joined them.

Turiana swiped at the rock pile, sending it smashing across the cavern, and Dar sat up, his face begrimed with dirt and blood. The golden dragon grabbed him in one claw and Hapwith and Sharlin in the other and hopped from the cave, then threw herself into the midnight air with a snarl and a hiss as Baalan bellowed a curse behind them.

Sharlin reached for Dar through the dragon's claws. He stirred, then looked back to her, from a battered face yet triumphant face. He held up a sword, but it was not his own.

"Dar!" The wind tore away her words.

"I found this . . ." he panted. "Beyond the Gates. It's the mate to my helm. It's from Thrassia."

"And," Hapwith muttered, "it reeks of magic."

"That it does," Dar shouted back. "It talks to me!"

Sharlin shrank back unhappily. Dar had found his destiny before she'd been able to set him free.

"Now," he added, "Turiana will have to listen to me."

Chapter 16

With a rustle of robes, M'reen mounted the thirty worn steps to the Wall of Looking in the dawn's first glow. The stone felt cold even through her boots. She wished for spring and hoped she might live that long, though the color of her mane told her she was old, very old indeed. But spring, to lie on the rocks and feel the warmth of the full sun basking her again, yes, for that she would endure much.

She turned her face to the sparse rays of the new morning sun. A cool breeze across her skin sent her scales to shivering, but she braced herself in it. All her life, she'd gone with mask and veil. She'd thought to be buried that way. All the lives she'd ever painstakingly chronicled had gone in mask and veil and robes and gloves. Now she felt as though she stood at a threshold for her people. If she could only know what she had done.

A dry rustle on the stone behind her. M'reen didn't turn. She knew it had to be a junior, waiting for her attention. She sucked in a deep breath of fresh, cold air, then moved.

"Yes?"

The junior gasped at the sight of her bare face, then bowed quickly. It was Itha, a male. His words scarcely fluttered his veiling. "It's true then, your grace."

"That I have shown my face to another people? Yes.
And where have you been? Hibernating in the stone
deeps again, instead of doing the work you were chosen
to do? You hope someday to follow in my footsteps, and
yet . . ." She let her voice drift away.

He looked up. With a defiant gesture, he tore away
his own veil and mask, and then lowered his hood. His
skin of burnt sienna glowed like copper in the sunrise,
and his luxuriant mane flamed at his neck.

M'reen smiled. She turned back to look out over the
valleys and plateaus. "It is easy to do now, after someone else has led the way."

Itha came to the wall beside her. "Not easy," he said.
"It is never easy to do a thing when its final outcome is
unknown. It was easy to walk these steps, knowing I
would reach the top and stop. It's not easy to unveil,
unknowing of the consequences of my actions."

M'reen nodded. "You're learning," she said. She lifted
a gloved hand then and squinted across the valleys.

Itha looked too. "What are you looking at?"

"There! Do you see something?" M'reen leaned over
the wall. She hissed. "By the egg! Itha, sound the
alarm. And find me a way, some way, of reaching the
girl Sharlin! That's an army of dragons coming across
the plateaus."

Sharlin slept late in the early-morning sun. She'd
awakened when Dar got up and then gone back to
sleep, the military drilling of dragons totally uninterest-
ing. And with Turiana working with Hapwith, there
was little left for her to do but worry. Even sleep was
better than worry—though as she turned and fretted,
she knew she wasn't really sleeping.

Into that hazy nonsleep and nonawakeness, she thought
of the pallan M'reen. The face once obscured by mask
and veil grew sharper and more distinct until Sharlin
could have sworn the being leaned over her. She put

up a hand to touch her cheekbone. The faintest fragrance of lyrith wafted over her.

"Danger," M'reen whispered. "Look into my eyes. You must see it, too."

Sharlin felt herself drawn in, and suddenly was overlooking the plateau city of ruins. Across the valleys, flung against the verdant hills, winged the rainbow colors of a hundred dragons or more. Unmistakably, a purple dragon led the army. She sat bolt upright, wide awake, and the image of the pallan shattered.

"Dar!" she screamed. Her voice echoed over the mountain slope.

Hapwith shrugged into the surcoat, its links rattling noisily and in danger of sliding off his sloped shoulders. "Are you sure this will protect me?"

Sharlin stuck a fingertip between the links and poked him in the ribs. "Well, it won't stop a stinger or an arrow, and your biggest worry is dragonfire."

His already pale face grayed. She laughed and pulled a battered old helm onto his head. "You won't be anywhere near the fighting, I'm sure."

"But you will be."

"Yes." She sobered. "I'll be riding Turiana. Chey will be with Dar. Pandor's agreed to watch you—and I don't care if he says his wings are fit to fly or not, you're not to let him!"

The bronze dragon had made his way cross-country, his newly healed wings a thing of beauty in his shining eyes, and though he had made a very short flight to get up the mountain slope, Sharlin knew the patched skin had not completely healed. In a few months, perhaps, the bronze could fly. But not today. And definitely not against Baalan. She felt a moment of sorrow that he hadn't stayed in the Nettings. To have come all this distance in all these days, to see the slaughter of his fellow dragons.

She slapped Hapwith on his shoulder. "You have the wards?"

"Yes, but—" The lanky man paused. "I'm not sure how well prepared they are. Turiana's temper is too uncertain now, and I'm no sorcerer."

"Let's hope they're better than nothing. Baalan will be using protection spells, we know that." With a sigh, she straightened and turned. She wore a bronze-worked breastplate and shin and arm guards, as well as a winged helmet Dar had found. He'd tucked her long amber hair into it before kissing her on the nose and taking Chey.

Turiana made a noise outside the cave. Sharlin hesitated, then picked up her small round shield and went out. The golden dragon put her head down to speak to her. Sharlin patted her gently even as she noted that the dark coloration took over nearly two thirds of Turiana's body now.

"You can change your mind, fair daughter," the dragon said.

"No. I won't let you go alone. I think I can help."

Turiana blinked slowly. "There are two of you to consider."

Sharlin's hand dropped a moment to the very slight rounding of her stomach, covered by a mail shirt, yet left open under the breastplate. She wore leather breeches and hip-high boots of falroth and felt almost invulnerable. "I know," she said. "But this magic shield will do you no good without someone to wield it."

Turiana nuzzled the shield. "Just remember, the spell is temporary. We'll not be protected more than half a day."

"I remember well."

"The others are up. Let's go." Turiana lowered herself so that she could mount.

Pandor looked at her, his eyes aglow. "I have spells too," the bronze dragon said. "I will be at both your backs."

Turiana snorted. She said a few words of dragonish. Sharlin felt a dizzying moment of complete and total darkness, and then they were aloft, over the plateau. Pallans waited at the ruins of their city gates. Sharlin caught a glimpse of the iridescent white-robed figure before Turiana swung about, and they faced her troops.

It took her breath away. From horizon to horizon, the sky was like an ocean filled with the gem-colored forms of dragons. Nearly fifty sculled and glided on the still air above the plateau. Turiana made a pleased sound deep in her throat, and made a graceful wingtip-down pivot back to the fore. Sharlin raised her shield.

Chey broke ranks, with Dar sitting high on his shoulders. The swordsman wore his silver half-helm and the bits and pieces of battered armor he'd collected through the years. The bastard sword he kept unsheathed in his hand, at the ready, and he saluted Sharlin with it.

For an eerie moment, she wondered if she should have told him, for she knew that there was no way he could have guessed yet. She thought of it now, and fear shivered through her. What if he died this day? What if she died? What good would it do to know?

What harm would it do?

Sharlin raised her hand and waved back to him. She made herself smile.

He cupped his hand to his mouth and shouted, "There's no sign of them. Where are they?"

Sharlin shook her head. "I only know what I sighted."

Turiana snorted. "Back to your wing, Chey," she began to order the brown.

There was a sound, a rumbling as if a great thunderstorm roiled across the skies, but the day was clear without a cloud in sight. Sharlin looked down to the valley and saw them, an inexorable wave of a hundred dragons or more, launching upward, at their throats and underbellies, to meet them.

*   *   *

It was like Dar's greatest nightmare, Baalan's forces coming underneath them, from the shadow of the valleys below. He had hoped the unmagicked dragons would be in a wing of their own, so he could peel off their own wing under Alzo . . . he'd only had a day to drill them that way, but now, as he looked downward, he could see that there was no way of telling whether they fought flesh or magic.

They had but one hope, and that was for him to cut off Baalan as soon as possible.

He hauled back on Chey's rein, trying to catch the brown's attention. But the dragons were all immersed in their efforts to gain the height necessary to protect their stomachs, whether they had powers or not. The wind beat with a hundred wings, roaring and tearing, the current a turmoil of motion. As Dar looked over, he saw a flanking movement.

More dragons, dropping down from above, and coming in at their side. He raised his sword. "Chey!"

The dragon ignored him. Finally Dar put the flat of his blade to the dragon's side and whapped him. The sting made the brown whip about, nearly unseating Dar. It also brought him face to face with the flanking wing.

Chey roared then. His angry noise brought a dozen dragons with him, and they charged the flankers, jaws opened and stomachs rumbling. Dar licked his lips, wondering if Turiana's ward against the flame-throwers would prove effective.

The beasts clashed in midair. Their magic bolts and thunderballs, fire, and other weapons froze, but their scaled bodies rang against one another. Talons slashed and fangs ripped, and the spined tails lashed. Dar leaned over and lopped off the head of a raging green. The sword that bit through rock found dragon equally pleasing. Ichor spurted. The sky filled with its substance, and as the bulk of the creature dropped, it took another out of the wing with it.

Dar settled back in the leathers as Chey dodged a savage talon. The swordsman got an eye-to-eye view of a pair of vicious white fangs as he ducked down and hugged his dragon's neck.

"Chey! Remember to give me room, too!" he shouted, but the hissing and spitting of the battling beasts drowned out his voice.

The forces pulled apart, each spiraling downward to join the main force. Dar saw with satisfaction that all of his beasts made it, while he'd seen at least five of Baalan's drop. Turiana's wards worked, for now.

He leaned over. Chey's ear flicked back. "It's brute force, for now," he yelled.

The brown nodded. He trumpeted to his followers accordingly, and they dove to the attack, but nowhere did Dar see the purple dragon he sought.

Hapwith shuddered. He stood with his neck craned back, the flat of his hand shading his eye as the sun climbed high, watching the carnage. Pandor braced him. The magician felt sick to his stomach. The sky rained blood and ichor and now and then a butchered beast to the stones below. The pallans had fled to the cellars of their stone homes, leaving him in the open. He dropped his hand and hugged himself. The wards in front of him, set exactly as Turiana had told him, looked like ordinary blocks of wood, except that they burned with a blue fire that did not consume them.

When they began to be consumed, the protection would begin wearing off. He was to stand and watch for this to happen.

The youth shuddered again. He had no stomach for this! If it weren't for Sharlin and the terrible guilt of what he'd nearly done to her, and what he felt he owed her, he would bolt.

Pandor nudged him. "They outnumbered us, but we begin to grow even," the bronze said, in his rolling bass voice. "Turiana is magnificent."

Hapwith looked up again quickly. He saw the fleeting streak of gold overhead. If he was lucky, perhaps he would be struck dead before the wards flamed up, and Sharlin was slaughtered. He clenched his fists helplessly.

Sharlin grasped the harness tightly. Turiana's flight grew ragged, and her flanks blew out and collapsed like a gigantic bellows. She leaned down and pleaded, her voice a tiny note in the din of the battle, yet she knew the dragon heard her.

"Land. You can't take any more of this. Land, and guide your dragons from there. Where will we be if we lose you?"

They dipped and bounced through the sky. Turiana reached out and slashed through a green's wings. With a scream, it crumpled and plunged to its death.

"I want Baalan!" Turiana said. She slowed, wings spread, rearing against the wind. Then with a cry of triumph, she kited downward. Sharlin looked down and saw the elusive purple streak, surrounded by dragons bearing riders.

She hugged the gold's neck. "Call Chey, Turiana. Please! Call for Dar!"

Hapwith jumped and looked at the wards in shock. When had they begun to flicker? How could he have failed to notice? He jostled Pandor. "The wards are giving out! You've got to tell Turiana!"

The bronze looked downward. His brows jumbled together. He rumbled, "I will try."

"Try? Try? She's carrying Sharlin! Pandor, that's what we're here for."

Pandor looked at him sadly. "The enemy has spells, too, little magician. I have been blocked since the fighting began. All I can do is try, or fly up to warn her myself."

"But you can't fly!"

"I flew up the mountainside last night."

Hapwith felt his blood go cold, and he began to shake uncontrollably. He stood on one foot and then the other, while the bronze closed his lantern eyes and mumbled to himself.

Chey stalled. His neck serpentined, and his orange eyes glowed. "We are a good team, Dar."

Dar swung, as a blue dragon swooped past, slashing at Chey's unprotected head. The sword barely connected. A gash opened up and the beast veered away, squalling. Chey looked back around.

"I suggest you watch what we're doing," Dar shouted dryly. His arms and shoulders ached, and his eyes felt burned from the sun.

They jerked around suddenly, as a screaming dragon drew their eyes, and they looked beyond. A gold beast reared against a purple one, and a bronze tumbled slowly from the sky, wings tucked in.

Chey roared. "That's Pandor!"

"And that's Turiana! And Baalan!"

With a singular rage, they dove to the attack.

He caught a glimpse of Sharlin's pale face. Her helm gone, her hair streamed in the wind. Crimson streaked her face. She screamed to him and waved him back, and it took him but a moment to find out what she meant.

Baalan roared, and a fireball cracked the heavens.

The wards had gone. Now magicks would be loosened and the sky itself would be hell. But he'd found Baalan. He kicked Chey.

"Cut Turiana out of there!"

The gold dragon reared against her mortal enemy.

Golden bolts dashed uselessly against Baalan's armored side. She heaved and faltered.

The purple dragon's black-dressed rider laughed. He raised a crossbow and aimed at Sharlin.

"Turiana!" Dar screamed. He heeled Chey downward as the brown protested, and they crossed the line of fire.

The bolt bit deep into the brown's foreleg, and he skewed away, with a squeal of pain. Turiana veered away as Baalan's fireballs crackled, but Sharlin had no place to go. She threw up her arm with the shield upon it.

Blue-and-purple flames smashed into the bronze plating. She crackled with the discharge. Her hair stood on end and her mouth screamed a soundless word as she pitched backward out of the harness, did a slow somersault, and fell from the gold dragon's back.

Turiana folded her wings into deadfall, scrabbling through the sky to reach her in time. Dar had no time to see if she made it.

Chey reared and dipped inward at Baalan's flank.

Valorek twisted and looked at Dar, even as the purple opened his jaws again.

"Leave him! This one is mine!" the witch king shouted. He slung the crossbow across the saddle and pulled his sword.

"No magic, Chey," Dar warned, as the two beasts encircled one another. "Just get me close enough for one good swing. With luck, I'll take both heads at once."

The dragons darted at one another. Dar swung, but Valorek's sword met his, and parried, and the blades belled. Dar's sword slid downward, catching the edge of the sorcerer's black cloak and ripping it from his shoulders. Their eyes met, and then Dar gasped in horror.

Valorek's torso melded into dragon flesh at the hips.

He had no legs left, but was half dragon himself. He threw back his head and laughed, howled, at the shock in Dar's face.

"Like it? Nightwing's last, cruel joke on me! When he dropped me off to die at the Pit, my form was carelessly left lying across the bones of old Baalan here. When the resurrection came, we found ourselves joined together, for better or worse!"

Before Dar could signal Chey, Baalan struck at him. Their necks entwined, wings unfurled, they glided in a deadly dance upon the wind.

His target loomed. "For Sharlin!" he cried. Dar leaned out and sliced Valorek from the serpentine neck.

The witch king's mouth opened and shut wordlessly, and then he pitched through the air. His severed torso turned over and over as he plunged down.

Dar shuddered and raised his sword to deal with Baalan. A whoosh, and the purple disappeared, and the air rushed in with a thunderclap. Once again the purple dragon had escaped.

Chey pitched in the turmoil. Dar clapped his heels to the brown's flanks. "Find her!" he cried, and they streamed downward.

The wind in his eyes brought tears.

Chapter 17

Chey flung his sails wide and braced their plunge at the last second. He swooped in over the ruins, turning and then dropping. Dar had already spotted the golden dragon on the ground, and the broken heap of bronze, and the sprawled body of his love, in the dust.

As soon as Chey touched earth, he flung himself off the beast. Hapwith looked up, his pale face streaked with tears, and he caught Dar up.

"Leave her!"

Dar threw him off. Turiana turned her golden eyes to him.

"She but sleeps, Aarondar. I caught her, with Pandor's help."

A white-robed form, with colors that played off the white like a prism, stood up from the shadow of Pandor's patchwork wing.

Dar caught his breath as he faced the naked countenance of the pallan. M'reen smiled.

"She passed out. It's best to let her rest. She'll be all right."

He looked at Hapwith. "But why—" He stalled to a halt. Beyond the youth, he could see Pandor, his flanks laboring with each husking breath.

He lowered his sword and approached the beast.

Pandor made an effort to lift his head, failed, and lay with his bulk quivering.

"I flew," he said proudly. "And though Baalan knocked me down, I flew well enough to get under Sharlin and cushion her for Turiana to reach before I fell."

Dar said nothing. Ichor and blood ran from the bronze's wide nostrils. The swordsman reached up and scratched the beast, and then said, "You were magnificent. I saw you."

"Did you? Thank you for the falroth skins. To have never flown again . . . You saved my life, cubling." His voice faded.

"And you mine."

Dar looked to Turiana. Her eyelids closed slowly, as though she could not face the question in his gaze. Already, the dragonhide under his scratching hand was growing colder.

Chey moved closer to the elder beast and hunched down. Pandor sighed. "I cannot seem to move my tail, cubling. Would you do me the favor? I like to . . . sleep . . . with it curled about me."

Dar sheathed his sword and picked up the spined tail, heavy and cold though it was, and tucked it about Pandor as he'd often seen the dragon resting. Those days at the Nettings seemed far away now, as though they had never happened. He put his hand palm down on the dragon's neck, wishing that Pandor had never left the safety of the seaport.

Turiana began a low keening. She sang a dragonish melody, in a voice that spoke of high winds, and mountains, and molten rivers of gold to warm the body. After a few seconds, Chey joined in, and Pandor relaxed.

He roused suddenly and turned his head to Hapwith. "To you I bequeath my powers," Pandor said. Then, with great effort, he nuzzled Dar. "And to you, I bequeath my love, though you need it not."

Dar threw his arm about the beast's neck and could

not answer him. Lastly, Pandor gasped, "Good night, my queen." Then with a rattle and a massive convulsion, the great creature died.

The spasm threw Dar to the dust. He got up slowly, then went to Sharlin's side and knelt. He brushed the heavy wing of her hair from her face, and touched her cheek gently, reassuring himself that she was still warm.

Above them, the screeches and hissing of battle still raged. He looked upward.

"I got Valorek, Turiana, but not Baalan."

The gold stopped her keening and straightened up. "Then it's time we met him."

"We're being slaughtered. I want you to tell the others to scatter, to retreat. We've taken a toll. There'll be another day to battle."

Chey left the side of his fallen comrade. His muzzle flared in rage. "Quit? Like cowards?"

Dar shook his head. "You and I aren't quitting. We're going after Baalan."

Turiana shook herself. "No. Chey, you order the retreat. Dar and I have work to do."

The swordsman considered the golden dragon. He'd seen her ragged flying and knew that her other battles had taken too much out of her. And though he was afraid, he swallowed it down. Turiana lowered her shoulder to make mounting her easier, and he swung up.

Hapwith patted his boot. "I'll stay with Sharlin."

"All right."

The brown and gold ran together, off the edge of the plateau, and took to the wind, their wingtips touching, and got the current. Dar skewed around.

"There he is!"

Turiana curved her neck to give him a fleeting look. "If we get through this," she said, "I'll take you to the Gates myself!"

Dar grinned. "It's a deal!" He unsheathed his sword and braced his legs in the harness as well as he could,

for the stirrups had been shortened to Sharlin's length.
He wrapped his left hand in the reins.

About them, the ranks of dragons opened up a corridor to let them through. The fighters broke away. He
caught a glimpse of Alzo chasing a tremendous brown-
and-black beast across the peaks, his blue hide sparkling. The horizon was dotted with the faraway forms of
the combatants as the retreat began.

Below them, plumes of smoke trailed up from the
verdant hills and valleys where many a dragon had
plunged to death.

Baalan spotted them. He arrowed toward them.

"Just get me close," Dar shouted to Turiana's alert
ears. "I'll take care of the rest." He cocked the sword
back, preparing to throw it like a javelin.

No. Hold on to me.

His palms went wet. Dar shifted his weight. With a
muffled curse, he rebalanced the weapon in his hand.

Turiana lunged at the purple, closing with him before
he could strike at her. The clash of their bodies nearly
unseated Dar. Teeth clashed. With talons spread, they
ripped at each other. Baalan's tail lashed around, and
Dar ducked. He felt the blow along his half-helm, and
the leather strap which secured it went taut.

He shook his head, seeing stars for a moment. The
two beasts dropped through the air, their weight plunging them toward the mountain below. He kicked and
wrestled at Turiana.

"Let him go!"

She spread her left wing, but her right was entangled
between their bodies. Baalan made a low guttural sound
deep in his throat, his jaws sunk into her breast.

She whipped her tail about, catching the dragon across
his eyes. With a screech, he let go of her, and they
were free-falling through the heavens.

Turiana gasped. She batted her wings madly to stall

their fall. Dar caught the dizzying glimpse of the ground
rushing up. Then the purple streaked under them.

"He's below us!"

The dragon panted. "He's too strong for me. The
gods help us, Dar—I can't do it!" With a sobbing breath,
she dipped her wing, soaring to the right. Dar swung as
the purple beast came up, talons wide and fangs bared.

He sliced clean through the ivory teeth and open
jaws. Baalan breathed, and flames engulfed them.

Dar ducked his face down as Turiana plunged with a
shriek. She carried them to their deaths.

From the corner of his eye, Dar saw the brown flash.
With a roar of his own, Chey appeared under them. He
sheered off. The wake of his passage gave a sudden
buoyancy to Turiana, and she gasped as she caught
herself.

The wind whistled past his face as her sails billowed
out. Her wings strengthened. Dar found himself able to
breathe again.

They plowed into the scarred dirt and stone of the
plateau. Dar threw himself free as Turiana tumbled
over and came to a shuddering halt.

Hapwith ran from the stone walls. Behind him staggered Sharlin, her hand pressed to her lips as though
she had been stifling a scream. Chey landed rapidly,
hissing, his head snaked upward, watching as Baalan
circled.

"I can't hold him," Turiana panted. "Chey, take them
and leave. Go as far as you can."

"No." Dar gripped his sword tightly and held it up.
"Lure him down."

The gold shook her head. "Go now, while you can!"

The plateau thundered as Baalan lowered his head
and lunged for them. Hapwith threw up his arms.

"I'll stop him. Turiana, Dar, Sharlin—get behind
me!" The lanky youth, his helmet bouncing on his head

and his surcoat rattling over his tunic, ran forward, arms raised. "I'll send you!"

"There's no place for me to hide," Turiana protested. "Save yourselves."

The magician laughed, his voice nearly drowned out by the roaring of the purple beast as he plunged down toward them. "Get mounted, and quickly."

Dar got aboard the golden dragon and pulled Sharlin up after him. The hairs prickled on the back of his neck. He sheathed the bastard sword as Sharlin threw her arms about his waist tightly.

"I love you," she whispered to the back of his neck, and he felt the sweet warmth of her breath.

Then, as Baalan came slashing down, talons spread, Hapwith with his arms akimbo stood between them.

"Go now!" he shouted, and opened the doorway. Thunder blasted, and the plateau disappeared into darkness.

Chapter 18

They flew, blasted into the nothingness of a transport spell. Sharlin ducked her face to Dar's shoulder, the bitter taste of vomit in her mouth. Her head ached horribly and her stomach turned.

Turiana spread her wings, trying to slow their descent.

They were in a nothingness that spread into forever. Her heart beat as a slow drum, and finally she screamed to the gold dragon, "Where has he sent us?"

"The only place he could have—the only place we've trained him for. Into your past, fair daughter—if he succeeded."

She hugged Dar tightly. Despite the winged dragon, they plunged downward, steadily, into a bottomless pit. When they emerged, Sharlin knew they would be entombed in the center of the earth.

Dar hugged her arms about his waist.

They continued to drop. Finally, Sharlin's nerve broke. She knew she would begin to scream and not be able to stop, when Turiana's body shuddered, and the nothingness of the dark air about them became a barrier.

They burst with a tremendous explosion into another night.

Sharlin caught a glimpse from the corner of her eye.

She saw a girl hunched on griffinback, as the discharge from their emergence blasted them, and sent them tumbling.

"Gabriel!" she cried and reached toward them.

Dar caught her arm. "It's too late!"

Shocked, she watched the black funnel of their passage swallow the two up. She pressed her forehead to Dar's armored shoulder. She sobbed. "Dar! We did it! We were the ones who struck Gabriel. And I thought it was Rodeka! I killed him." She clung to the man in front of her as though he were life and sanity itself. With that burden, she bore another, alone. She had brought Dar with her, into a time where he was never meant to be. Hot streaks ran across her face.

Turiana sped across the skies of Rangard. Below her the countryside blurred, even in the night.

Dar looked down. Day, night, day, night. He saw the seasons pass, even as they plunged downward. They were still going through time, but now forward! He watched as the fields ripened, and armies trampled them, and then smoke consumed them.

He knew that well. The farmers would sooner burn their lands than let the conqueror profit. Sharlin cried softly at his back.

The scorched earth faded into late autumn, and then Turiana glided, turning leisurely, and the night blossomed into dawn.

"We are here," the dragon said.

Sharlin glanced up as Dar answered, "We're too late to stop Rodeka . . . we knew that, from the pallan history. But, by all the gods, we're still here!"

They dropped to a small, sunlit meadow. On a mountain slope overlooking the plateau where a blue-gray stone fortress reigned the morning, the gold dragon finished her journey. The two dismounted, and all three stood shivering in the dawn.

"Dhamon," Sharlin said softly. She would have gone to her knees, but Dar reached out and put his strong arm about her waist.

He kissed the side of her face. "When I saw you fall—" He stopped abruptly, unable to tell her that he'd thought his heart had died then.

She put her hands about his. "I thought I was going to die," she said. "And then Pandor came up from below me." She swallowed. "Dar, I have something I have to tell you—"

"Not now, children," the dragon queen interrupted. "We have urgent business to attend to. This is a conquered land, but there are enemy patrols about. I smell goblin. And I fear I must find a cave or a hollow."

They looked at her suddenly. A charcoal pallor washed up her throat and across her muzzle. Her flanks heaved.

"My time is very near," said Turiana.

Dar sat on the ground and wiped his blade clean of black blood. Sharlin dropped down next to him, mopped her brow on the sleeve of her blouse, and said, "She's bedded down now."

He looked down the gnarled path they had climbed. He'd surprised the one goblin patrolman. "The woods are riddled with goblin snares and traps. Either they catch a lot of game up here or . . ."

"What?"

"Or this mountain is one of the strongholds of whatever resistance Rodeka's troops face. Those snares are meant for something big and clever, not another softfoot for their pots."

"Do you think . . ."

He looked into her eyes, blue-gray and tired, and saw a tiny hope in them. "I think that some of your people are fighting back."

"I hope so." She brushed a gentle kiss across his lips

and sat back before he could respond. "I sought Turiana for that purpose. And now look, she's holed up back there, about to lay a clutch, and maybe die. All for nothing."

"Maybe not." Dar sheathed his sword. It whispered a goodbye as it always did when he sheathed it. One day he would get used to that ghost voice in his mind, telling him when to strike and parry. He thought of Turiana. "How's she doing?"

"In pain. Baalan hurt her. We've all hurt her, I guess." Sharlin brought her knees up and hugged them, and put her chin down to her kneecaps. "She asked if you would be with her when the time came."

Uneasiness washed over him. The last thing he wanted was to be trapped in that narrow, smelly hole of a cave they'd found with a dragon who was turning vicious. But he nodded, because he also remembered the understanding they had. If Turiana lost her battle against Nightwing's darkness, she expected Dar to kill her. "All right."

"What do you think happened to Hapwith and Chey?"

"I don't know. We were Baalan's target. They could have made it. Whatever happened, it's beyond us now." Dar took off his helm and laid it in the grass. His brown hair waved slickly to his head, but the dawning breeze riffled through it. He reached for her. "We haven't been alone in a very long time."

Sharlin felt her insides tighten up, then she surrendered into his arms. Perhaps she would tell him later.

They must have slept. Sunlight dappled his flanks as she awoke in his arms. Sharlin lay very still for a moment. She looked closely at him, trying to memorize what she saw in him, sensing that this was one of those times that might slip away otherwise. A few freckles dotted his shoulders, and a stray hair or two faintly curled against his skin. He lay on his back, and her fingers were still entwined in the diamond of wavy hair on his chest. She pulled her hand back slowly. In the afternoon, she could see the boy he had once been in his face . . . red-cheeked and eager, hair that the sun brought a faint tinge of gold to, though the years had darkened the color to brown. A strong chin and straight nose, and broad forehead full of eagerness and determination. Sleep took away the fierce joy that she often saw in him. She was grateful that he slept well, the demons of his earlier nightmare gone, at least for now.

Sharlin smiled and moved away. She already knew that their son would look a great deal like him. Not quite as fair as she, but sturdy and handsome as he was, a soldier who'd once been a dairy farmer's son. He had put away the pouch he used to carry on his belt, the pouch that contained the ashes of his parents.

He woke as she withdrew from his side and grinned. He lay back and watched her dress in her battle clothes.

"I'll have to steal you something appropriate."

"Just ask Turiana—" Sharlin stopped then. She'd forgotten the gold dragon nesting up the hillside. She fastened her breeches, then put on her full-sleeved shirt.

Sharlin pulled on her hip-high falroth boots and mail shirt, but left the breastplate lying in the grasses and lastly strapped on the wrist sheath for the dirk.

He began to dress then. Dar left nothing behind. He said little as he shrugged into the guards and body armor, and Sharlin watched him. If he had trouble with Turiana, he would need as much protection as possible. He strapped on the sword and stopped when he saw the expression on her face.

"What does it say to you?"

"The sword?" He shrugged. "Not much. Mostly whether to strike or not. Just a word or two."

"Not 'Hail, master,' or anything like that?"

"No." He smiled broadly. "Are you jealous?" He pulled her close and opened the neck of her shirt to kiss the red birthmark on the side of her throat.

She flushed and tossed her head to keep her hair from her face. "Of course not. Why would I be jealous?"

"Just asking." He released her and held out his hand. "Let's check on our dragon mother."

It was ominously silent as Dar reached the cave mouth and began to pull away the loose brush they had covered it with. The shelter was little more than a hollow of dirt and stone, but it went deep, and Turiana had been able to fit into it.

Sharlin paused. "Dar, I don't like this. Suppose she's . . . while we slept, that she . . ."

"We'd have heard. She'd have let out a yell for us, don't worry." All the same, Dar blocked her view as he ducked into the grotto.

Turiana swung her head around, scuttling about on her stomach as he entered. She gave a little snort. "Welcome, Aarondar. Where is my fair daughter? I'm close now, yes, very close." Then, in a cold voice, the beast added, "Are the two of you through rutting in the field?"

It took him aback. Sharlin made a shocked sound.

"We fell asleep," Sharlin murmured.

"No doubt." The dragon slit her eyes. "I know who my friends and enemies are. Make no mistake of that!"

Dar put out an arm, barring Sharlin from coming closer.

The dragon gave a short cry and rolled to her flank. It was then, in the shadows, that he saw she'd gone entirely dark, except for her head and a thin starburst down her back. Sharlin gasped, and he knew she'd seen it, too. "Get out of here," he said urgently to her.

"I want to stay."

Turiana put her muzzle up, stretching her neck in a

moment of pain. She gasped, "Water, Sharlin. Please fetch me some water."

"I heard some downslope," Sharlin said. "It won't take me long."

Dar removed his half-helm. "Use this."

The dragon thrashed. "Who are you? By what right do you trespass my kingdom?" Cold, her voice again.

Dar took Sharlin's elbow. "Get out of here!"

"Let the maiden stay. I once had a taste for maidens."

Sharlin froze. The malevolent yellow eyes pinned her in place and drained her will from her. Her hands grew slack. The half-helm wobbled in them.

Dar moved her physically to the mouth of the grotto, where the sun flooded in warmly, and she found herself shivering in spite of it.

"Who are the two of you?" the dragon demanded. "Leave now, while you can! You trespass more than you dare!"

Dar said, "I'll take care of her. Just get the water."

Numb, Sharlin turned and ran. She skidded over the soft dirt and grasses, heading toward the sound of running water. With hands shaking so hard she could barely hold the helm, she rinsed it and then filled it with the sweet brook water.

Returning, she could hear the voices in the cave. She could swear there were three talking: Turiana, Dar, and a third . . . cold and sly . . . and dangerous. With a deep breath, Sharlin approached the hollow.

"I have it."

The dragon's attention snaked to her. "Bid her go." And then, "Come closer, Sharlin, and hold it steady for me."

She looked at Dar as she walked close and held the helm for the dragon. Turiana dipped her soot-black muzzle down and sipped the liquid until the helm was dry. Then she looked at Sharlin, and their eyes met.

Madness reigned in those golden lanterns, a madness that shook the girl to her very soul to see it. She put her hand to her mouth in fear, and the helm clattered to the ground. Dar stooped and picked it up.

Turiana husked, "Go now, while you can. You mustn't see any more of this."

"Dar—"

"Leave him with me. I must have him, don't you see, for if Nightwing wins, you will have brought a greater evil to Dhamon than Rodeka." Then the eyes narrowed. "Run, little softfoot, while you can. I will deal with you later."

He moved to her elbow. "It'll be all right."

She wrenched her eyes away from Turiana to look at him. "Dar, I—"

"Sharlin!" gasped Turiana. "You must go and go now. But first, come close. Come close and touch me once more."

She shook. Involuntarily, she stepped backward, afraid.

"You . . . must," the dragon panted. Her flanks heaved. "I want to give you my powers."

Dar stiffened. Sharlin shook her head, then remembered what M'reen had told her. The powers of the pallans could be taken off and put on again, like robes, she'd said.

"You can't do that," Sharlin protested. "If you do, you'll have nothing left to fight Nightwing with!"

"I must. If Nightwing succeeds and Dar fails, then you'll have a tiny respite until he searches out new powers. It's my gift to you, Sharlin. This is my repayment to you of the lifedebt I owe."

Dar murmured at her cheek, "I'm here. I think I can protect you."

Sharlin hesitated, then moved forward. Turiana opened her jaws and gently took her hand in them.

"Look into my eyes," the dragon commanded.

Sharlin did so, and was swallowed whole.

For a moment, she felt only pain, a pulsing pain that centered in her stomach. Then, as the golden glow obliterated her, she knew that she was feeling a part of Turiana.

She had a sense of what it was like to ride the wind. To rule luck and chance with magic. To chase a gunter down and devour it while the blood was still warm. Sharlin/Turiana both shuddered and exulted in the memory. A sense of timelessness took her in. She knew what it was like to see the seasons flowing past in a river of Time, and to be comforted by its sameness.

She rode the memory of the dragon until the next convulsion, then both gasped with the pain, and Turiana let go of her hand, breaking the contact.

Sharlin felt tears upon her cheeks and looked at the dragon in amazement. The beast closed her eyes, shuddering.

"Now go!"

Dar caught her at the mouth of the cave.

"Save her, Dar," Sharlin said, still filled with the wonder of what had happened.

"I'll do my best."

She turned and fled.

In the sunlit glen, she looked where two lovers had lain, and her senses were filled with the smell of the bruised grasses. Sharlin hugged her elbows and knew that she couldn't wait there. She was close enough to sense still what Turiana felt.

The grove beckoned. She strode toward it, seeing and yet unseeing. Was she still Sharlin or partially Turiana? What had she become? And why now, so close to home? Why now had she so suddenly become so confused over who she was and what she wanted?

In a daze, she staggered toward the woods she had once known well, as if seeking a shelter from the storm

of her thoughts. She stumbled into the damp under-
growth of the thick forest until she lost her mind, and
her body carried her forward unknowingly.

Bramble-torn and moss-stained, the girl wavered. She'd
been lost for so long, she had no idea where to cast
about for her direction. She ducked under a branch and
strode across the clearing, and then the snare closed
about her ankle and whipped her into the air.

Sharlin's eyes opened wide as her body flung her
head down into the air. She bounced for a moment,
then twirled at the end of the snare. Her heart pounded
furiously, and her mind cleared. How far had she wan-
dered? The sun slanted low through the woods, and
Sharlin spat out a curse. She could have been killed,
wandering through the forest, her thoughts snatched
away from her by what Turiana had tried to do.

Sharlin craned her neck and looked at the ground.
Goblin-ensnared as she was, chances were very good
that she could be killed.

Her arms dangled from her shoulders. She pulled
her right one up and saw the wrist sheath still firmly in
place. Sharlin pulled the dirk, then began to curl back
up the length of her body, trying to reach her ankle.

Three times she tried, gasping, the muscles of her
body protesting and straining, and three times she failed.
Her head throbbed as though it would burst as she
tried a fourth time and then lost it, her body snapping
back downward and the dirk falling from her hand.
"Dammit!"

She spun a second. Her eye blurred. Then she knew
she'd have to try again, and this time, hope to unknot
the rope.

That was when her watery vision saw the figures
standing at the edge of the glen, moving in toward her.

Her heart stopped. Sharlin held her body very still,

waiting to die. Then she saw that these were not goblins but men that approached her.

Dirty and ragged, she saw their haggard faces. Farmers, perhaps, at one time, for one of them carried a harvesting sickle as a weapon, and another a hoe at his shoulder.

"Cut me down," she pleaded and reached toward them.

"By gar," one breathed as he moved nearer. "It's a woman."

She felt another kind of fear then that only a woman knows. With a dizzying, distorted sense, she saw their patched clothes and lean bodies. Rusty blades were stuck into their belts, and slack packs rested upon their backs. The others murmured as they came close, and she could smell their rank scents. What if they weren't rebels, as Dar had supposed, but only bandits . . . renegades, grubbing whatever kind of existence they could out of the land?

Sharlin felt sick. She held out her hand. "Cut me down. We fight the same enemy."

They sucked in their breaths. The one carrying the sickle swung it, and Sharlin cringed before she sensed that he struck at the snare and not her. She crashed to the ground.

They made no further move to help or hurt her as she quickly got to her knees and searched through the leaves and mold for her dirk. It flashed silver as she picked it up.

"It's na the queen," the sickle wielder said finally. "Ah've seen her before. She's older."

Sharlin got to her feet warily. Could she risk telling them who she was? "Do any of you know King Balforth? Is he still alive?"

Their faces were closed to her. She looked at the five of them, then saw a sixth in the brush, in the shadows, watching her.

"Can't any of you tell me?"

The sixth came through. He was tall, though middle-aged, and he wore the remnants of a good suit of mail. "She's not Rodeka," he announced. "Though the black arts are devious. King Balforth lives," he said to her, "in the mountains, same as we do."

"Lives?" Sharlin returned to the soldier. "Or *fights?*"

His eyes hooded a moment, then he nodded brusquely. "Tell me who you are."

"I'm from the house of Dhamon," Sharlin said, and pulled down the neck of her shirt and mail so that he could see the curve of her throat clearly. "Do you know the sign?"

His eyes widened then, and he went to one knee. "I know of the sign, though I've only seen it one other time. Who are you?"

"My name is Sharlin. I'm the daughter of King Balforth," Sharlin told him, and hoped that her naming wasn't her death warrant to be delivered to Rodeka.

The soldier signaled his ragged troops. "I'm Milard. Bring her with us." He paused. "These woods are full of traps and patrols," he said. "We can't stay here or we'll be found sooner or later, and it's getting late. I'll take you with us, but you must go blindfolded. I'll leave you your dagger."

Sharlin swallowed tightly, then nodded. If they were to trust her, she also had to trust them.

A smoke-scented, greasy cloth was wrapped about her eyes. Then a work-worn and creased hand took hers. "Hold on t'me tightly, milady," the man said. "Ah'll guide you."

It was the sickle holder who'd cut her down. She responded to the pressure on his hand and let him urge her into a brisk walk through the woods.

"What's your name?"

"Dalby, milady." He paused, then said roughly, "If

yew are th' princess, then you'll remember my woollies
for the fine yarn they sent you."

She swallowed. It was from a time far away, but she
nodded. "Yes, you're a crofter, one of the best."

"I was, before th' goblins ate my herds." His hand
tightened on hers. "But their time will come," he added
and lapsed into silence as Milard said, "Keep your
voices down."

They wound their way first downhill, then up. Sharlin
stumbled, then found a sense of balance that kept her
even footed. It was as though the blindfold limited her
eyes, but not her other senses. And the falroth boots,
with their invulnerable hide, kept her from many a
stray root and rock. Dalby did his best to keep her from
whipping branches and errant thorns as well.

Sharlin sensed the night from the cool breeze through
her hair as they emerged from the forest and stood.
There was rock beneath her boots. A ridge? A pass?
She waited for Dalby to tug her forward again.

Dalby let go of her hand as Milard said, "I'll take her
from here."

Her pulse quickened as she realized they were in the
encampment. What would she find when they took off
the blindfold? Had she been saved . . . or betrayed?

Another few steps, and then a turn. Pebbles crunched
under her feet. The wind grew high, then died down.

Milard stopped, and she bumped into his mailed
shoulder, then righted herself. She smelled the smoky
scent of a burning torch.

"We found this girl in the woods. She bears a birthmark and says she's from the house of Dhamon, milord."

The blindfold was jerked from her eyes. Sharlin
squinted, then rubbed her eyes to clear her vision, as
the low light of the smoldering torches hid the man
sitting beyond her in the shadows.

He got to his feet. He was tall, and broad-shouldered,
though they sloped as though from a heavy burden.

Fair-headed, his hair hung to his shoulders, and a matted beard curled upon his jaw. He lurched a step closer to her.

"Sharlin?" he asked. His voice was deep and husked, rusty as though he hadn't used it in a long time, or perhaps had used it too much, hoarse and wearied.

She stared, disbelieving, then cried aloud and ran to the man who held up shaking arms. "Father!"

Chapter 19

Turiana twitched. She turned to Dar, illuminating the entire grotto with the glow of her eyes, and said, "Stay close with me now. It begins."

He hesitated, then stripped off his wrist guards and rolled up his sleeves. It had been a few years since he'd helped his father with calving gunters, but he'd not forgotten. The bronze guards, a symbol of war and death, he kicked through the dirt to the side of the cave, as he prepared to bring forth a life, of a sort.

The dragon strained. She lifted her tail up and to the side as Dar leaned close. Eggs, dozens of them, opalescent and leathery, the size of his fist, rained from her vulva, in a river of a liquid that smelled hot and musky. Dar saw a much larger egg, the size of his head, caught in the opening. He hesitated at first, then reached out and gently cupped his hands to either side. The egg was stuck fast, and her bruised flesh began to swell, gripping it tighter.

"Push," he muttered, as he tugged on the stubborn egg. "One more time."

Turiana grunted. She kicked a hind leg back, the spur and talon narrowly missing him. Dar flinched. Her womb pressed on the backs of his hands. He felt the convulsion and knew it could crush the egg she tried to pass now.

"Breathe deep. Breathe deep, and let go."

"Curse you, wormling!" the dragon spat. "I've done this before. *I know.*"

"Then do it!" His fingers were growing numb, yet still he tried to slide the egg forth from the wedge.

She convulsed once, and then the egg came free in his hands. He laid it in the dirt of the cave floor, amid the dozens of smaller eggs.

Turiana turned to it and nuzzled it proudly. It shone, too, with the same pearly sheen of the others, but this held a bronzed tone.

"A dragonet," she murmured. "Perhaps to grow one day in the likeness of Pandor."

"What about these others?"

"Unfertilized. They will be the food of the dragonet. Those that escape to the rivers will become falroth." As the dragon confirmed what Sharlin had told him days ago, Turiana looked adoringly into his face. "It would have been crushed but for you."

Dar tried to wipe some of the fluid from his hands, and failed. "How many more?"

"Hundreds," the dragon answered placidly.

Dar stifled his response, but he knew that before morning, he would be up to his hips in eggs and goo.

As the encampment filled with an army of sorts, Sharlin mopped up the last of a thin stew and fed it to her father, sharing a trencher with him as she'd often seen her mother do.

Although torchlight often played tricks, she feared that the careworn lines she saw in his face were not an illusion of the light. Neither was the rapid graying of his once wheat-gold hair. He swallowed his bite painfully, then put his arm about her shoulder and hugged her tightly yet again.

"If this is a joke of Rodeka's," he said softly, "it is the most cruel."

'It's no joke, Father," she reassured him.

He still wore his plain iron coronet with the single blue-eyed stone, but little else that she remembered was the same. He'd always been vastly taller than she . . . but now, careworn and stoop-shouldered, the bottom of his jawline met her forehead.

She took his hand. "Now tell me about Mother and Erban."

He shuddered and would have withdrawn his hand, but she grasped him firmly.

Milard approached, interrupting his deliberate response, and bowed to the two of them. "We have a raiding party ready."

Balforth nodded. He made as if to stand and leave Sharlin there, but she was anchored to him.

"Raiding party?"

"It's all we can do. We harry at them. It does little. Rodeka's arts are terrifying, but she stays holed up in the fortress and leaves rarely."

"Draw her out! Father, what's wrong with you? Make her fight for Dhamon."

His glance flickered to her. "We gave up the kingdom for you. We thought she had come during the night and taken you. We found one of our own men, traitor, slain outside the eyrie. Criticize me if you will, Sharlin, but remember that I did what I did in your name!"

She flinched as though he'd struck her. "But you have me now. You can strike back."

"No." His blue gaze wouldn't meet hers and she stood.

"Why not?"

"Because your mother and Erban stayed with Rodeka, thinking to meet you in her care."

"You let them go?" Sharlin dropped her father's cold hand. "How could you do that?"

He sighed. Raising his hand to his forehead, he massaged his brow in weariness. "How could I not? Your mother wouldn't hear of leaving you behind, and . . . and I did not seem to be able to stand up to Rodeka's sorcery."

"I left to find help for us against her siege. I told Erban what I was going to do—"

"He gave us a child's fancy tale of a golden dragon and magical aid. What was I to think?" For a moment, her father's voice thundered in the old way. Men all over camp stopped what they were doing and watched, and she saw renewed hope in their faces.

Was this what she had read in them? Defeated because their lord felt defeated? Uncertainty because he was uncertain? Hopeless because he no longer held any hope? Then, Turiana or not, Sharlin knew she had brought back help for her kingdom.

Her voice echoed in the box canyon that held them. "Look at me! I'm not dressed in a lady's skirt, Father. This is armor. I came ready to fight for Dhamon. I won't give it up easily. Are you ready to give your life for your people?"

He sighed. "Sharlin, you know that I've always been ready to make that choice."

"Then why do you think Mother or Erban is any less ready? Or me!" Thinking of Turiana, she pivoted and threw her hand out at a blank slab of granite. A golden bolt burst forth, and the rock powdered. Shaken, she lowered her hand. Turiana *had* done it. A weakness echoed inside of her, then recovered. She did hold some of the dragon's powers.

Around her, the men began to gather and clamor at her. Balforth looked at her, with wide, stricken eyes.

"What have you done?"

She looked at him. "I've done whatever I've needed to do, in order to come home and bring victory to you. If we're going to go out tonight, let's do it to bring Mother and Erban home. Let's go out to win."

He stood, wavering, and she sensed that he was a man torn, disintegrating inside, and that she was helping him to his final destruction. Her next words caught in her throat, so she simply took his arm and helped him remain standing.

The men quieted, waiting for their king to speak.

He lifted his eyes from the ground finally. The torchlight gave him a color to his cheeks that he did not have. He said, "Gather your weapons. I know of a back way. Can you do that again, Sharlin, if you have to?"

She did not have the stamina of a dragon queen, but she knew she could pull forth the bolt maybe two or three more times, and she nodded. If it took more force than that, then she knew Rodeka would win the final battle anyway.

The dragon's hissing filled the earthen cave with a warm steaming and ceaseless sound. Dar felt deafened as he waded calf-deep through the eggs surrounding him, going to her womb once more. As he did so, he made a tiny move to loosen his sword in its scabbard on his left hip. Turiana was losing her battle against Nightwing's venom, as the laying weakened her, and though she now tolerated Dar for the aid he was giving her, he didn't think he had much longer to live.

His fingers pulled at the hilt.

Strike not.

Dar dropped his hand away, then used the back of it to mop his forehead. It was going to be hard enough to do what he had to do without the sword's advising against it.

The eggs moved fluidly against him. Seven more large eggs he'd helped. They lay nestled among the roe of their lesser kin, one black, one gold, three green, one blue, one bronze, and one mottled, as though unsure of its coloration.

Turiana nosed at them even as she hissed. Her entire

body was now jet-black, with the exception of her broad
forehead and around her two eyes. When she turned to
look at him, it was as though she peered at him from a
cloud of darkness obscuring the rest of her.

She spasmed weakly. He knew that movement. Wearily, aching between the shoulders, he moved to aid
her. "Again," he said, spotting the large egg caught in
the birth canal.

"I know, you vile little turd," the dragon said. She
shuddered. "Where is that whore with my water?"

The purple sheen of the pearly shell glistened at him.
Thinking of the evil Baalan, he considered crushing it
between his hands instead of helping it into existence
with the others.

She rode a sturdy little mountain pony, a mare with a
thick stubby coat and a mane that threatened to drag
the ground. Milard rode to the fore, and her father
paced her. All the men rode similar beasts. Sharlin
smiled slightly. She had fond memories of riding Gabriel over the mountains and seeing these creatures
running wild below.

"Father," she said, twisting in the crude hide saddle,
"What happened to the eyrie?"

"Most of the griffins are gone. My spies tell me she
has two or three left. The others escaped the first time
she tried to use them."

Sharlin tried to grasp the information and put it to
use with what she knew of the Rangard she'd shared
with Dar. He'd fought wild griffins, but the stories of
war-griffins broke to carrying people had been dismissed
as legend. She felt saddened. Even if she beat Rodeka
now, that part of the legacy of Dhamon would be lost.
And she also knew that her bloodline had faded from
the world and was no more. But that could happen to
any house, through marriages of alliance, or not bearing
a son to carry the name. For a moment, she lamented

the destruction of the pallan temple which had held her history etched upon it.

But then, if she had read it all, and knew this moment whether she rode to victory or defeat, would she still have the courage to do it?

"You've grown," her father said, and placed his hand over hers on the pony's reins.

"It's been a year and a half," she said.

"And Gabriel carried you far, far away, or you wouldn't have been that long in coming back to us."

"No."

"Tell me more about this swordsman who aided you. Where is he now?"

She looked at him and saw the stern, disapproving face of a father staring back at her. Sharlin grimaced. "You'll like him when you meet him. As for where he is now . . ." She glanced back at the mountains they were leaving. "He's not far from where Milard and the others found me. He's aiding a companion who was wounded."

"And this companion. Does he—sorry, she—have anything to do with the powers you've acquired?"

"Everything. The companion, father, is the golden dragon Turiana."

He sucked in his breath, and his hand moved from hers as the ponies clopped along the barely seen trail. "Then Erban was right."

"Yes. I found her and I've brought her back to help us, but she was wounded making the crossing. Dar helps her fight for her life."

"Then her journey was in vain."

She reined her pony to a halt. "Do you really think so?"

His gaze tried to move from hers, then the king said quietly, "No. Never, if she brought you back to me. But the stories all say she's dead, and has been for a hundred years."

"The stories are wrong." Sharlin kicked her pony

back into a trot, unwilling to tell him more of the story than that. And how was she ever going to tell him of Dar and that she carried Dar's child? Without her mother's presence, she didn't think he could take that blow. He still thought of her as a girl, his, a maiden, though she rode side by side with him, dressed in better armor than he was, and with more power to command.

Milard stopped on the track and held up his arm. Behind them, the straggling trail of fighters also halted. Balforth reined out and around them, and Sharlin followed.

"What is it?"

"This is where the foresters lived."

Sharlin remembered well the lumbermen. She had loved to visit when the sawmill was working, and the sound of sawblades moving to their chanting voice filled the air. She looked, and saw a dead forest. Trees of ghostly gray filled the clearing. The log houses looked empty—and worse, dead.

"What happened?"

"The goblins cleaned them out." He kneed his pony forward.

As they neared a log cabin, he held his torch out, illuminating the scene for her in an eerie orange light.

A three-rock altar had been stacked in front of the door. Its stone surface was rusted brown with an old stain that the wind and the rain had not been able to wash away.

Sharlin felt a hard lump rise in her throat. "What— what is it?" she asked, afraid she knew the answer.

"This is where the foresters, every man, woman, and child who didn't escape, were sacrificed last winter." The torch quivered in his shaking hand, then he abruptly spurred away his pony from the site.

Sharlin felt a tingle of the power, like a spiderweb over the village. She thrust out a hand and brushed it away, golden sparkles crackling from her fingertips, unknowing of what she did, except that she must cleanse it.

The stone altar cracked and fell in upon itself. The air, which had been deadly silent, gave way to the rustle of the night wind, and the cry of a hunting bird. She gasped at the sudden drain, at the fatigue she felt, then straightened in her saddle. The power was not without price.

This was what Turiana could do, should have been able to do, if Nightwing had not raped and poisoned her.

With another sorrow weighing her, Sharlin turned her mare and followed her father into the night.

As the last, silvery egg nudged its way into his hands, Dar held on to it. His back felt as though a battle ax cleaved it. The night must be nearly spent. He felt the same. As he waded knee-high through the opalescent roe and clutch of dragonets, he held the egg as his only protection against the dragon queen.

"Let me see it," she whispered weakly.

He approached cautiously. To get close enough to strike her was also to put himself within her striking distance.

"Silver," she mused. "The last is silver. I have never seen a silver dragon, though . . . years ago . . . I heard tales of one." She nudged it. "May you grow and prosper," she whispered.

Then the narrow glare of her yellow eyes turned to him. "Drop it," she said.

He did, and drew his sword as she snapped toward him.

Strike not, the blade told him, and he hesitated, even as she struck. Dar screamed as the fang pierced his thigh and she took him in her jaws. She shook him as a dog shakes a mouse. The sword disappeared in the roe.

He balled up his hand and punched her between the eyes. Startled, the dragon let him go, and Dar jumped up, catching her behind the neck. He wrapped his arms and legs about her, heedless of the spines which threatened to puncture him in a handful of different, all vital places.

She shook her head. He rode her, knowing that if he let go, she would strike him again. Too weak to hiss, she scratched at him with her hind claws, then stopped, for it upset the ocean of eggs that surrounded her.

"Turiana," he said. "It's me. Remember who you are! You've survived the laying—now fight to survive Nightwing!"

The dragon paused, then began to shake again. He clenched his teeth together as his ears rang. His only hope was that she might be so weak that he could jump off and recover his sword before she got to him first. He gripped her throat tighter.

She stopped again. "I hear you, Aarondar," she husked. "Tell me more."

The sound of the golden dragon's voice brought a small hope to him, hope that there was more to Turiana than her magic. "Help yourself," he said. "You are more than magic. You're more than a beast of the earth. Remember your soul."

And then he began to talk to her. He told her of the great morning when she arose from the dragon graveyard and battled a bitter enemy. He spoke to her of the mornings the three of them had spent together, and of Pandor and his sacrifice. He sang to her the song that Chey had sung him of the horde-thieving goblin and the dragon's revenge.

And when his voice grew hoarse and faltered, she sprang in the air, straight upward, her wings flailing, and she nearly threw him. Dar clutched to stay aboard.

He bumped his head on the low dirt ceiling of the grotto, but she didn't have enough strength to smash him. He felt her pulse racing through her neck. When she landed, she took great care with the eggs.

Her face had lightened. The gold of her coloring came through the dark as though a glow fired her from within. Dar saw it and took a shuddering breath.

"Listen to me," he said. "I'll tell you about your nest when we went through it, Sharlin, Hapwith, and I."

And he told her that. Of the medals and works of art given to her in gratitude. Of the many monuments to a dragon's benevolence. Of the beauty she had hidden away. Of the greatness of heart she must have had, and used, to mold Rangard with. That he knew why she had been the dragon queen, and why she must live to be one again.

She lay down under him, shivering violently, as if in an icy land. But her hide burned with a fever that he felt through his armor. His leg throbbed and ached, and he could tell it bled slowly. It would give out on him soon, and then he would be hard pressed to keep hold of her.

But suddenly his impending death became much less important to him than hers.

And as he talked, he watched the gold aura of her head growing like a sunburst.

Sharlin put her hand to her mouth and turned her face away, determined not to gag. The stench of the hanging bodies filled the pathway, but Milard and her father rode past unheedingly.

She'd passed three of these groups so far. Rodeka's rule had brought about this savagery. She breathed through her mouth and hoped not to see another demonstration until they reached the fortress.

Her home hugged the top of a plateau. It was the same and yet far different from the plateau where she had talked with M'reen. It was the same in that the mountain's top had been sheared away flat. Different in that the valleys and mountains overlooked were halfway around the world from each other. Even the air smelled different here. The trees and shrubs were different. The tiny flowers that grew late into autumn, and even splintered rock to do so, she had never seen anywhere else.

Orange and red and even pink leaves foretold the coming of winter. Soon the trees were be bare, and snow would lash the mountain peaks. Then the fortress held the land of Dhamon like a lonely warrior, for in the valleys, the villagers had the shelter while the fortress braved the wind and ice alone. On the far side of the plateau, the gentle slope was guarded by walls.

It was those walls, the bastion of the goblin army, that she and her father faced now.

Sharlin licked her lips. Obscene signs and paintings in the dried rust-brown of what had once been blood decorated the ancient stone. Uneasily, she knew why her father had never had the courage to storm the old house. She felt the oppressive darkness of Rodeka's power lying over everything she saw.

This was not the home she'd returned to in her lyrith dreams.

It had been burned bare, by fire, not the summer sun. Orchards that should now be laden with fruit were charred sticks. Fields lay fallow. The goblins ate flesh, and all the wild creatures of Dhamon had fled. Even the prolific softfoot had been scarce during her night's ride.

Balforth stirred beside her, as though he'd been waiting for her thoughts to end. "Well, daughter? Are you still eager for a battle?"

Smudge pots glowed behind the walls. She had tried counting the hunchbacked creatures surrounding each

pot, to estimate the force, but had given up. She looked
to her father.

"There is no way to win back Dhamon without fighting." She reined her pony aside to Milard. What would
Dar do? What did he do now, enmeshed in Turiana's
struggle to lay her eggs and survive? "Does every man
have a weapon?"

"Yes, princess." His eyes flickered briefly to her father then back to her. "And we're ready!"

Her pony stamped, and she thought of softfoot again.
If she could use Turiana's sleep charm to lay the goblins
down . . .

"Wait for my signal," she ordered Milard. The captain nodded. She squeezed her legs, urging the mare
forward, closer to the walls. Soon she would be out of
cover and exposed.

"Sharlin!" her father said softly.

"I'll be all right. If you come with me, be still."

An unreadable expression flashed across his face, and
she realized that in that moment, he knew she was no
longer his girl-child. Nor would she smile at him to
soften that realization.

The pony stopped. She looked out over the slope.
Due north, the fortress hugged the windy side of the
mountain. She saw lights flicker within. Strange that a
woman who had brought forth so much darkness lived
within light, she thought. Then she put aside her
thoughts and searched for the power of sleep given her
by the golden dragon.

When she stirred, she found her father bolstering her
in the saddle. She looked out.

The walls were quiet.

"I did it," she whispered to herself. Again the terrible weakness possessed her, and she pushed it aside.
"Tell Milard they're asleep. But they can be wakened,
so we've got to move quickly and quietly."

"How long will they sleep?"

She shrugged as her father let go of her. "I don't know. I've never done this before."

With a startled look, he left her and returned to his army. Milard came back with him.

The captain looked in astonishment over the battlements. Then he flashed her a grin of triumph. "We have them!"

"Perhaps not all."

"Then may I suggest that a small force go up. We need only to get out the queen and Erban, and we're free to fight."

Balforth nodded. "If necessary, we can take the griffins."

"But there are only three left."

He looked at her steadily. "You, your brother, and your mother."

She nodded abruptly in understanding, and kicked her mare forward. She'd loved Dar long enough that he'd given her that understanding of a soldier's sacrifice, and mentally she thanked him for it.

They rode through the fallen troops. Her nose wrinkled at the smell of goblin. They had fallen in their tracks, literally, leather armor and warty skin vulnerable, bared tusks gleaming to the night sky in charmed sleep. Her little mare balked once. Milard dismounted and took her by the reins, and led her and his own mount up the slope.

They wended their way through the mountains of goblin flesh. Sharlin's heart faltered. If they had to fight through this . . .

She pushed the thought from her mind. They wouldn't fail. They couldn't fail. Even as they walked, she burned aside the web of darkness that cloaked the plateau. Turiana's powers were like a torch of liberty that she held before her, and its flame consumed Rodeka's evil.

They faced the foot of the fortress. Balforth took charge, bringing the two of them around to a secret exit. A great boulder lay across the barred door. Sharlin remembered the door well, moss-covered and old, scarred by wind and ice. Now she looked at the boulder. If she had had Dar's sword . . .

But she didn't. She gathered up her anger and fury and aimed it at the rock, and Turiana's magic speared through the night, a gold fire that powdered the boulder into dust.

Coughing, they raised the counterweights, and the door creaked open. Balforth paused.

"You know the way."

Sharlin nodded. "I remember."

"Then Milard and I will hold the door here. You're on your own inside, daughter. Take care. Use the griffins to leave, do you understand?"

She nodded again. Impulsively, she hugged him tightly, and he whispered into her ear, "I don't think I can bear losing you twice."

"You won't."

Sharlin took out her dagger and made her way up the pitch-black well of steps.

Chapter 20

She kept to the inside wall of the stairwell. The stones were fetid and slimy, but she remembered that the stairs were rigged. Every fourth or fifth step to the outside would give way. Only the house of Dhamon knew that and would survive a journey up or down the lightless well. Her falroth boots creaked and she gripped the dagger in her hand so tightly the metal warmed to a blaze in her palm.

Her heightened senses told her something waited beyond the secret panel at the top of the stairs. She felt its dark brooding. Her pulse quickened. What would it be? A demon perhaps, or even Rodeka herself?

A tiny drop of sweat beaded on her upper lip, and she licked it off. It left a salty taste. She looked upward. If she only knew the depths and limits of Turiana's power. Then she made a grim smile. With or without that magic, she'd still be making this climb.

At the last step, she paused and, with her left hand, felt at the blank wall in front of her. There would be a lever about here.

And the stone ground away.

Sharlin reeled back, as the evil and the scent assaulted her. The great beast grinned at her, his hairy knuckles brushing the ground and his tusks curving outward from thin, black lips. The goblin guard reached for his slicer with a grunt.

She drove her dagger into his bulging belly, the stomach that swelled out greedily from under his surcoat. With both hands, she ripped upward. Blood and intestines gushed out. The creature bellowed. She ducked under his swiping hand, and as she danced to the side, he tried to grasp the contents of his stomach. He slipped in the wash of black blood and went down.

The crash seemed to echo through the hall. Sharlin bit her lip as he convulsed, then leaned down and, with a twist, liberated her dagger. The goblin she left dying in agony behind her.

His death answered one of the questions in her mind. Her sleep charm clearly had not bothered the fortress inhabitants.

She dashed to the right. Her mother and Erban should be in the children's wing, where she and Erban had been quartered. She had no doubt that Rodeka would have taken over the better-furnished and more strategically placed quarters of the king. Her feet had wings of their own. She was home, home, and knew exactly where she was going and what she had to do.

With a pant, she slowed at the thick oak door that secured the wing. It was locked from the outside. She looked at her bloodied dagger, with its stiletto point, then wiped it on the top of her boot. She picked the lock, worrying at its inside, uncaring of what the jimmying did to the edge of the dagger. It had served its purpose.

The lock fell open. Almost as a second thought, she brushed aside the intangible black webbing about the door, a golden fire streaking along the wooden frame and then sizzling out. She put her shoulder to the door and moved it open, surprised and grateful that it had not been barred from the inside. It fell open with a voice of its own, deep and murmuring.

The wing was dark. Not even a night lamp flickered from the wall sconces. It smelled cold and empty, and she would have wondered if she had chosen properly, except for the locked door and the magical warding.

Sharlin felt the dirk's blade. Nicked and curled now, it was nearly useless. She returned it to its wrist sheath. Erban would have a sword or two secreted away, unless Rodeka had found them, hoping that one day he would be big enough to fight his way out—if he lived long enough. She remembered her brother as a tousle-headed boy, feisty and teasing, with a love for weapons and fighting, a kind of game that noble blood won at.

She wondered how the year and a half of imprisonment had changed him, if he lived. Rodeka had used Dhamon blood summoning her through lyrith dreams. Whom had it come from—Lauren the queen or Erban the son?

A slim door halted her search. This had once been her room. She looked to the floor. Even in the darkness, she could see a pathway of smoky footsteps upon the planking. Rodeka had walked this way often. Sharlin felt contempt and anger curl her lip, and scrubbed her face with her hand.

Then she lifted the latch and opened the door.

Her room had been stripped bare. All that she'd grown up with as a princess and firstborn of King Balforth was gone. The stone window where the pale light of the moons shone in was uncovered. A pile of filthy hay lay in the middle of the room, covered with threadbare and patched blankets, and her mother and brother lay curled in sleep upon them. With a catch of her throat, Sharlin moved forward.

She didn't remember the network of lines upon her mother's face that even sleep did not ease away. As she leaned down, she felt like a coarsened copy of the fine-featured Queen Lauren, a woman so slender and delicate that the homespun gown she wore hung on her like a sack. Sharlin hesitated, afraid to wake her.

Erban snorted, and stirred. He'd grown. He would be tall, like their father, but heavier, stockier. She saw now, and knew without asking, that her mother had given him the greater portion of their meager existence, for he bloomed. And Sharlin knew, too, that she'd better take precautions when she awakened them, or Erban would make enough noise to rouse the fortress.

With a smile, she lowered her hand and covered his mouth.

He came awake fiercely, kicking covers and hay everywhere, and she nearly lost her hold on him.

"Erban! It's me!" she whispered piercingly and felt as though she wrestled a falroth.

He went slack. His pale blue eyes opened. Then they widened with recognition.

She removed her hand, and he grabbed up with an immense hug, pulling her down on top of him, nearly crushing their mother.

Sharlin looked to her. Queen Lauren sat up, both hands shaking and pressed to her pale mouth, while her eyes welled up with tears. Then she reached for Sharlin and they embraced. Her mother's heart beat in her thin chest like a frightened bird trying to escape a net.

"It's all right," Sharlin said. "I'm here to bring you out."

"I thought . . . I thought she'd killed you," the woman said.

Sharlin took a corner of one of the meager blankets and wiped the tears from her face. "She lied to you."

Erban had gotten to his feet to dress and now stuffed a foot into a boot that had to be too small. He grunted as he did so. "All her magic is lies," he said angrily. "Where's the dragon? I told them you were bringing back a dragongod." He went to the window, one boot on and one dangling from his hand, as if he could see the beast hovering outside. "Where is it?" Then he turned around. "They're all asleep out there."

Lauren got to her feet, with Sharlin's help. She stood, shaking still, her frail body quaking.

"Get dressed, Mother, please." Sharlin pulled Erban back from the window. Ten years of age, and he looked her in the eye.

"Stay away from the window. I want to get you out of here quietly, before the attack."

His brows went up, silvery gold in the moonlight. "Attack? I've been waiting for this!" He felt along the stones of the turret. A piece of loosened mortar fell out under his probing. A little more working, and he pulled forth a short sword and held it aloft triumphantly.

"Got any more like that?"

His face fell. "Just this one." His hand gripped it convulsively, then he held it out to her. "You can have it."

Sharlin pushed it aside gently. "No, you keep it. I've other weapons." She turned. "Mother, are you ready?"

"Yes. I think so." She dabbed at her eyes again. She wore an old pair of Erban's trousers, belted at her wasplike waist with a rope. The tunic was grease-stained and torn, and she had pulled on a blanket for a cloak.

Sharlin felt her own eyes blur rapidly. This was the Queen of Dhamon! The cords on her neck strained.

"How are we getting out?"

"Through the stairwell, unless the guard's been discovered. If so, then down through the kitchen. I want you to get to the eyrie and take the griffins."

Erban frowned. "They've gone pretty wild."

"If a Dhamon can't ride a griffin, who can?" Sharlin shot back. "This is no time to hesitate."

Lauren came up and grasped her daughter by the arm. "No, it's not. But give me a moment, anyway." She reached out and pulled her close, stroking her hair with a worn hand. "Where have you been, my little love, and how are you?"

Sharlin felt her mother's trembling. She guessed, without being told, where Rodeka had found her blood for the spellmaking, for her mother's fair skin had gone more than pale.

She lifted her head. "I've been halfway across the world, and farther. I took Gabriel to go find Turiana, the golden dragon. He was struck by magic. He died, but not before he bore me to safety. Then pallans took me in—"

"Whats?" interrupted Erban, but Queen Lauren nodded.

"I've heard of them. A mysterious folk."

"They, too, kept me safe. And then I was given a map, to the dragon graveyard, and I knew I'd find Turiana there. And Dar came with me, and we shared the map—"

"Dar?"

"Aarondar. He's a—well, I guess you'd call him a free swordsman."

Her mother looked at her closely, and Sharlin felt a blush warm her cheeks.

"Is that what you'd call him?" her mother said softly.

Mother and daughter looked into each other's eyes, and Sharlin burst out, "Of course you'd know. I love him. He brought me back."

"Then where is he now?"

"With Turiana. She was wounded. Mother . . . he doesn't know it yet, but I'm carrying his child."

The queen hugged her fiercely. "I thought so," she murmured softly. "I prayed it wasn't a child of rape. Take care of yourself for me."

They parted. The queen took a deep breath. "Now," she said, "I'm ready to go."

Sharlin took the lead, her dagger at the ready once more, though she knew it wouldn't be of much use.

The fortress seemed shrouded in sleep, dark and quiet, and that prickled at her. She'd seen many lights from down below.

Her home—what had been her home—now felt like the giant maw of a trap, waiting to close on her and crush her.

Erban bumped into her from behind. He grumbled. "You said this was no time to hesitate."

Sharlin waved him silent with a curt gesture. His lower lip went out, but he shut up.

Sharlin knew that the guard had been found. Perhaps it was dragon sense, perhaps it was all that Dar had taught her through the time they had shared with each other. But she knew it had to have been, and that to return to the stairwell was folly.

She turned. "We're going to the eyrie," she said. She thought she heard a tiny sound of dismay from her mother, but wasn't sure, as she led the way.

The entire fortress was webbed with the black smoke of Rodeka's footsteps, and the webbing of her magic. Sharlin brushed it aside gently, weaving and reweaving as she walked, though it made her tremble and her forehead bead with sweat, as though she carried the weight of the world upon her shoulders. She needed to rest, but could not. She would sleep for a handful of days when she got them free, but not before.

On the landing above the kitchen, she paused. She listened for the familiar creak of the cook making bread dough for the morning, and heard nothing. Even the heat of the huge stoves did not filter through. Dead. All dead, all gone.

With a swallow to ease her dry throat, Sharlin took them downstairs and through the kitchen. She saw, then, the dust and disuse. Erban gagged as they passed the body of a softfoot, pinned to the butcher table, its entrails torn out and strewn across the cutting board.

This slaughter had not been for a meal. Rodeka had been reading her fortune in its death throes.

Lauren placed a hand on her son's shoulder to brace him, and they continued onward.

Sharlin found the door. She motioned Erban, and together they eased aside the heavy crossbars. Spider-webs parted with a sticky sound as they did so. No one had been through here since the day Rodeka took up residence. And, true to her fears, the door squeaked loudly as they opened it.

The eyrie stood in a beam of moonlight, a quick sprint across the courtyard. Sharlin leaned out. She saw no guards. The hair rose on the back of her neck. The trap seemed to stretch and grow to its utmost tautness.

She patted Erban. "Go on."

Her mother hesitated, and Sharlin looked at her. "Now," she emphasized.

The queen nodded. They ran across the courtyard, boots rustling through dried grasses, and Erban flung open the door.

Three griffins sat on their perches. Their hooded heads turned at the invasion of their eyrie, and they clacked loudly. One bated his wings, filling the mews with the sound of his unrest.

They looked well enough. Sharlin felt a little of the knot ease in her breast. Perhaps they were going to get away with this.

She moved to a griffin and motioned to Erban. "Get the leathers."

He pulled riding harnesses down off a peg.

The leonine haunches grew tight and the beak of the griffin opened threateningly as she brought the back of her hand up against its chest and gently ruffled the feathers there. The beast squawked, then settled. Erban came up behind her as she swiftly prepared it for a rider. She left the hood on and went to the next.

It struck her before she could move her hand out of

the way. Sharlin sucked the blood from the welling wound. Erban eased around her and soothed the griffin. He saddled this one.

Sharlin got the last. She led the two through the blind darkness of the eyrie toward the doorway, and her mother followed. Erban mounted his and tore off the hood.

With a cry of triumph, the griffin spread its wings.

Sharlin and her mother moved quickly into the courtyard, fighting to keep their griffins quiet, as Erban's mount burst from the shed and he fought to stay on.

The griffin's piercing whistle was echoed by a short, dark laugh.

"Now I have you, my beauty. Everything else is just history." Rodeka appeared from the shadows of the fortress, her dark hair hanging to her waist, still bound with thongs of copper coins and feathers, her robes hanging tightly from her full waist and then flowing to her bare feet.

Sharlin's heart sank as she recognized the type of feathers they were. Then she turned on her heel.

"Fly, Erban!"

He whipped his mount with the flat of the short sword as it fought his command over it, then the beast took to the air, even as goblins rounded the corner of the building and lunged at it to stop it. Its leonine paw whipped out. A goblin went rolling in his own blood.

The queen's griffin reared, shaking its head wildly. The loosened hood went flying. The beast raked the skies. Lauren cried out, once, as the vicious beak snapped at her neck.

Sharlin screamed as her mother fell to the courtyard. Her life spurted from her severed neck. The griffin shook itself and launched with a scream, scattering the goblin guard as it flew.

Rodeka pointed at her. Sharlin answered with a bolt of fury that burned with the coin of Turiana's color, and it drained the last of her trembling strength. As the last griffin reared and dragged her, Sharlin went down. Her ears roared with the darkness.

She heard the sorceress murmur, "All the rest was worth it."

Then nothing.

Chapter 21

The brilliant sunrise of a clear late-autumn day in a pure blue sky was nothing to compare with the sunburst within the cave, Dar thought, as he wearily climbed down from Turiana's back.

His body shook uncontrollably. The dragon moved her head slightly to lower him.

He touched among the ocean of eggs carefully. The liquid that bore them was beginning to thicken. They shifted only slightly, and he had to push through them to wade to where he thought he'd dropped the sword.

Here, master.

Dar plunged his hand down to his shoulder and grasped the blade.

Turiana nudged him. "I must cover them with dirt to keep them warm, once I leave the cave."

He nodded and trudged ahead wearily, squinting at the brightness of the day.

The golden dragon sang to herself at his back, as she scratched and covered the precious spawn. Then she emerged behind him, and it was as if the sun rose again, for she shone more molten than before. Like topaz, she sparkled.

Dar ducked his head and sank to the grasses. He stank. The fluid goo that now held the eggs together in a shimmering mass threatened to stick him together as well, limb to limb.

Turiana nuzzled him fondly. "Well done, fair son," she rumbled.

He ran a hand through his hair. His thigh ached, and a crust of dried blood itched him. "I'll wake Sharlin and tell her," he returned wearily. "Then I'm going to bathe before I turn into stone."

The dragonish sound of laughter tickled his ear. Then she froze, her fangs bared, and crouched above him, guarding.

The woods filled with men. Dar looked up and saw the desperate faces, pale in the morning, their hands clenched about makeshift and poorly wrought weapons.

As he staggered to his feet, he knew the man who approached him from their midst. They'd met, he knew, in a dream.

King Balforth inclined his head. "I know you," he said. "And you must be Sharlin's Dar."

"How did you find me?"

At his back, a burly, much younger version of the king struggled with a griffin, curbing its hissing and striking. The boy answered, "The griffin knew."

Turiana made a sound, and the beast quieted.

"Sharlin told us of you." The king looked toward the dragon. "I never thought to live to see a god."

"Where is she?"

Balforth sighed wearily. It rattled through the man's chest and Dar felt a stab of fear run through him.

"Rodeka has her."

Dar stood fully dressed in the icy brook and poured the water over his aching body. It cascaded from his half-helm, and he sputtered, as Balforth sat on the banks and watched him.

"How could you leave her behind?"

"We heard the griffins. We thought they'd been successful. Not one of the guards raised an alarm, so we gathered the ponies and left the way we'd come. It wasn't until later that . . ." The king paused a moment, gathering himself. "It wasn't until later when Erban found us that we learned what had happened."

Dar vigorously massaged his scalp, then poured another helmful over. His leathers were going to dry hard and his metal rust, but he didn't have time to bathe properly. "And what do you suggest we do now?"

"The dragon appears to have recovered."

"Exhausted, but recovered." He slicked his hair from his eyes. Balforth eyed his hairless face but said nothing. Dar grinned. It was the custom of his country to use an ointment that generally kept the face hairless for a lifetime, but he knew the king wondered if he was going to have to turn the remnants of his army to a lad too young to grow a beard. He paused. He couldn't very well tell Balforth that Turiana had given over her powers. From what the dragon had told him, she couldn't even flame if she had to.

He waded from the brook and stood, water pouring from him. "What do you think about a direct attack?"

"Scouts tell me the goblins awaken slowly. The ones that have roused are still fairly groggy. Rodeka's not as vulnerable as she was last night, but she's still open."

"And the main bulk of her army is elsewhere?"

The king grimaced. "She's in the process of conquering a kingdom to the south. Most of her human soldiers and wizards have gone in that direction. But I won't attack now for the same reason I couldn't last night. She holds a member of my family hostage!"

Dar hesitated. He didn't know what Sharlin might have told the king. He'd witnessed the transfer of power, and yet, like Turiana, he didn't know if it had been successful. Sharlin's wandering off and getting ensnared didn't sound as if she'd been in her right mind. Yet her attempt to breach the fortress and get her family out did. "There is that in Sharlin which can protect her, if we create a diversion."

"You mean the magic?" Balforth thrust himself abruptly to his feet. "I gather she's untried and unused to it. The sleep charm she cast last night nearly knocked her from her saddle. I have little confidence in it."

Dar didn't like the sound of that. He looked through the grove to where Turiana munched on a leg of gunter, and Balforth's men stood around roasting the remainder, at a reasonable distance from the golden creature. He picked up the sword and scabbard and lashed it on, and adjusted the swing on his left hip for an easy pull.

"If you don't trust magic, then are you willing to try an attack? Goblins are notoriously dragon-shy. I'll take care of Sharlin if you take care of the army."

Balforth hesitated yet again, and Dar eyed him. From the spirit he had grown to love in Sharlin, he had never thought to find her father a coward. He had to remind himself the man had lived in exile in the woods and mountains for a year and a half, living on the hope he could free his family one day, and then his wife had been cut down last night while escaping. Dar tucked his helm under his arm. "If the sleep charm is still wearing off, we should press the advantage."

The king nodded abruptly. "I understand. Milard!" he shouted up the slope, and the men hurriedly scoffed up the last of their meal. "Get ready."

They brought their shaggy ponies out of the thickets and mounted up, tired but determined, with hope shining in their faces.

Turiana stretched. Dar reached up and scratched under her jaw, and she looked lovingly down at him. They watched from the edge of the burned-out grove as Balforth led his men toward the fortress.

"Rodeka doesn't know I've lost my powers. That is our one great advantage. She may even be flattered that I have come to challenge her."

"If she recognizes you."

"Hah! Even a sorcerer of your people couldn't fail to recognize me." Turiana shuffled in the ashen dirt. "The goblins will run, of course, when we fly in."

"Straight into Balforth's arms, I hope." Dar thought of Chey's love of roasted goblin and was sorry that brown dragon wasn't with him. "And what's to keep Rodeka from blasting you when you face her?"

The dragon caught his gaze in hers, and he felt the strength of his bones melting away. He caught himself when she wrenched her auric eyes away from his.

"A dragon does have some natural abilities," she said smugly.

"If Rodeka lets you get that close."

"Oh, she will." Turiana nudged him. "Mount up. They're nearly in place."

With a groan, Dar pulled himself up. When this was over, he was going to take Sharlin and hibernate for a year. The shock ran through him that he might never hold Sharlin again . . . and even if he did find her, what would their future be? They were stranded in Dhamon.

He shook off his uneasiness. He had a future with his love; he knew it, the fact of it burned in his chest. He could no more deny it than strike off his arm.

He took hold of the leather harness and said, "I'm ready."

"Good, Aarondar. It is . . . nice that you have acquired a taste for dragonriding." Turiana snorted in amusement, and gathered herself for flying.

Sharlin woke. Her head throbbed, and she found herself unable to move, strung on crossbraces and hanging from her wrists. She put her head back, trying to ease her neck and pull her hair from her face so that she could see. She knew now what a fly felt like in the center of the spider's web.

Rodeka caught her movement. The witch queen sat

in a chair lined with furs. Each fur still held the skull of the beast that had worn the pelt in life, their eyes replaced with gems that glittered maliciously.

The woman stood up. She was older than Sharlin, but ageless in grace. Her dark hair had not a single strand of gray in it. The sun had never put a wrinkle about her hard eyes. Her skin was still of the purest white, and as she held out a hand to Sharlin, she gestured with fingers that had never blistered or calloused with hard labor.

Sharlin thought of her own hands, still scarred from digging through rock and dirt to free Dar. Then she put her chin up, knowing she wouldn't have traded any of those scars, if it had meant leaving Dar behind.

The sorceress halted in front of her. "I see you've awakened."

"Of all the things said about you, Rodeka," Sharlin answered, "it was never said that you were not observant."

Rodeka smiled. It did not reach or warm her eyes. "You show a great deal of courage in the face of adversity. This is why I came to conquer the house of Dhamon. Imagine my disappointment when I found little of the renowned traits in the other members of your family."

Knowing she was being baited, Sharlin couldn't hold her tongue. "Your traits are generally reviled," she returned.

The witch queen's eyes narrowed. She flung a long, dark wave of her hair back over her shoulder. "I will not forget or forgive what you say here. If you wish a merciful death, you'd better remember that." She walked to the brazier, and Sharlin recognized then that they were in the great hall of her dreams . . . barren, wrecked, with a diagram crudely painted on the flooring. The brazier smoked gently. At its side sat a small table.

Sharlin looked away quickly. She recognized the table as one her mother had often used to hold her embroidery when she sat working at night. But it was not covered with embroidery now. There were small knives and flaying hooks, and other things whose purpose she didn't want to guess.

Sharlin tested her bonds slightly as Rodeka picked up a knife and examined it.

The sorceress looked up. "You have power," she said, "but I've bound you. You're good, quite good. You're well protected. I couldn't harm you if I wanted to." She smiled, showing neat, clean teeth. "But I can if you want me to, and you will, before this is over."

"Why should I let you hack away at me?"

"Because I want my powers extended. I intend to summon a being here which will help me."

"A dragongod?"

The candle-lit lanterns about the hall flickered, and Rodeka's eyes caught their glitter. "Perhaps. Is that how you got your powers?" She reached under her robe and held up a jeweled talisman on a chain, big as a cackle egg, that glowed and pulsed with a life of its own. "Power is like one of these gems," the sorceress said. "Good or evil. It's a life you mine out and polish, shape, to be your own. Sometimes it's your power and sometimes it's a power you can suck away from someone else. As you did."

Startled, Sharlin looked to the woman, although she didn't want to.

Rodeka gloated. "You thought I wouldn't know? You have power, but you don't know how to use it. Well, I do. And I'll have yours and my benefactor's before this morning is over. Which"—and she cast a glance to the ragged tapestries hanging over the windows— "it nearly is." She struck at Sharlin.

Even as she flinched, the ropes suspending her from the frame parted, and she fell limply to the floor.

Rodeka stood over her. "Get up."

Sharlin chafed her ankles with hands that were also numb, then slowly got to her feet.

"Come with me. I want to show you why you'll let me hurt you. Why you'll let me suck away your power, and beg me to do it quicker."

She took Sharlin's arm in her hand. The grip was hard and tight, and Sharlin felt the pain clear to the bone, but she bore it in silence. The witch queen walked her quickly through the fortress and to the back door, which overlooked the slope with the guardian walls.

Please, Sharlin prayed. *Please let my father not be there.*

Rodeka kicked the door open.

Wave after wave of goblin soldiers looked back, awaiting their mistress' bidding.

They lay on the ground, asleep to all appearances, except for a few who walked back and forth with an exaggerated stagger.

"They've awakened," Rodeka said. "And they're ready for whoever might come." She pointed. "My powers and my scouts tell me that your father and whatever pitiful army he has gathered is waiting out there. Are they stupid enough to come charging up the slope to save you?" The grip tightened. "Well, tell me, princess of Dhamon! Are they that stupid?"

She grit her teeth. "Perhaps."

"I thought so." Rodeka looked at her. "Give me leave to sacrifice you, and I'll spare them. With your Dhamon blood, I've no need for theirs. I have another kingdom waiting for me now, to the south. It's time to move on anyway."

Weariness washed through Sharlin. Dar and Turiana waged a battle of their own. This was her destiny. She knew, as had Hapwith, that this was not where Rodeka died.

But at least she had saved her brother and could possibly save her father.

Sharlin nodded. "All right," she whispered. She felt

spent. "Do whatever you want with me. Just let my family and my kingdom go."

"It's done!" Rodeka grinned and lashed her wrists together. With a show of force that her slender figure denied, the woman lifted up Sharlin, hands over her head, and hung her from the edge of the massive door. Her feet dangled above the ground. The sorceress laughed. "Just so that you can watch the slaughter. But never fear. Your father and brother will be spared."

Nails raked her throat as Rodeka pulled open the neck of her shirt. Sharlin trembled as the woman caressed the curve of her skin.

"Did you ever wonder about this mark?" purred Rodeka. "It's a birthmark. All born to the line of Dhamon carry it. Like tiny punctures. Or, for that matter, did you ever wonder where your house got its name, Dhamon? Likely not. It's entirely probable that all of you have forgotten. Then let me tell you."

Sharlin wanted to close her eyes and ears, shutting out the hateful voice and the sight beyond her of the goblin soldiers beginning to rise up at the barriers, but she couldn't. She jumped as the knife point dug into her neck. A warmth began to trickle out, down the front of her breasts. It was crimson.

"It was said your great-great-or-whatever-grandfather wrestled a demon to its defeat. He was bitten in the process, rather badly, but the demon healed him and granted him a kingdom for his freedom. This," and Rodeka gestured with the stained knife, "is the kingdom. The demon was a master of the wind. You hear it all the time in Dhamon, howling through the mountains, and along this plateau, but you've never feared it, have you?"

Sharlin moved her head slightly. The bloodletting was nearly painless, except for the fear. She didn't want to die!

Rodeka stroked her cheek. "Now that demon will

come to me, and I will have its power. The power of
the wind, in all its fury. Even a dragon will not be able
to face me then!"

Behind her, Sharlin watched as gold streaked the
sky. With a shout, the goblins got to their feet, and
roared to the attack.

Then she saw the sky and realized the golden streak
was Turiana, and she bore a rider on her back.

Rodeka must have seen something in her eyes. She
whirled, sacrificial knife in hand, as the goblins screeched
in fear.

The golden dragon swooped low, talons out. She tore
through the pack of soldiers before they even raised a
spear to her. Wheeled and slashed through again. Behind her, in a wave of determination, rode her father's
army.

Sharlin gasped for breath. "I deny you," she whispered. "I want my life back."

Rodeka twisted back to face her. "Then grasp for
your power, my princess, and feel it run through your
fingers like sand! They won't get through my troops in
time to stop me."

Sharlin closed her eyes. She reached for Turiana's
power. It escaped her, and she felt herself floating
through the air, as though she, too, had dragon wings.

I'm getting giddy, she thought. With a shuddering
inhalation, she fought to slow the tide of her blood. She
fought to find Turiana's powers and unbind them from
Rodeka.

With a roar and a puff of smoke, Rodeka's apparition
appeared before her. They soared, the two of them,
skyborne in a night of illusion. Like a giantess of smoke,
she blocked Sharlin's flight.

The sorceress pushed her cupped hands toward Sharlin
with a mocking laugh. In her pale palms lay a fortune in
gems, each pulsing with its own fire and light. "Power,"
she said. "You must mine it and then polish it!"

Red, yellow, purple, blue, green, dazzling white, and the last, a common mud-brown flint.

"Dhamon! I summon you, with all your might, to come to me. See what I offer you."

The witch queen looked at Sharlin from half-veiled eyes. "The ruby is your mother . . . her blood I used to draw you first. This rough diamond is that gangly youth, perhaps, whose ghost I drew. This sapphire with a flawed star for its soul, can you guess who this is? Ah . . . you give up too quickly. King Balforth, of course. And this emerald here, with a soul as deep and abiding as the forest, might almost be your brother Erban. And for yourself, which do you pick? You must know your power before you can use it!"

The front of her mail shirt and underblouse grew damp and splattered with every beat of her heart. Sharlin felt it, even as she flew higher, trying to get beyond Rodeka. She hovered in two worlds, life and death.

The sorceress laughed softly, hauntingly. "Pick the one you want before I grind them all to dust." And the woman began to press together her cupped hand, and Sharlin gasped, knowing that she was close to her end.

Why could she not pick, as Dar had? He had chosen to love her, and then also chosen to accept a destiny. He was whole, as she hadn't been for months. Despite all the signs of the futility of her effort, she had come home through time. Despite all the signs of his love, and her love for him, and the future that they might hold together, and his son, she had not made the same commitment. Instead, she had fled into the past.

She looked at the flint in Rodeka's palm. The brown of determination and steadiness—and fire.

Sharlin reached for it. "I pick the stone that brings fire!" she said in triumph, knowing that she had chosen Dar's own fierce joy in life.

As soon as she touched it, she was engulfed in golden flame.

*   *   *

Turiana swung about and swooped low. Then the sparkle of flame drew her, and the incredible surge of power.

"There she is!" snapped the dragon, and Dar raised his bloodied sword higher.

Rodeka stood in a pool of crimson, a woman in pagan robes, with copper and feathers in her hair, blown as if by a tremendous wind. Sharlin hung from a wooden door, covered in her blood.

As Turiana reared to a halt, Dar vaulted from her back. Before witch and dragon could meet, he swung the sword even as it sang to him, *Strike now!*

"No!" screamed the woman, as Dar cleaved her in two.

The stones underneath his feet shattered in a blast, and her robes fluttered to the ground, empty.

Sharlin moaned and raised her chin. "Dar," she whispered.

The swordsman dropped his sword and gathered her in his arms, lifting her hanging and limp body down. He fell to the ground under her as Turiana lifted her voice in dragonsong, the keening of grief filling the air.

She put her cold hand in his warm one, and smiled at his tears.

"I'll be all right," she said softly. "Tell Turiana to stop wailing, please. I just . . . need to rest."

Chapter 22

"Stay awhile longer." Balforth reached out and stroked the amber hair of his only daughter.

She smiled. "No. I've been here overlong, I think. And Turiana has terrorized the kingdom enough."

The aging king looked to the swordsman who stood behind her, and Dar returned his stare without expression.

Balforth sighed. A very faint blush of pink had returned to her cheeks, she who'd been so deathly pale when he reached her and Dar that morning that he'd been sure she was going to join her mother. He supposed that knowing she lived and was loved would have to be enough. Fathers should be used to the idea that they give their daughters away. He dropped his hand. "And why is this kingdom of yours so far away that I'll never see you again?" he said gruffly.

Sharlin leaned forward and kissed him. "It's across two oceans," she said, knowing that it was across one of water, and another of time. Her heart ached, because she couldn't tell him what she knew of the future, and didn't want to. The house of Dhamon would become no more than a pallan history. What of Erban? She didn't know, and as she turned from her father to her brother, she whispered fiercely, "Take care of yourself!"

"I will." He beamed. She knew he'd already trapped

251

three of the griffins and returned them to the eyrie. His work would be cut out for him this winter, starting anew.

Dar backed her, as he had quietly, the last few weeks. As soon as they were alone, she would tell him her news. She could hardly wait much longer, for the taut roundness of her stomach would tell him if she didn't. That, or Turiana, who had known all along and was dying to tell Dar herself.

Behind them, the dragon queen trumpeted querulously. She carried packs on her back of gifts from Dhamon, and three of the sacks bulged with dragonet eggs, close to hatching. Now that she had her powers back, full-fledged, she was anxious to return.

Sharlin felt the dragon urging her to hurry. Baalan awaited. Dar shifted.

King Balforth sensed that the time had come. He gave her one last kiss across her forehead, and looked at Dar. "Take care of her, swordsman."

"I will. On that you have my solemn word." Dar took the man's hand in his, and they shook.

Erban jostled between them, and pumped Dar's hand as well, and said, "When you die, will you leave me your talking sword? Turiana can bring it to me."

As Sharlin gasped, Dar threw back his head and laughed. He pounded Erban's shoulder. "The sword goes where it will," he said. "You'll have to make do without it. But you have the griffins."

"True."

Turiana rumbled. Dar took Sharlin's hand and drew her away. She waved to them.

"Remember how much I love you," she said, her throat catching on the words.

Balforth took his son in his arms and they embraced each other, as the older man answered, "I will never forget."

At the last second, Sharlin broke away from Dar and

came running back. As she hugged her father, she whispered in his ear, "And you're shortly to be a grandfather. A boy. Like Erban, only with Dar's hair and eyes. And I'm going to name him after you."

The tired blue eyes filled with tears then, and she tried to wipe them away. Her father managed to say, "And give me a girl later, after your mother."

"I'll do my best."

"Then what other immortality can I ask? Go on now—your future's waiting for you." Somewhat roughly, he pushed her back toward Dar.

They mounted the dragon, Sharlin in front. As Dar swung on and gripped her waist before he picked up the reins, he said, "Are you sure?"

She tucked his arm snugly about her. "Yes. Very sure. If Turiana can manage it."

"I can do anything," the dragon said smugly. She unfurled her golden wings to the wind.

"Say," Dar added, "are you putting on a little weight there?" He jostled her waistline.

"There's something I've been meaning to tell you," Sharlin answered, as the golden dragon took flight, and headed to the blue sky, and the Rangard of another tomorrow.

ABOUT THE AUTHOR

R. A. V. SALSITZ was born in Phoenix, Arizona, and raised mainly in Southern California, with time out for stints in Alaska, Oregon, and Colorado. Having a birthplace named for such a mythical and mystical beast has always pushed her toward SF and fantasy.

Encouraged from an early age to write, she majored in journalism in high school and college. Although Rhondi has yet to drive a truck carrying nitro, work experience has been varied—from electronics to furniture to computer industries—until she settled down to work full-time at a word processor.

Married, the author matches wits daily with a spouse and four lively children, of various ages, heights, and sexes. Hobbies and interests include traveling, tennis, horses, computers, and writing.

The earlier adventures of Dar, Sharlin, and Turiana can be found in *Where Dragons Lie*, published by Signet.